THE little maid slipped into the room. She approached the bed with a nervous smile.

"What is it, Bronwen?" I asked, though I knew she had no English.

She giggled a little, and brought out a folded paper from the old-fashioned pocket hanging under her apron. I stared at it suspiciously.

"Is that for me?"

She pointed at me, and giggled again. Then dropping the note upon the coverlet, she fled.

I picked it up. For no known reason, I found I was afraid to open it. My hands were shaking.

With an exclamation of impatience at my folly, I controlled my hands, and unfolded the message.

It was brief and to the point. It merely said, in printed letters, "DANGER! LEAVE WALES."

Fawcett Crest Books
by Jill Tattersall:

CHANTERS CHASE

DARK AT NOON

THE WITCHES OF ALL SAINTS

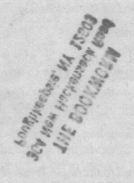

DARK
AT
NOON

Jill Tattersall

FAWCETT CREST • NEW YORK

DARK AT NOON

Published by Fawcett Crest Books, a unit of CBS Publications,
the Consumer Publishing Division of CBS Inc., by arrangement
with William Morrow and Company, Inc.

Copyright © 1978 by Jill Tattersall

ISBN: 0-449-24211-0

THIS BOOK CONTAINS THE COMPLETE TEXT OF THE

ORIGINAL HARDCOVER EDITION.

Printed in the United States of America

First Fawcett Crest printing: December 1979

10   9   8   7   6   5   4   3   2   1

"O dark, dark, dark, amid the blaze of noon..."

Milton

Prologue

The winter snows were beginning to melt in the mountain ranges with the increasing warmth of spring. The Afon Ystwyth, never a gentle river, was tumbling now in full spate down the rocky falls towards the valley. The roar of its tumultuous passage completely obliterated the sound of the stagecoach rattling along the last mile of its journey to the Castell Marten Arms, en route for Holyhead. The first warning of the imminent arrival of the Highflyer came from the long horn carried by the guard, who raised it to his lips just as the coachman reined in his horses for the dangerous corner above the waterfall, and let out a blasting note that echoed from the rocks around.

At once, a bustle of activity transformed the old stone inn below. Fresh horses were led out into the cobbled yard, while ostlers came forward to fold back their rugs, revealing gleaming harnesses and well-groomed flanks. Bronwen and Megan peeped smiling from the upper windows, safely out of sight of Mrs. Jones, who stood ready on the doorstep in clean cap and apron to receive the passengers for the few minutes allotted for their refreshment. But the Holyhead Highflyer was never to require the change of horses, nor the home-cured ham and October ale for which the Castell Marten Arms was justly famed; for as if the sounding horn had been a signal, the nearside leader had shied violently, forcing the other horses to the edge of the road, and causing the offside front wheel to run up over a rock. A moment later, the top-heavy coach had tipped beyond hope of recovery. With a sound to rival the thunder of the river, it overturned into the *pistyll*, dragging down the screaming horses with it and hurling the coachman and the guard into the abyss.

There was a witness to the disaster: a person on horseback who stared down from a place of concealment in the ring of rocks above the road, motionless, as if entranced—or perhaps stunned by the horror of the sight. But when the horse began to whinny in sympathy with its unfortunate fellows, the rider came suddenly to life, turning the horse sharply and slashing at it with a whip, urging it on recklessly over the stony mountain shoulder and into the shelter of the mists that clung to the upper heights. There for a moment horse and rider loomed, briefly magnified by the vapour—and then vanished as suddenly as if they had been plucked away by the Devil himself.

By that time the tumult in the *pistyll* had died away, apart from the intermittent screaming of one of the horses, mortally wounded by the broken carriage pole. In the swollen river a shoe and a reticule joined a sodden sheep carcase as it swept over the rocky falls and through the whirlpool beneath. A few moments later a man's hat and a tangled shawl followed, plucked out of an eddy by the current and tumbling over each other as though they too were eager to join the Afon Ystwyth in its headlong rush towards the sea.

In the foam-flecked amber pool below the cataract, twin shapes turned slowly, one upon the other. The eddy tugged at torn black cloth, while two shades of long brown hair, darkened by the water, mingled with the twisting river weeds. Then the icy stream pulled the bodies apart, and a crested ring slipped off one of the pale fingers to go spiralling down to a shallow patch of silver sand, where it lay glinting in a watery shaft of noon sunlight that had pierced the massing clouds above.

One of the bodies was now travelling with the current. It passed between the boulders and floated several feet downstream until it was halted by a tree trunk, half-submerged. There it lay submissively, while the water rippled through the folds of the ruined mourning gown, giving the drowned corpse an illusory appearance of vitality.

In the other body, also that of a young woman, some life

remained. The movement of the restless river had nudged the bleeding head onto a rock, and the parted lips, though pale and cold, were open to the air. The body was numb, half-frozen by its immersion in water frigid with barely melted snow. It had been for several minutes beyond feeling, but gradually the fading sunlight began to revive it, and a voice penetrated at last to the half-conscious brain...

Chapter One

"*Diw, Diw,*" a far-off voice was saying, a shocked and mournful birdlike cry that seemed to carry no meaning with it. Then I became aware of other voices, hissing and sibilant, and equally incomprehensible. Hands began to pull at me, and I knew that I moaned against their touch even through the numbness of that deep black cold...

Time passed.

I became conscious of red flowers blossoming along my closed eyelids, and after a while I realized that the spring sun was warm upon my face. I was aware of the pungent smell of blood and trampled grass and rotting weed. An odd and horrible scream was cut off abruptly by a sudden violent concussion of sound—a shot? But then the growing sharpness of pain became unbearable, until it swallowed me completely.

Darkness deepened, and lightened again. There was an ache to which I tried to draw attention, but though I managed to murmur a few words, it seemed that those about me were deaf—or spoke another tongue.

"Water," I begged, but it was wine they forced between my icy lips, rough wine that made me choke at first and then, agonizingly, vomit. I was conscious of shame, and humiliation... but then at last came a measure of comfort with the feel of a warm cloth sponging me gently, and a soft voice murmuring in the familiar English of the home counties:

"There, poor child, there:.. the doctor will be back to see you presently. He's just setting the harper's leg, poor fellow..."

There came a sudden draught, and the stamp of booted feet. I felt shock, disturbance, a premonitory fear.

"Oh, pray hush, my lord!" cried out the woman who was tending to me.

"Which one was drowned?" demanded an authoritative voice, cutting across the motherly woman's protests. "What was her name? And who is this?"

I realized I was within doors, lying on a bed, in a room that now seemed full of voices, swinging up and down the scale. The newcomer silenced them abruptly.

"You are wrong, Nan Jones," he said, and his voice sounded raw with rage, or pain. "It does concern me nearly—more nearly than perhaps you know. Did they tell you papers were found with my brother's name upon them, and that it seems that Gerry—Gerry is dead?"

I lost some moments then, adrift in a tumbled sea of misery and confusion. When I returned to my senses, it was to find his lordship talking still.

"Not in the accident, I tell you," he was crying impatiently. "He died a few days ago of an illness."

"Master Gerry—dead?" It was the woman's voice, astonished, shocked. "Dead? And of an illness? Lord save us! What will my lady do?"

"She will bear it," he said roughly. "As she has borne so much . . . You had not heard it, then?"

"No, upon my soul. Ah, you will miss him, Master Lucian, for all your differences."

"There's more," he said with difficulty.

"What more?" The woman sounded almost as if she were afraid; and I was conscious of a faint curiosity to hear the answer.

"It seems—it seems that Gerry married, the very day he died."

"Married, my lord? And we knew nothing of it?"

"Ay, but never mind that now. What concerns us at this moment is that his widow was on the coach—or so I assume, for who else would be carrying the certificates of his marriage and burial?"

"His widow . . . !" I felt her touch me gently. "So you think this poor girl may be she?"

"It must be either this one—or the corpse. The two of them are in mourning, look you; and both found in the

11

river—one drowned. Before I ride to my mother with the news, I must know if Gerry's widow lives."

The anger in his voice seemed to hurt my head, and I heard myself moan aloud. The hand with the washcloth soothed me, and the woman remarked softly, "The young lady stirs, my lord, as you see. Why don't you ask her yourself?"

He approached. I felt the bed sag under his weight as he leaned his hand upon it. "Mrs. Marten," he said clearly. "Mrs. Marten . . . do you hear me?" After a pause, he went on with a trace of uncertainty, "Victoria? Answer me, Victoria!"

With a supreme effort, I opened my eyes. The first thing I saw was the dark bold face of the man who bent over me, and I was aware of fear. My head ached, my hand stung, my ankle throbbed—I was in pain, but there was something worse. Something was troubling me, something terribly important, but I could not think what it was. I sensed that the room was quite full of people, and that they were all looking my way, but I could only stare at the black-browed, tight-lipped face looming immediately above me. It was an arrogant face, to match his voice, and hard with the effort of self-control.

"Mrs. Marten?" he demanded again.

I gazed helplessly into his narrowed dark eyes.

"Mrs. Marten?"

Gradually it occurred to me that he was addressing me—but was that my name?

"I—I don't know," I murmured. "I—don't think so."

I felt myself falling back into the well of darkness, but he seized my left hand in a hard rough grip and raised it from the bed.

"No ring!" he cried out in a tone of great relief. "She is not married, then. It must be the other one who is—who was the widow."

Someone cried out at that, in an incomprehensible babble of sound. A moment's silence followed, and then his lordship said wearily, "You say that young Idris found a ring, and it was in the river? Where is the boy? Let him come forward and tell me himself."

A shrill voice responded excitedly. My kindly nurse soon interrupted the lad. "What is it, sir? What's that he is saying? Was it—Master Gerry's ring?"

"Ay, Nan, no doubt of it. I have it here. It seems the boy saw it gleaming, on a patch of sand under the water."

"You are quite sure of it?" she asked anxiously. "It has the crest upon it?"

"Yes, yes, there is no doubt, I tell you. But no one knows which of the young women was wearing it, of course. Ah, Dai Glynn!" he cried in a tone of relief. "What news have you?"

Another man's voice answered him wearily. "Owen Pennant has just died," he announced, in that strangely musical lilt. "Only this lady and the blind harper, Samson, have survived the accident. Samson will mend, I hope, but he'll never walk straight again."

"Can he speak? Would he know the names of the other passengers?"

"He's in no state to be questioned yet, my lord. And he might know their names, but he is blind, remember. I doubt if he'd fit the names to their owners with any certainty. But what does it matter? The dead will be claimed soon enough, I dare say. But what do you here, Castelmarten? Did you come upon the accident by chance?"

"I was riding the hill, as it happened, looking to see if any of my sheep had wandered into ap Owen's flock—and then I saw ap Owen himself upon the road."

"Ah! Sir Caerleon ap Owen is the nearest magistrate, of course. Jones would have sent for him at once."

"Ay. He told me the news and we rode down here together. When we arrived, they had just found the reticule with the papers in it."

"Why, what papers do you mean?"

It was my nurse who answered him. "Papers with Master Gerry's name upon them, Dr. Glynn. He is— Master Gerry is—dead, sir, it seems."

"What! Gervais Marten dead? The fittest young scamp I ever attended! Well, this is a shock. Another shock. It will be long before this day is forgotten in the valley. How did

13

it happen? Was there a letter? Any explanation of it?"

"Only this." There followed the rustle of paper and an exclamation from the doctor.

"A marriage certificate! 'The Honourable Gervais Wynn Ivan Williams Marten to—to Victoria Clarissa Merridew, of the Parish of St. Michael's, Upper Buzzard, Dunstable.' Why, I've never heard of her! Have you, my lord? And both dated less than a week ago! This is passing strange!"

"Certainly I find it so."

"What, did you know nothing of it?"

"Nothing, until this day."

The woman spoke. "Master Gerry was ever a wild one, God rest him. But he didn't ought to have done this. This will make my lady grieve . . . let alone him dying so sudden and unexpected."

"Gerry married," the doctor mused. "And to a stranger! I always thought—well, never mind that! And is he really dead? I can scarce believe it yet. But this bears hard on you, my lord—to learn such news, and in such a way. No explanation either? No letter, you say?"

"The stagecoach was not carrying mail. You remember the bag was brought up last week by Prys-Roberts, lawyer. These papers were found in a lady's reticule. The inference is that one of the passengers on the coach was travelling to us with the news."

"Well, well. And it is quite possible, I suppose, that one of the two young women on the coach was actually Gerry's wife—his widow?"

"That," said his lordship with what I interpreted as barely controlled impatience, "is what I am endeavouring to establish. Is this—person fit to answer questions? Would you say that she is sensible, from the medical viewpoint?"

A cool hand touched my forehead, raised my eyelids in turn.

"She is pretty well conscious—still confused, no doubt. She will make better sense tomorrow." The doctor patted my shoulder and moved away.

"She won't tell us if she is, or is not, Mrs. Marten," his lordship complained. "And the other young woman is

14

dead, so we'll have no help from her. But they did find another reticule in the river, which had a letter in it. It is over there, drying out by the fire. Pass it over, Jones. Yes, it's in a bad state; but the direction is clear enough, do you see? *'Mary Ramsey, in the care of Mother Cliffe,'* and ... yes, *'Springwell Court, in Lichfield.'* But as to the content, 'tis well-nigh illegible."

"No, wait a moment," said the doctor. "What's this? *'sorry ... death ... Cliffe—Mr. Cliffe,'* it is. *'Need you here ... your aunt sadly ...'* This piece is very much spoiled, in truth. Ah, this is better. *'leave privily ... the law would say Mother Cliffe ... have ... custody'* Ah, I have it, *'Mother Cliffe should have the custody of you ...'* hmm. *'a week on Tuesday'* Today is a Tuesday! *'at the Red Lion ... affec. uncle, Owen Tho—'* it must be Thomas, I suppose."

"Thank you, Glynn. That is a great deal better than nothing."

"Well, my lord, it does explain why both the young women are in mourning, certainly—one for her husband, the other for this Mr. Cliffe, whoever he may be—but it scarcely helps you to determine which is which."

"It gives me a name, and that of a relative, besides the place where he was expecting to meet her."

"Ay, the Red Lion. But it doesn't tell us which Red Lion, my lord."

"It will be the Red Lion in Holyhead, I dare say, which was the final destination of the stagecoach from Llangollen. Mary Ramsey!" he cried suddenly, close to my ear. "Mary Ramsey! Rouse up and speak to me!"

Something—was it water?—flicked my face.

"No," I moaned, turning my face aside. "No ..."

I was begging him to go away and leave me alone, but I had not the strength to put it into words.

"Do you mean that you are not Mary Ramsey?" he demanded.

"Leave me ... leave me alone ..."

"Only tell me your name, and then I swear I shall leave you in peace."

But I could only sob and turn restlessly until the woman

15

caught hold of my hand and stroked it, soothing me.

"Where did they find the reticule?" asked the doctor suddenly. "The one with the papers in it?"

"By the coach—the string had caught in the door handle. So that is of no help to us. Victoria! Victoria Merridew!"

"See now, my lord," said my nurse gently, "why don't you leave the poor child be 'til morning time? She'll be in her senses then, doubtless."

"You don't suppose I enjoy bullying a person in this state?" he demanded savagely, while I shrank beneath the bedclothes. "I want to know if Gerry's widow lives, for my mother's sake." But to my relief he turned away as if abandoning the attempt to force the truth out of me. "Now," he said briskly, in a different tone, "we must send at once to the Red Lion, to this man Thomas, to tell him that his niece was in an accident, and to bring him here to identify her. Whom can you spare, Jones?"

"Ivor Griffiths, sir. Ay, let us send Ivor on the Eagle, for he rides like—like Dick Turpin himself."

I cried out at that, frightening myself.

The silence following my cry was broken only by the creaking of boots and the singing of the river not far beyond the window.

"Bring me a pen and paper," said his lordship eventually, sounding as if he were utterly weary of the whole business. "Have you sealing wax? Very well. I will write a few lines only, nothing to alarm this fellow Thomas overmuch, but enough to make sure he comes . . . There," he added presently, sealing the missive with his ring. "Take this, Ivor. Choose a good horse, and make sure that you are back by morning—and with Mr. Thomas. Let us hope this young woman will be still alive by then. What do you say as to her chances, Glynn?"

"Why, sir, her wounds are light enough—the ankle, the hand—both will mend easily, I dare say. And the head wound is not dangerously deep. But as to the concussion to the brain within—that is another matter. If I had seen her fall, I should know better what to expect. Internal bruising in that area is an uncertain, a chancy thing. Quiet, my lord,

16

quiet and rest are what I prescribe for her—and the ministrations of good Mrs. Jones."

"Very well," said his lordship curtly. "Out, all of you!"

There was a sliding, shuffling sound as various persons left the room. At least my hearing was unimpaired, I thought, though my sight was still uncertain.

"And how long, Dr. Glynn, do you think Miss should stay?" asked Mrs. Jones. "I mean, I was thinking that if—if she is my lord's sister, then it will look better for her to be cared for at the castle."

"My sister!" cried his lordship. "Good God, I suppose you could call her so, if she was in truth married to Gerry."

"Indeed, you could, sir," the doctor agreed. "And certainly it would look better, when Mrs. Marten is fit to be moved, to take her to Castell Marten."

"Perhaps it would look better, but I am loath to do it."

"I am sure my lady would think it proper, sir."

"No doubt, Nanny, but ap Owen won't want her leaving until her statement has been taken; and besides, her identity is quite uncertain yet."

"Nanny, indeed," said Mrs. Jones. "It seems I must remind you that times have changed, my lord. I am Mrs. Jones to you, these days."

"You know I always think of you as 'Nanny,'" he said, and I was surprised that his voice could sound so warm. "However—Mrs. Jones—I must point out that our only knowledge of Gerry's marriage comes from a single paper that might even have been forged, for all we know. Where are those documents, by the way?"

"I returned them to the reticule," the doctor said. "I believe young Bronwen tidied it away somewhere."

"Never mind it now," said Mrs. Jones. "'Tis in the cupboard, like as not. I'll find it later. But as I was saying, my lord, I was Master Gervais's Nanny too, and know what is due to his memory, if he did indeed marry her. Though how he could do such a thing, with never a word to any of us—!"

"It is all of a piece," said his lordship coldly. "Exactly what one might have expected of him."

"And then to die so sudden," mused Mrs. Jones.

"Terrible, terrible. I believe I am only now beginning to realize that—that I shall never see him more. What did you say he died of, sir?"

"An inflammation of the lungs, following influenza. Now that certainly does not sound like him, does it, Nanny? I would have said that Gerry had the constitution of an ox."

"He was never a sickly child," she agreed.

I found I could no longer ignore my raging thirst. "Water," I whispered.

Mrs. Jones assisted me to drink. "You can't move her yet, in any case," she remarked, settling me back against the pillows. "What do you think, Dr. Glynn?"

The doctor approached. He asked a few questions of Mrs. Jones. Then I felt his hands on me again, strong, sure, impersonal.

"She will do better here for a day or two, my lord. And you are surely right that Sir Caerleon ap Owen would wish it too, for no doubt they will hold the inquest here, where the bodies are, and she should be available to give evidence. I'll look in on her as often as necessary and will send word to the castle when I think she can bear the drive."

"And when Mr. Thomas has seen her," his lordship pointed out. "We can do nothing until then, in case she is his niece. If she is not, I'll pay your fee, of course."

"I'll bill you, if she lives—and I see no reason at present why she should not. Pray excuse me, my lord, while I instruct Mrs. Jones as to her proper care..."

The voices faded, and soon I slept.

Towards nightfall, I woke again. I was hot and feverish and turned restlessly in the soft bed. Mrs. Jones gave me tea to drink and bathed me with cool water. Later in the night, I half-opened my eyes to find her leaning over me, holding a candle high, watching my face.

"Gervais?" she asked. "Gervais? Gerry?"

She was testing me, I vaguely realized; but "No...no!" was all the answer I could bring myself to make.

Mrs. Jones sighed and shook her head. She set down the

18

candle and, settling herself again in the bedside chair, picked up her knitting.

I slept, and dreamed,and woke again.

Once I started up with dry mouth and pounding heart, certain I had seen a masked face at the mullioned casement. But after a while, when nothing further happened, I persuaded myself it must have been a nightmare, the product of a fevered mind.

And yet it had seemed real—frighteningly real—that glimpse of a face in its black disguise. At least I was almost sure that somewhere I had seen a man in such a mask; but I could not remember where or when.

For a long while I dared not sleep but stared through my half-drawn bed-hanging at the casement window. It was unlatched and rattled gently in the wind, its soft white curtain billowing into the room.

It must have been the moving folds of muslin which had set off the nightmare in my mind, I decided. In any case, no one was there now; and Mrs. Jones was dozing lightly by my side, so I was safe enough.

A few moments later, I went back to sleep.

Chapter Two

Dawn came, and the day broke shining bright.

"Rain before nightfall," forecast Mrs. Jones. She rose stiffly and placed her hand upon my forehead.

"Your fever's down a trifle, miss. How do you feel? Did you sleep?"

"Yes, ma'am. But... where am I? How came I here?"

"Ah, you are properly conscious now, my dear," she returned comfortably. "Where are you? Why, at the Castell Marten Arms, to be sure. You were travelling by the stage and met with a nasty accident, not half a mile away, at that bad corner up above the cataract. You were thrown out of the coach and rolled down the rocks into the river. You suffered a blow to your head, and a nasty cut on your right hand. Ay, and a twisted foot—but no bones broken, I'm very glad to say. You were lucky not to be drowned, like—ahem! Ay, all things considered, you may count yourself fortunate, my dear."

I said with an effort, "I cannot seem to remember... I wonder why I was travelling? Was I alone?"

Mrs. Jones looked somewhat disconcerted. "Well, as to that, my dear, there was another young lady with you on the coach, but I can't tell if you knew her or no. Ah!" She turned to the door with an expression of relief. "Here is Bronwen with hot milk for you, and a little thin gruel. Let us see you eat it, my dear, and you will feel better for it soon."

I ate and drank obediently, but I was by no means satisfied with the answers she had given me.

"What did I have with me?" I persisted, when the tray had been set aside. "I had luggage, I collect?"

She pursed her lips. She was a pleasant-looking woman

in late middle age, somewhat pump, with small sharp blue eyes and curly greying hair under a neat starched cap. The autocrat had called her 'Nanny,' I remembered; and an excellent Nanny she must have been.

"Two bags of young ladies' clothes were found in the coach," she said cautiously, "and a reticule. Another reticule was found in the river; but we don't know which of them belongs to you."

I stared at her. "Where is the other girl?" Then I brushed my left hand across my eyes as recollection came. "She is dead, is she not?"

"Ah well, there's no sense in deceiving you, my dear. Ay, she was drowned, poor soul. The river is great with melting snow at this season of the year..." The woman sighed. "They are to hold an inquest on her and—and on the others who died—and they don't even know what name to bury her under, the poor young thing. She was either Mary Ramsey of Lichfield, it appears, or—or the Honourable Mrs. Gervais Marten."

"Oh..." I felt very tired. Speech was an effort, so I remained silent for a while, listening to the steady ticking of the clock, handsomely cased in some dark wood, and the crackling of the fire, and farther off, the river hissing and singing between the boulders.

"I suppose the river has a name?" I ventured at length.

Mrs. Jones let out a breath, as if she had been holding it expectantly. "Indeed, it has," she said. "It is the Afon Ystwyth, the winding river. And wind it does, not so much up here; but farther down in the valleys, there it wanders like the River Jordan."

"Afon Ystwyth?" I repeated wonderingly. "That is not English, surely?"

"No, no, my dear. You are in the heart of Welsh Wales here."

"In the heart of Wales! But you—you must be English?"

"I was born so, indeed; but my dear Edrys Jones has made half a Welshwoman out of me, I like to think. Though I must own I still find the language puzzling, especially when they speak it fast....I was born in Northamptonshire more years ago than I care to

21

remember," she continued comfortably, taking up her knitting, "and went to work as a nursery-maid for a Welsh family, connections of the vicar here. After one thing and another, I was recommended to her ladyship, to be a nurse to the young gentlemen, when her old Nanny Richards died—to Master Lucian, that is, who is now Lord Castelmarten—he spoke to you yesterday in this very room, if you remember—and to his younger brother Gervais. Ay, well, I was many years at Castell Marten, and when the butler, Jones, retired, he asked me to marry him, and his lordship—the old earl, who died last year—he put us in here to manage the Arms, which was always Mr. Jones's ambition."

"Castell Marten—is that two words or one?"

"Ah, strangers are always confused by that, my dear. It seems that in past times folk did not care for their spelling as they do now, and it was written any way one pleased. Now the custom is to write one word for the title, and two for the place. There is the village too, you know, hard by the castle—the village of Castell Marten."

Now I had learned something, I thought; but not what I longed to know. It was time to voice a fear which had been growing in me by the minute. I gathered up my courage and said hesitantly, "Mrs. Jones, everything seems to have a name, even the river . . . but I—if I have one, I—I don't remember it."

I could see she was dismayed, though she strove to hide it. She picked up my unbandaged hand, and held it warmly.

"Oh, you poor thing," she cried. "But sure, you have a name. His lordship will find it out for you—or more likely, it will come back on its own."

"Thank you," I said, a little comforted. But I had not told her the full story yet, that everything was gone— everything that had ever happened to me, before I was taken from the river. Not only had I lost my name, but I had lost all the past. It was a lonely, frightening feeling, and one that made me as dizzy to contemplate as if I had awoken to find myself in a fog, upon a precipice.

"There, there, my dear," said Mrs. Jones, patting my

hand. "It may be we will know more today, when Mr. Thomas comes." She cocked her head on one side, listening. "Perhaps this is Ivor with him already." She glanced at the clock. "No, 'tis over soon to expect them, I fear." She went to the window. "Ah, the doctor's gig! I hope he will be pleased with you."

I looked with interest at Dr. Glynn, who knew at least as much about me as I did myself. He was a dark, strong-looking man in early middle age, with a shock of black hair and shaggy brows over bright eyes. He had a warm smile, revealing white teeth, and the backs of his hands were very hairy. His smile died, however, when he heard that I could not even remember my name. He questioned me closely, shook his head, took my pulse, and remarked that my fever was rising again.

Mrs. Jones, seeing no doubt that his obvious apprehensions were affecting me, neatly changed the subject.

"Did you meet your friend?" she asked him. "Were you able to get the ointment, sir?"

To my surprise his face lit up like a child's. "Ay, indeed, ma'am. And she gave me not only a fine salve for the wounds, but—look here! A special pillow, stuffed with herbs, to help this young lady sleep."

He began to dress my arm with the assistance of Mrs. Jones.

"Are they for me?" I asked. "It is very kind of—your friend, Dr. Glynn."

"Yes, isn't it," he assented eagerly. "She has certainly no need to do such work—never takes anything for it, of course, but it interests her greatly. She has made a study of plants and of medicine, you see. Talented she is, indeed. I told her about your case—we chanced to meet in the village last evening—and nothing would do for her but to hasten away to her stillroom and get to work. You will find her remedies excellent, I predict. Indeed, I often wonder what my patients would do without her."

"You had better ask her to tell you her secrets," muttered Mrs. Jones. "For you and your patients may well have to do without her, I believe."

The doctor raised his dark eyes to hers. "That is as it

may be," he said gravely, his brightness quenched.

Mrs. Jones smiled slightly. "Love laughs at locksmiths, we know that—but parents have a way of bringing their daughters to heel, sir. I happen to know that—a certain match has been arranged for Miss Carnaby which is far more suitable, if not absolutely agreeable to both parties concerned."

Dr. Glynn abruptly finished his ministrations. "This young lady is not yet able to leave," he said curtly. "You can spare the room a while longer?"

"Ay, if need be, I dare say."

"But it is your best bedchamber here. You will not want it occupied overlong. I shall inform you immediately I think her fit to travel. Now let us visit Samson."

He gathered his things together, avoiding my eye.

"Samson has a slight fever, sir," Mrs. Jones remarked. "But you will not hear him complaining of it—not he! I have a soft spot for the old fellow, bless him."

"Yes, he is one of a dying breed—the blind harpers of Wales—" The doctor flung up his head at a sudden clamour in the yard, dogs barking, an autocratic voice calling orders, the ringing of spurs on the cobblestones.

"It is his lordship," cried Mrs. Jones. "You go to Mr. Samson, and I will meet his lordship in the hall..."

She bustled away, and the doctor after giving me a few quick words of advice, soon followed her.

A moment later I was surprised to hear Lord Castelmarten's voice coming quite plainly from the direction of the fireplace. The chimney must connect with that leading to the hearth below, I deduced.

"Well, Mrs. Jones," I heard him say. "What news have you of our drowned rat? Has she recovered her memory yet?"

"Hush, my lord—not so loud, for you know how sound carries in this house, and perhaps she's drowsing, for she was restless in the night."

"Her memory, woman!"

"Now don't you 'woman' me, Master Lucian! No, sir, I fear she can't recall her name."

He muttered something, and she reproved him sternly.

"Very well, Mrs. Jones. What's your opinion, then? Do you think she's Mary Ramsey—or Mrs. Marten?"

"Well, 'tis hard to say, of course. She seems a lady, sir—but then Master Gerry would not care a fig for that. Liveliness was what attracted him—ay, and a pretty face."

"One could not call either of those poor creatures pretty—or lively."

"Now, my lord, that's not very nice, when one is dead and both were terribly cut about. I dare say when Miss upstairs is herself again, she'll be quite a beauty, with those great eyes."

"Come, Nanny, all your geese are swans, as I remember. Besides, whether she is or not has nothing to do with it, for if Gervais knew that he was dying, he would have allied himself to the first little nobody who came to hand, whether pretty or no, only to disoblige me."

"Now, my lord, why should he do that?"

"So that Aunt Gwynneth's fortune would go to his widow and not to me—for he never cared a rap for the estate, and a good deal for spiting me."

"Pray hush, my lord!"

"Why, I only speak the truth, as you know well."

"No one knows the truth, my lord."

"Oh, in this affair—! No, indeed. But I shall find it out, never fear. I mean to discover exactly what happened after Gervais left for England, if it takes me the rest of my life to piece it together. Why, I swear that if it were not for Mother, I would ride off tonight to—to wherever it was—"

"Upper Buzzard, in Northamptonshire," Mrs. Jones reminded him placidly. "I have relatives not far from there. I think I will write a letter to my niece, and see if she has anything to tell us. How is her ladyship, sir? She took the news hard, of course?"

"Yes. It cut her deep, woman of courage though she is—"

"She is that, sir, and has had much to bear. The loss of your little brothers and sisters alone, to say nothing of his late lordship . . . and of course your aunts would not have made it easier for her."

"No," he said grimly. "It was an afternoon I would not

care to repeat. Yet somehow, Nan, I believe my mother was not utterly surprised. It was—almost as if she had somehow expected Gerry to come to a bad end."

"We do not know what end he came to, sir."

"True—though he was reckless enough for anything. Has that fellow arrived here yet? The uncle—Thomas—that Ivor went to fetch?"

"No, my lord, not yet. 'Tis many miles to Holyhead, and much of it an ill road, as you know."

"Ay. And somehow I've a notion he will claim the corpse. It would be too much to hope that Gerry's widow died so conveniently."

"Conveniently, sir?"

"Don't look so shocked, Mrs. Jones. What do we Martens want with Gerry's widow hanging about our necks for years to come?"

"It would be . . . awkward, I suppose. And then there is the fortune, as you said," she added, sighing.

"Yes, indeed. You see, Nan, there seems a good chance that it will devolve on me if Gerry's wife is dead—assuming that she made no will. That money would be useful, Nanny. Very useful, I must own. And then, there is another notion that occurred to me. It is only a conjecture, but one that kept me wakeful half the night. I was thinking of it when I asked your opinion of your patient. But now I'll put it more directly. Do you think it possible she could be shamming?"

"Oh, sir, whatever made you think of that?"

"Why, I saw her eyes open once or twice while we were talking and I could swear she understood us, though she feigned unconsciousness. It struck me that when she learned of the confusion, she saw a chance to profit by it."

"I—I don't follow you, my lord."

I could hear Lord Castelmarten begin to pace the flagstones of the hall below. My heart beat fast, but not so loudly as to drown his words.

"I may be wrong," he was saying, "but let us suppose that she is the girl from Lichfield, Nan, and not Gerry's wife. Let us assume she made up her mind to pretend to be his widow, knowing that none of us had ever seen her. All she would have to do would be to feign losing her memory for a while. Then, when she had learned a little about Gerry she could seem to recover a trifle, just enough to 'remember' that they had been married. If we had no proof to the contrary, we would be obliged to accept her as a member of the family and she—why, she would have gained an honourable name and a comfortable position for her lifetime."

"Welladay!" cried Mrs. Jones. "What a wicked thing to think of!"

"It is a wicked world, Nan. Even if this girl knew nothing about the fortune Gerry was soon to inherit, she would have guessed that an earl's brother would not be precisely a pauper."

"Well! I'm sure I don't know what to say—but that I can't believe that poor young lady upstairs could think up a plot like that, so weak as she is."

"She isn't put to the trouble of thinking of it, Nan. All she has to do is to keep quiet and let events carry her along..."

At this point I was overtaken by a fit of weeping. I was wiping tears of rage and weakness from my eyes when Lord Castelmarten flung open the door of my chamber.

"Good day, Mrs. Marten," he said, with a sardonic look.

How I hated him! "I have no name," I muttered, and blew my nose.

"Oh, that will never do," he said lightly. "We shall have to give you one." He turned to Mrs. Jones, hovering rather anxiously at his elbow. "What shall we call this young person, Nan? Ophelia? Mary? Moll?"

He turned suddenly. He was trying to catch me out, I realized. Moll, of course, was a contraction of Mary ...Mary Ramsey.

"Becky?" he went on. "Vicky? You look wistful," he said angrily. "Shall we call you Niobe? Or Persephone, torn between two worlds?"

"She looks a little like Rosie, to me," remarked Mrs. Jones.

"Rosie?" repeated Lord Castelmarten blankly.

"Ay. My niece, Rose. There's a nice easy name, just to call her for convenience, until she finds her own."

"Rose," the earl mused. "A white rose, then—or perhaps the faintest palest pink. A wild rose, neither Lancaster nor York. Yes, perhaps Rose will do."

Mrs. Jones came to my side. "What do you think, miss? It is for you to choose just for the time being, you know."

I looked at her with gratitude. "I like it," I said. "It is strange . . . I find I know quite well that roses are my favourite flower."

"That's settled, then. Now just let me dry your face . . . there, that's better. And let me brush your hair again, for you've disordered it."

"One moment, Mrs. Jones," said the earl, approaching me. "There is another task, of far greater importance, that must be seen to without delay."

He reached into his waistcoat pocket with two fingers and withdrew a ring—his brother's ring, I supposed. He picked up my left hand and pushed the signet onto my wedding finger, where it hung loosely.

That is the proof, I thought. The proof that I am not Mrs. Marten . . . but the earl merely lifted my hand and stared at it, his thick dark eyebrows almost meeting on the high bridge of his autocratic nose.

"It's a deal too large," he muttered. "That is why it came off in the river, I dare say."

"It does not fit her, sir," Mrs. Jones declared bluntly.

He shook his head. "It is as my brother wore it, Nan. I tried it on the corpse last night. It was hard to tell for the fingers were so swollen, but I fancy it would have been too large for her also. If it *had* fitted this young lady, then perhaps . . ."

He broke off. I was looking at the ring, wondering if I had ever set eyes on it before. It was heavy, a valuable piece, richly chased. I peered inside it for an inscription, but there was none. It was worn smooth and looked very old, for even the crest on the outside was worn down, obscuring the details of the device: a dragon, I thought, and a tall flower, a lily, perhaps. It was with reluctance that I returned it to Lord Castelmarten. It would have been comforting, I thought, to have had something of my very own . . . but the ring was a family heirloom, of course; and I was not yet proven a member of that family, nor was I sure I wished to be.

"Hark!" Mrs. Jones exclaimed. She hurried to the window. "It is young Ivor at last, my lord, and he has a fellow with him."

"Mr. Thomas, for a certainty." The earl turned to me. "Well, Miss Rose, this may be your long-awaited uncle. Only a few moments now, and we'll see whether he lays claim to you or no."

Mrs. Jones sat me up a little on the pillows, and tidied my hair. I waited with a sense of expectancy approaching pain as the sound of footsteps drew nearer, first across the hall, then mounting the stairs.

The door was flung open. The host of the inn stood there, round and smiling.

"Nan!" he cried excitedly, and then, observing Lord Castelmarten, "Beg pardon for interrupting you, my lord—I did not know you was here. But Mr. Thomas is come, look you, and wonderfully impatient he is to see the young lady here!"

"Show him in," said his lordship tersely.

A thin grey-faced little man was pushed across the threshold. He stood a moment, swaying with exhaustion. Mr. Jones gave him a nudge and he approached the bed, peering at me from red-rimmed eyes.

Suddenly he held out his arms.

"Mary!" he cried. "Our little Mary, after all these years!"

Chapter Three

I shrank away from Mr. Thomas, and was conscious of a childish desire to bury myself beneath the bedclothes.

Mrs. Jones put out her hand to prevent Mr. Thomas from embracing me.

"Excuse me, sir, but the young lady is hurt."

He hesitated, rocking on his toes. "Mary, Mary—!" He shrugged his outstretched arms, and dropped them by his sides. "But you don't remember me, of course."

"No," I said weakly. "I am sorry, sir, but I don't remember you."

"She has lost her memory," said Lord Castelmarten bluntly. "But you remember her, it seems. You have no doubt in your mind that this is your niece, Mary Ramsey?"

Mr. Thomas turned to stare at him. "But—the groom—Ivor Griffiths, is it? He told me this was the young woman who was in the accident. The accident to the coach from Llangollen, that is. So it must be Mary, then. Of course, I have not seen the child since she was five or six, and she is a grown woman now—twenty, I suppose, or twenty-one. Lost her memory, has she?" He sent me a bewildered look. "But who else could she be? She has brown hair, just like poor Tom—her father, sir, and my brother—only it was paler then, when she was little. And her eyes were of a brownish colour, as I recall..."

"You are not absolutely certain, then?" demanded Lord Castelmarten. "Not positive? Did your niece have any identifying marks?"

Mr. Thomas slowly shook his head. He seemed to have shrunk since entering the room, and he was not large then. "None that I remember." He stared about him in perplexity. His narrow dark eyes lighted at the sight of the veiled bonnet and black shawl which still lay across the chair where Mrs. Jones had cast them.

"Do those belong to her?" he cried. "Well, there you are, then. That settles it for certain. My niece was in mourning, look you—mourning for her foster-father Cliffe—"

"There were two young women on that coach," explained the earl with ill-concealed impatience. "Both had reason to be in mourning. The other girl was killed in the accident, and this one has lost her memory. We hoped you would be able to make a positive identification; for we are at a standstill."

"Well, well! Young Griffiths did not tell me that—only that it was a bad accident, and several lives were lost. There is a tragedy then . . . another young lady! What did she look like, may I ask?"

"You may see her for yourself presently," Lord Castelmarten promised, coldly. "Her body is here in the inn, with the others, pending the inquest. You will see that her hair, too, was brown, and her eyes darkish in shade. The combination is not unusual. Come, Mr. Thomas, search your memory, and then look closely at this young woman. Perhaps something will strike you—some resemblance that could help you to determine if this is in truth your niece."

Mr. Thomas licked his lips. He peered at me again, more nervously now that there was a chance of my being a stranger, after all.

"Well . . . she could be Mary, I believe," he murmured. "There is no great look of Elizabeth, mind you—her mother, that is. And I could not say that she favours Tom, except in the matter of her colouring. But it might be that she takes after the Ramseys, her mother's family. I never set eyes on any of them," he added with a certain emphasis.

"Her father was your brother, you say?" queried Mrs. Jones. "His name was Thomas?"

"Ay, Tom Thomas . . . But he's long dead now, poor fellow."

"Yet your niece's name is Ramsey?"

31

He turned to Mrs. Jones, and I could see him relax a little under her gentle gaze.

"They were not married, you see. Our Tom worked for Squire Ramsey... as soon as they found their daughter was with child, they disowned her. Proud people, the squire and his lady. And Tom was turned out without a reference—he was only an under-footman there, you understand. But the worst of it was, they would not even give Elizabeth permission to marry—she was under age, of course."

Mrs. Jones hissed in her breath indignantly. Mr. Thomas nodded.

"Ay, it was very wrong of them. Not Christian, at all. Heaven only knows what they expected to become of her. What happened was, poor Tom brought her to us, naturally. Times were hard, so he went to sea, and soon enough he was washed overboard and lost, poor fellow. Elizabeth and the child stayed with us some years, and then—"

"And then?" prompted Mrs. Jones, as he paused unhappily.

"Why then—they had to leave. There was no room for them, you understand. We had six children of our own by that time—it was before the cholera."

"So you turned them out," said Mrs. Jones sternly. "What became of them after that?"

"Why, Elizabeth wrote to us a few years later, to say that she had found work in Lichfield with the Cliffes and that she had been able to keep the child—Mary—with her. She was not well, she said, but her master had promised he would be a foster-father to Mary if—well, if the occasion arose."

"You were quite satisfied, I see," said Mrs. Jones. "What happened next? For Mary wrote to you, I know."

He looked startled. "You know? Oh yes, the fellow told me they found my letter in her reticule. Well, yes, Mary wrote to us from time to time, after her mother died. She told us she had taken on her mother's work. She was always wanting to leave the Cliffes and come to us, though we could do nothing for her then—but matters are different now, and I was able to offer her a home at last."

"One moment," said Lord Castelmarten, who had been staring at me while I listened blankly to all this. "She seems fully conscious now. It is possible that something you have said may have touched off her memory." He leaned over me. "Come, ma'am. Can you remember nothing from your past? The least thing may mean something to Mr. Thomas here."

I closed my eyes, and he reached for my shoulder and shook it slightly.

"You must help us, ma'am. Anything—anything at all!"

"It is as if my mind were dark whirling layers," I said reluctantly, "... stabbed with flashes of light—but I don't want to look into them—"

"Try!"

"There is a dusty place. And an old man's hand, groping..." I began to cry. "There is a b-basket of-of blackberries spilled on the g-grass..."

"Hush, child," said Mrs. Jones. "His lordship does not mean to harry you. For shame, sir. You can see how weak she is, how this distresses her!"

"It is important, ma'am!"

"She never will remember, if you harass her so."

"Oh, very well." He turned back to Mr. Thomas. "What sort of people were these foster-parents, do you know?"

"Working people, sir. Ragpickers by trade."

"Ragpickers!" Lord Castelmarten appeared to be almost as startled by this as I felt. He glanced at me. "That alters the matter, for this young woman is plainly an educated person."

"Oh, Mary knows her letters, sir. Elizabeth was brought up in a fine house, with a governess and tutors. She taught her daughter to read and write, and French, and—all manner of things. Tom was only the footman, look you, but Elizabeth was a lady born."

Lord Castelmarten frowned. "I see."

"Yes, sir, Mary could write a pretty hand. She didn't know us—could not remember us, but her mother had taught her that we were her only family and she wrote to us, as I told you, sir, from time to time—not often, for she had to work long hours. Mother Cliffe is a rough woman and beat her apprentices. One died—but it was hushed up somehow. But the work, Mary told us, was not heavy."

He gave me a sly apologetic smile and picked up my left hand.

"See, sir, the skin is smooth enough. Rag sorting would not spoil her hands, though she hated the work and was afraid of Mother Cliffe. She had an affection for Mr. Cliffe, who protected her, she said. But when he died she wrote again to ask if we would shelter her. She promised she would do anything for us..."

"And you accepted her offer?" said Mrs. Jones. "You told her you would welcome her?"

"Oh yes, indeed. We had not thought it would be possible, bound as she was to Mother Cliffe, but when she said she would run away to be with us—well, there's grateful we were, and that's the truth. My wife has the arthritis cruelly now, and not a child left to help her with the work. We have had to take in lodgers, and there's a deal to do, with all the cooking and the washing...Mrs. Thomas has the girl's duties all planned out. I hardly know how I can face her if I don't come home with Mary!"

He bent over me, his thin nose twitching. "Mary!" he hissed. "Don't you remember your Auntie Blod? She has your room all ready for you—a home waiting for you!" He added a few words in Welsh, and sighed when I shook my head. "No, they wouldn't be speaking Welsh in Lichfield, I suppose, and Elizabeth never had more than a few words of it."

"One moment," cried Mrs. Jones excitedly. "You say she wrote to you—would you recognize her hand, if you should see it?"

"Ay, that I would—"

"I spoke to the doctor on that head," said Lord Castelmarten flatly. "Her right hand is injured...Dr. Glynn says it will be many days before she can pen a normal script. I think no further purpose can be served up here just now, Mr. Thomas. I propose to take you down to view the body. Perhaps you will recognize it." He felt in his pocket. "And I will take the opportunity to try my brother's ring on the corpse again—the fingers may be less swollen now . . ."

"A ring?" said Mr. Thomas. He shook his head. "Well, if that fits one of them, it will prove something—for Mary had no ring, that I can promise you. If one of them had a ring, it was not Mary. She had nothing of value to call her own, I am quite sure of that. I had to send her some money for her fare—and great trouble I had to do it." His mouth turned down as he reflected, no doubt, upon the possibility that his pains might have been wasted after all.

"But your brother's ring?" he queried suddenly. "May I ask, sir, what your brother has to do with this?"

Lord Castelmarten looked as if he might refuse to answer; but Mr. Jones laid a hand on Mr. Thomas's arm and murmured a few words in his ear. They ha⌐ a profound effect upon Mr. Thomas.

"I beg pardon, sir—my lord! I did not realize your lordship *was* a lordship! Did not understand your lordship was so intimately concerned! No wonder that you do not want me to claim this young lady as my niece—you wish to prove her to be your brother's widow!"

"Not at all," said Lord Castelmarten curtly. "I am as anxious as your are to disprove it!"

I lay there after they had gone, trying to calm my agitated mind in order to review the facts that had been made known to me. Someone had taught me thus to order my thoughts, I knew, but I put that reflection aside for the time being.

What, then, were the facts I had learned about myself?

First that I had been travelling on the common stagecoach from some place that sounded like a person clearing his throat. Llangollen. I had been travelling alone, but presumably somebody knew that I had left; and surely someone must be awaiting my arrival somewhere? I had only to be patient, I told myself, and the mystery would eventually be resolved.

But it had already gone some way to resolving itself, I recalled. I must be one of only two people out of the millions in the world—and the other one was dead. Either

35

I was Mary Ramsey, escaped from Mother Cliffe and on her way to Aunt and Uncle Thomas; or I was the Honourable Mrs. Gervais Marten, journeying to the home of her late husband in the hope of being received by Lady Castelmarten as her unknown, unexpected, and apparently unwelcome daughter-in-law.

The one outlook struck me as extraordinarily depressing; the other as embarrassing in the extreme. And even more confusing was my mounting conviction that I had nothing whatsoever to do with either of the identities so arbitrarily assigned to me.

Mrs. Jones was the first of the party to return. She looked pale, but gave me a reassuring smile.

Mr. Thomas was behind her, mopping at his forehead. "A terrible experience... terrible!" he panted.

"Your own?" asked Lord Castelmarten unsympathetically, appearing in the doorway, "or that unfortunate's?"

"Terrible!" Mr. Thomas repeated, unheedingly. He stood at the foot of my bed, but did not meet my eyes.

"Of course, no one could expect me to swear to Mary after all these years," he said rapidly, "but it seems to me, all things considered, this one is the more likely to be Tom's daughter, of the two."

"And it seems to me," said Lord Castelmarten coldly, "that you are at all costs concerned to provide a slave for your wife, no matter whom."

"But I thought, my lord—and beg pardon for mentioning it—that your lordship was most eager to have the matter settled, and the girl identified? Surely the best solution for us all would be for me to take this one—Mary—as soon as she is well enough to move?"

"Only a positive identification will satisfy me," declared Lord Castelmarten stubbornly. "What if you do take her, and she turns out to be my brother's widow after all? I have no mind to be obliged to explain to Mrs. Marten, if it is she, how it was I allowed her to be claimed by you and used as a domestic drudge. I have no faith in your affirmation that this young woman is your niece. She may be, or again, she may not be—and it seems apparent to me

36

that you could as easily have persuaded yourself that the poor corpse downstairs was Mary Ramsey, had it profited you anything. No, sir, the matter must now rest until further proof is forthcoming. I shall dictate some enquiries to my secretary this afternoon and send them by express to both Lichfield and—where was it?—Dunstable."

"Not Lichfield, my lord, I beg you," Mr. Thomas cried. "It may be that Mother Cliffe could have the law on us for enticing away one of her apprentices! Let me beg you, sir, to begin your enquiries at Dunstable."

"Very well," said the earl after a moment's reflection. "It is with Dunstable that I am most concerned, after all. I shall send my letter to the Sugar Loaf tonight."

"Very good, my lord," said Mr. Thomas humbly, "but may I ask what your lordship is hoping to accomplish by such a letter?"

"Why, I will send it by a messenger who will find out a description of the young lady who took a seat upon the heavy coach to Birmingham from there. He will, I trust, be able to discover which house she lived in and who her people are. Thus we may hope to arrive at some relative who will have sufficient interest in her to come to Wales to make the identification."

"It will have to be a very particular messenger," said Mrs. Jones. "Tactful and—well, my lord, I have suggested asking my own family in those parts to make enquiry for you, but it does seem best to send someone who has already seen this young lady. There may be a portrait there, which would prove the matter at once—"

"Nan," exclaimed Lord Castelmarten, "you are quite right! It is not a matter for a messenger. I will go myself, just as soon as I can be spared." He turned back to Mr. Thomas. "That will not be for a day or two, and naturally several more must pass before I return with any news; so you had best go back to Anglesey, and leave your address with us. You may present my condolences to your wife and inform her that in a few weeks she may hear more of this business. She need not give up hope just yet of having her niece eventually restored to her, I think," he added, with one of his sardonic glances in my direction.

"Very well, my lord." But Mr. Thomas appeared to be reluctant to depart. I wondered if he feared his wife unduly, but then, after shuffling from one foot to the other, he finally gathered up his courage to enquire of Mrs. Jones if I had run up a great bill during my enforced stay at the Castell Marten Arms.

"I mean," he said apologetically, "if she has to be kept here very long, and so long as there is a possibility that I might have to foot the bill, I wonder whether some arrangement could be made to find another place to lodge her? This room is overlarge for one person," he suggested. "And the weather is not so very cold at this time of year—she does not absolutely require a fireplace in her chamber, for example, nor a featherbed—"

"I have booked the room for the young person so long as she shall need it," declared Lord Castelmarten impatiently. "Be at ease, man. I swear you will not be presented with the bill, whether she be your niece or no."

Mr. Thomas murmured that he was vastly obliged. He took a last despairing look at me, as if hoping even now that I might sit up and declare myself to be Mary Ramsey. When I did not do so, he shook his head, and left.

Mrs. Jones sighed with relief. She smiled at Lord Castelmarten. "Oh, I am so glad you did not let him take her," she said impetuously. "I am sure she could not be Mary Ramsey—and even if she were, I should not like to think of her going to such a place as that!"

"Don't allow yourself to become too fond of this young woman, Mrs. Jones," the earl advised her. "Remember that she may very well end by going to Mr. Thomas, after all."

But even Lord Castelmarten could not dampen my sense of reprieve, which no doubt contributed, together with the herb pillow, to the excellent sleep I enjoyed that night.

The next morning I awoke feeling much improved; and Mrs. Jones remarked upon the change in me.

I smiled at her as I sat up in bed. "Yes, I feel much more like myself—" But how did I know that, I wondered, when

38

I did not know who I was?

But I turned my thoughts away from that question and looked with the first consciousness of pleasure at my surroundings. Bronwen was just drawing back the curtains and spring sunshine slanted into the room, making a vase of yellow daffodils seem to glow against the dark oak panelling. There was a cheerful fire crackling in the hearth, a white sheepskin rug before it, bright brass winking everywhere.

Bronwen made some remark in Welsh, drawing my attention to the window, which was paned in thick glass and framed an extraordinary view of high grassy moors sprinkled with massive boulders, and a great mountain beyond, iced with the sharp white of untrodden snow.

I felt my mouth actually drop open with astonishment. I would never have believed a mountain could rise so high into the sky. I knew with every fiber of my being that I had never seen such a sight before. How was it that I had not noticed it earlier? For now I knew that it was there, it dominated the room. And it was not just one mountain, I now realized, but a whole range of them gleaming in the sun, blue in the shadows, peak upon ragged peak. And then the air misted and thickened, the sunlight paled, and one by one the mountains disappeared as if I had dreamed them.

"Ay," said Mrs. Jones, who must have been watching me, "clear skies don't last long in these parts, alas. The clouds will come down now, and by noon we will have a downpour."

She was right, for when Dr. Glynn visited me, he was shaking the rain from his greatcoat as he entered; and Mrs. Jones set it to steam by the fire.

"You look a great deal better," the doctor declared, rubbing his hands. "My friend will be glad to hear of it. She is taking a particular interest in your case."

He examined me, and told me he believed it would not hurt me to move to the castle on the morrow. I saw the relief in Mrs. Jones's face, and checked the protest I had been about to make. No doubt she was a busy woman and

I was taking up most of her time. Besides this room must be the best they had and so long as I was in it, it could not be let.

"What shall I wear when I get up?" I asked Mrs. Jones, when Dr. Glynn had gone.

"There's not a deal of choice," she told me. "The gown you travelled in is spoiled beyond repair. There are some plain muslin gowns, a rag cloak—that would be Mary Ramsey's, I suppose. Two pairs of boots, as I recall, and some more elegant in kid. A few gloves, a knitted shawl, several nightgowns, and two stuff mourning gowns. You can tell they belonged to persons in different stations of life—the bonnets especially show it—but both lots of clothes are patched and mended. Would you like to try on the boots? If one pair is more comfortable than the others, that might tell us something."

But the boots, like everything else, were inconclusive. The kid half boots were certainly the most comfortable but that may have been because they were made of fine soft leather, and the others were thick and heavy. The rougher boots were a little large for me, but then they were probably intended to be worn with thick woollen stockings.

"You had better take the lot," said Mrs. Jones. "Dear knows, the other poor young woman won't be needing them. They are holding the inquest today, by the way."

I was alarmed by the thought of giving evidence, but I need not have worried. Sir Caerleon ap Owen would not hear of my attending the Coroner's Court below, but came to my bedside to take my statement himself. He was a portly man with a red-tipped nose, surprised-looking eyebrows, and a somewhat abrupt manner. He very soon assured me bluntly that my evidence was useless.

"But if your memory should return, madam, I shall expect you to notify me of it."

"Certainly, sir. I shall be glad to do so."

He looked sharply at me. "You do not mean to leave the district for the present?"

"No, sir. I have been invited to the castle . . . for the time being."

I must have sounded rather forlorn, for he smiled kindly then.

"Of course. I am sure Lady Castelmarten will welcome you as a daughter. Well, well. I must not tarry. They are waiting for me below. Poor Jones is anxious for the burial, as one may imagine. It is a bad corner there by the *pistyll*, and I will direct the parish to put up a fence. Good-bye, Miss—er—Mrs.—"

"Good-bye, sir," I said quickly, to spare him.

Mrs. Jones went with Sir Caerleon to show him out, and a moment later, Bronwen slipped into the room. She approached the bed with a nervous smile.

"What is it, Bronwen?" I asked, though I knew she had no English.

She giggled a little, and brought out a folded paper from the old-fashioned pocket, hanging under her apron.

I stared at it suspiciously.

"Is that for me?"

She pointed at me, and giggled again. Then, dropping the note upon the coverlet, she fled.

I picked it up. For no known reason, I found I was afraid to open it. My hands were shaking.

With an exclamation of impatience at my folly, I controlled them, and unfolded the message.

It was brief and to the point. It merely said, in printed letters, "DANGER! LEAVE WALES."

Chapter Four

I was alone for much of the afternoon and had a great deal of time to wonder whether I should tell Mrs. Jones about the note. In a world where I found myself with so few landmarks, Mrs. Jones seemed almost in the position of a mother to me and I was anxious to have no secrets from her. But I could not help reflecting that my confidence would probably distress her, and that she would be unlikely to throw any light upon the provenance of the note. On the other hand, she might be able to do so. My head ached with indecision. I was glad when Mrs. Jones bustled into the room at last, though I had still come to no conclusion.

"The jury has reached a verdict," she announced. "Misadventure . . . no blame attaching to the coachman. It was lucky for him he only had one ale at the last change—or lucky for his widow and his reputation, rather. Now those poor corpses can be buried—not that it has affected trade, I must admit. But the thought of them out there in the cold room, well, it wasn't nice, was it? And they are going to put a railing round the corner where it happened. Lord Castelmarten said he'd pay for it, which I thought handsome in him with all the demands there are upon his purse. You haven't met the Miss Dyffryns, yet, of course—his lordship's aunts."

I found myself relieved to be distracted from my dilemma, and asked her to tell me in more detail about the family with whom I was so soon to make my home.

She sank into the easy chair, and picked up her knitting. "My lady's family moved in with her, more or less, when she married Castelmarten . . . let me see, about thirty years ago. There was her old father, and the four sisters, but the eldest Miss Dyffryn died a few years since..."

"Has the present Lord Castelmarten any other brothers or sisters, apart from Mr. Gervais?"

"Alas, no. Her ladyship had but the two sons when I came first to Wales. There were others born, both before and after, but it was only those two which survived. Ay, there was only a year between them, and they were very much alike—to look upon, that is, but not in character. Oh dear me, no. Master Gervais had all the charm—charm you into anything, he could, if you didn't keep a careful watch upon yourself. 'Tis hard not to spoil a child like that. And the tricks he'd play, he and Master Edward...now, there's another will take it hard, the news of Gerry's death."

"Master Edward?" I repeated. "Who is he?"

"The Vicar's son, young Edward Vaughan. The two families were very close. My husband's sister, Sionedd, she was nurse to the young Vaughans, to Master Edward and Miss Sarah, and she often brought them up to our nursery in the castle, in the old days. Master Edward was naughty, too—a mischievous young gentleman, always playing pranks, he was very like Master Gervais in that." Mrs. Jones heaved a sigh. "There was a quarrel, last winter, at the Vicarage. Ay, Master Edward quarrelled with his parents—with that mother of his, rather, for she protected him at every turn when he wanted to be out enjoying life—and I wasn't surprised, after the first shock, when I heard that he had run away to be an actor. He never wrote, not that I've heard. Miss Sarah must have suffered dreadfully pining for him, before she turned to Master Gerry, in her brother's place. I used to wonder if they'd end by marrying—not that Master Lucian would have countenanced it, I dare say, for a Vaughan would have been no match for a Marten, and besides—"

"Besides what, Mrs. Jones?" I prompted, as she hesitated.

She shook her head. "'Tis only that his lordship seemed to take against her, somehow—though she's a pretty young lady and very nicely mannered. Well I do hope that the news of Master Gerry's death was gently broken to Miss

43

Sarah, for she'll be sadly grieved, I fear."

And she would be jealous of me, doubtless, this unknown Miss Vaughan, I warned myself. Could it have been she who had sent me the note, hoping to drive me far from Wales?

"'Tis hard on all of us, come to that," continued Mrs. Jones. "Master Gervais getting married—and then dying—and not a one of us knowing the least hint about it. You would think his own brother would have been informed."

I remembered the reticule with the papers in it. "It seems likely that his widow was travelling here for the very purpose of informing the family," I suggested.

"Oh! Ay, that would be the way of it, no doubt. But you'd think she might have written first—discovered how they felt and if they would receive her, before she ventured so far from home."

"Perhaps she had nowhere else to go, poor thing. And surely she could count on their welcoming her in such circumstances."

Mrs. Jones looked at me curiously, and I realized how objectively I had spoken.

"I don't feel as if I were she," I owned. "Nor as if I were Mary Ramsey, for that matter."

"No, my dear. But for Lady Castelmarten's sake—"

"Oh no—you cannot expect me to act a part! Besides, if I did, and then a different truth came out, how terrible it would be!"

"Yes, you are right, I dare say."

"How bewildered she must have been," I mused, my thoughts reverting to Victoria Merridew. "Married and widowed immediately after. One could not expect her to have been thinking very clearly when she set out on her journey."

Mrs. Jones shifted on her chair. "What bothers me is, what was Master Gerry doing in Dunstable? For he has no connections there, that I've ever heard of—and I surely would have known. London was his destination. He set out for London a few weeks back, just as soon as the road was open, but we never heard that he arrived. Of course the posts in these parts come when they please, and that's not very often. They are reliable enough as far as Shrewsbury, or Llangollen, but after that the service is quite unpredictable, for there are weeks at a time when the stagecoach does not run—often the mails have to wait for a chance traveller to take them, and a bag may have been lost. Perhaps it's not so strange that we did not hear from him . . . but I'd give a deal to know where he spent those weeks. Of course," she mused, "the Vaughans have family in those parts: the Morton-Johnses, where I used to work long ago. Miss Sarah has only just returned from visiting her Cousin Lucy . . . but she surely would have mentioned it if she had met Master Gervais there."

"Perhaps she has mentioned it," I suggested.

"Ay, she may have done. But she could have known nothing of any marriage of his, or illness, or surely it would have been all over the *cantref* by now."

"Mr. Marten did have that connection with Dunstable, however," I said. "I suppose it must be possible that he visited his great friend's cousins there, for news of Mr. Vaughan, perhaps? Why," I exclaimed, "they may even have introduced him to—to the girl he married!"

Mrs. Jones shook her head. "Miss Sarah would have told me," she insisted. "She always liked to show me that she knew Master Gerry better than any of us . . . but it does seem strange that she should have been visiting there just now, after years when the families did not meet."

Our conversation was interrupted then by Megan summoning her mistress to the kitchen. When Mrs. Jones had left the room, I pushed back the bedclothes and swung my legs out of bed.

I felt very shaky when I stood, and soon found that my bandaged ankle would not bear my weight. But I was curious to see those papers that Mrs. Marten had travelled so far to bring to her husband's family, and forced myself to hop and hobble to the cupboard where Bronwen had put away the reticule.

I found it easily enough, on the topmost shelf. It was not elegant, appearing to have been homemade of some bulky grey stuff, but it was strong, and suitable for travelling. I pulled open the drawstring, and examined the contents.

First there was a handkerchief, embellished with drawnthread work, quite neatly done. Next came a worn purse containing four golden guineas and a few groats, and a tiny sachet of lavender seeds emitting a faint nostalgic scent. Pushed against the side of the bag were two roughly folded papers stained in the same way with brown faded marks in one corner.

I opened them out and found, not a death certificate as I had somehow expected, but a certificate of burial, in the Parish of St. Michael's, Upper Buzzard. I ran my eye over the text, written in cramped copperplate. "The Hnble Gervais Wynn Ivan Williams Marten...age twenty-four...inflammation of the lungs...influenza..."

I thought I heard footsteps on the stair, and thrust the paper back into the bag. I glanced at the other, the marriage certificate. "Victoria Clarissa Merridew, spinster, of this parish..." there was no time to read further, and I thrust it also deep into the reticule.

But then I paused. There was something hard at the bottom of the bag—something almost in the shape of a figure 3, about four inches across, sewn into the lining.

I heard Mrs. Jones call out to someone in the corridor, and tossed the reticule back on the shelf. I was hobbling across the room, when Mrs. Jones opened the door.

I stood still, transfixed by guilt.

"My dear child!" she exclaimed. "What in the world are you about?"

I opened my mouth, but could think of no good answer. Then I saw that she was no longer looking at me.

"And what's this?" she said. "Receiving letters, are you? And may I enquire—from whom?"

She passed me and bent to pick up the note Bronwen had brought me, which I had hidden beneath my pillow. It must have dropped out onto the floor when I got out of bed.

Mrs. Jones was looking at me with enquiry. It did not take a great deal to arouse her suspicions of me, I realized. She had championed me against Lord Castelmarten, but

46

after all, her first loyalty would be to him. He had poisoned her mind against me . . . and I found I could not bear the loss of her regard.

"I don't know who it is from," I cried, dropping down upon the bed. "I wish you could tell me! Read it, I pray you. Bronwen brought it in to me . . . I have been trying to find the courage to show it to you."

Frowning, she unfolded it.

"Well! And who would send you such a note as this?" She too sat down, and raised her piercing eyes to mine.

I shook my head. "How should I know? I know nothing—remember nothing! But you can ask Bronwen, if you speak Welsh."

"Ay, that I will."

Mrs. Jones went to the bell, and pulled it. "Bronwen brought it up, you say? What time was that?"

I was glad to get back between the sheets and tell Mrs. Jones what little I knew. When I had finished, she fell silent until Bronwen appeared.

Mrs. Jones summoned up her Welsh and asked some incomprehensible questions. Bronwen giggled, and twisted her red hands in her apron. Mrs. Jones seemed to repeat herself, and Bronwen replied. Soon Mrs. Jones dismissed her, and turned back to me.

"It seems that the tapster gave the note to her—he found it on the mantelshelf in the public room, with the direction upon it as you see, written in Welsh—'To the English young lady upstairs.' Now, I wonder who could be responsible for that?"

"The question is," I said slowly, "whether you think I should pay heed to it, or not?"

"Ah," said Mrs. Jones, with a puzzled look. "That is a question, indeed it is. But even if it is not some prank, you should be safe enough at the castle. And at least you are warned. You will take care?"

I gave a shaky smile. "I shall try." But how much care could I take of myself, in an unknown castle, in the company of several strangers, one of whom at least I knew to be bitterly antagonistic to me?

47

On the other hand, I had nowhere else to turn . . . there was no alternative but to accept the reluctant hospitality of the Martens, and see what transpired.

The next day Mrs. Jones assisted me to dress in well-patched stockings, bodice, petticoat, and the finest of the mourning gowns. It was unpleasant feeling that I might be wearing a stranger's clothes; but at least Mrs. Jones no longer seemed to suspect me of deliberate imposture. I valued her good opinion of me, I realized; indeed, it was not too much to say that she was the only friend I had in the world at present, and I told her so.

"Bless you, child," she cried, putting her arms about me. "You will soon be making friends enough, I trow. But perhaps you'll not forget Nanny Jones, and come to see me sometimes?"

"I will, I promise—why, this inn is the only home I can remember!"

"Fancy that! Well, you will know where to find us, if you need us."

Mrs. Jones gave me a kiss, and handed me my gloves and reticule. I fumbled in the purse and brought out one of the guineas, for her to distribute among the staff. She did not want to take it, but I prevailed on her to do so. Then she helped me begin to descend the stairs into the low-beamed hall with its great fireplace. Mr. Jones bustled in from the yard, his cheeks like two red apples from the sharp air. He announced that my bags had been put into the chaise and all was ready for my departure.

I held out my left hand, and thanked him for his hospitality. He blew his nose, shook my hand, patted me upon the shoulder, and led me to the waiting chaise. A smart postilion touched his tall white hat, and took up the reins. Mrs. Jones blew me a final kiss, the door closed behind me as I settled into my seat, and the horses leapt forward. The carriage swayed as the traces tautened, and then we were trotting up the muddy, stony track. A moment later the road sounded hollow under the horses' hoofs, and I glanced out of the window, to flinch at the swirling confusion of the swollen Afon Ystwyth below, as we crossed the ancient bridge.

48

The journey was not long, but I found it tiring. I stared with little interest at the red and grey stone village of Castel Marten, situated on a spur of green hillside within a loop of the same winding river. A little higher up stood a church, opposite a gloomy looking Vicarage, while above all the red half-ruined castle sprawled over the summit of the hill.

The post chaise rattled over a bridge and under a mighty arch in the castle wall, to halt in a wide cobbled yard.

Instantly there was a confusion of grooms and stablelads—far more than were needed to attend to one carriage. They were curious to see me, I supposed; and who could blame them? But I was relieved to be rescued by the appearance of a sober individual, clad in black, who announced himself as Hughes, the steward. He helped me to alight, and bade me lean on him.

I was glad of his offer, though it was not far to the great front door, which looked as though it could withstand a dozen sieges. A liveried footman held it open. Within, a narrow hall led to a wider one, impressive with chequered marble floor, high beams, and a cavernous fireplace. A dark-haired woman, also black-clad, stepped forward and curtsied to me.

"This is Ysolt, ma'am," said the steward. "She will look after you—she speaks English."

I summoned a smile and a greeting for Ysolt. She had a still, smooth face; I could not hazard a guess as to her age, and her thoughts were just as hard to ascertain.

She inclined her head, but there was no way of knowing if my presence pleased or repelled her.

"I will take you to your chamber, ma'am," she said in a soft singing voice. "It is only on the first floor, just above us. I hope the stairs will not tire you overmuch."

My foot was aching badly, but between Ysolt and the banister I managed to climb the stairs with several pauses, during which I gazed wearily at the large tapestries and dark paintings that enlivened the stark white of the castle walls. When we reached the great gallery, a little spaniel ran forward, barking.

Ysolt held him away with her foot.

"Her ladyship's spaniel, miss. He doesn't care for strangers, isn't it, but he will get used to you."

"Oh, pray let him come to me—I like dogs."

I dropped to my knees and pressed my face against the spaniel's silky neck. My mind trembled on the edge of memory—then it was blank again.

"Ma'am," breathed Ysolt, a faint note of warning in her voice.

I looked up. Lord Castelmarten was striding down the gallery towards us. He looked overpowering in his dark mourning clothes, I thought: tall, ominous, and powerful.

He stopped before me, and held out his hand. Bemused, I put my left hand into it, glad that it was gloved. I had not been able to put on the other glove over the dressing on my right hand, but had decided to try for the best appearance possible—and now had my reward.

Lord Castelmarten pulled me to my feet.

"Welcome to my house," he said, his face as expressionless as that of the maidservant. "I see you have lost no time in making friends with my mother's dog."

Somehow, he made it sound like an accusation.

"I like dogs," I said again, defensively.

He raised an eyebrow. "You remember that?" Without pausing for my reply, he turned to Ysolt. "You had better show Miss Rose straight to her room, and let her rest a while. My mother wishes to see her at three o'clock." He snapped his fingers at the dog, which ran instantly to his side, and bowed slightly to me before striding away.

Ysolt supported me down a short passage that led off the gallery into a panelled chamber.

"Let me order you a cup of soup, mistress," she suggested, assisting me onto the ornately carved fourposter. "'Tis weak you are . . . weak as a new lamb. I'll just take off your boots, there, and pull the eiderdown over you."

A footman entered with my bags. Ysolt spoke to him in Welsh, and then began to unpack. I knew her face would not betray what she thought of the garments she was transferring so neatly to the clothes press, but still I preferred to disassociate myself from the proceedings, and looked instead with careful attention about the room.

I had a feeling I had never before lain in so grand a chamber. The walls were rough enough above the panelling, which only covered them to a height of five feet or so, huge blocks of stone mortared in place, and the ceiling was heavily beamed; but the barbaric effect was offset by mullioned windows framed in elegantly traced Gothic arches, and by the floor of polished oak, scattered with glowing eastern rugs. The windows, some way beyond the foot of my bed, faced east, so Ysolt told me when I enquired. They looked out across the valley to the rolling forested hills of the Welsh Marches.

"What is that door over there?" I asked, looking to the right-hand corner of the room.

"There's sharp eyes you have," murmured Ysolt. "'Tis carved with the panelling, so not many notice it."

"But where does it lead?"

"Only to an old stairway, no longer used. One of those spiral stairs, it is."

"And where—?"

"Why, mistress, it leads both up and down... down to the Banqueting Hall, and up to the old Chapel and the other rooms on the floor above. But now that..."

"Now that—what, Ysolt?"

Very faintly, she flushed. "Nowadays, since Mr. Gervais left, the upper floor is no longer used. Do you see the grandfather clock there? My grandfather made it."

"It is very beautifully made, and it is going, I see. But I did not hear it strike."

Ysolt shook her smooth dark head. "The chimes were removed from all the clocks at Castell Marten, after Pen Maen burned."

"Pen Maen?"

"That was my lady's home, before she married. The place burned down shortly after the wedding. Her mother died in the fire, and her father never recovered from it."

A knock on the door heralded the arrival of the soup. Ysolt helped me to sit up, and placed the tray across my knees.

"What do you think of the bed, mistress?" she enquired softly.

It was amazingly carved, every inch of it rich with

51

biblical scenes and symbols, the four posts representing Matthew, Mark, Luke, and John. It was a wonderful piece, and I told her so.

"The Welsh are fine carvers in wood—wood and stone..."

I took a sip of soup. It was excellent, thick and strong. A strident cry sounded harshly from below my window, startling me.

"One of my lord's peacocks," Ysolt explained, steadying the tray. "My Lord Dyffryn, that is to say."

"And who is Lord Dyffryn, pray?"

"Why, mistress, I was just speaking of him!" She shook her head in wonder at my ignorance. "He is my lady's father, and was Lord Dyffryn of Pen Maen. Now he is a hermit and lives alone in the ruined Keep—has done so ever since my lady married the late Lord Castelmarten. Quite a curiosity, is Lord Dyffryn. Learned gentlemen used to travel far to talk with him—gentlemen from England, and not only that, but from Russia, and from France..."

"They don't come any more?"

"The country is at war, mistress," she said in surprise. I was silent. "Every year, my lord sees fewer visitors," Ysolt went on. "Ofttimes, even when they come, he will not receive them. They see him, though," she added, with a trace of pride. "They wait for days, sometimes, only to catch a glimpse of his beard."

"His beard?"

"He has never cut it, mistress, since the fire... 'tis the wonder of the *cantref*."

"If... if I am Mrs. Marten," I said slowly, "then Lord Dyffryn must be my grandfather-in-law! How strange he sounds! Shall I ever meet him?"

"Who can say, mistress?"

"He does not eat with the family?"

"No, mistress, indeed. Twice a day one of the footmen rows over with some food for him, and he lets down a basket from the walls for it. Sometimes, when the fancy takes him, he does wander about the grounds here, talking to the birds—especially in the spring, when the peachicks hatch. But for the most part he stays hidden in the Keep. Master Gervais used to seek him out sometimes for a game of chess—and his lordship too, of course, though he had less time to spare."

I recalled the glimpse I had had of a moated tower just before driving through the archway on my arrival at Castell Marten.

"Is the Keep that ruin on an islet, near the gatehouse?"

"The tower in the moat, ay, mistress. My lord lets down the drawbridge when he wishes to cross over. There is a stair leads from my lady's parlour—supposed to be secret, it is, but we all know of it, and the way in through the bookcase nearest the fireplace. It is the only way to pass between the Keep and the castle. Even with a boat, there is no landing place."

Ysolt closed the cupboard door, and glanced at the clock. "It is time to prepare yourself for her ladyship, if you are to see her at three."

"I am already wearing my best gown ... I will just wash my face and hands, and tidy my hair."

Ysolt poured water from the copper jug into the basin.

"Who else is there living in the house?" I asked her.

"Only Lord Castelmarten, and my lady, his mother. Miss Gwynneth is dead now, my lady's older sister; but Miss Enid and Miss Esther live here, of course."

"It seems as if the Dyffryns decided to make Castell Marten their home, when they married into the family," I observed, washing the fingers of my bandaged hand.

"Lucky it was for them they had somewhere to go, after the fire," Ysolt agreed.

She gave me a sideways glance. "Now I am gossiping too much, isn't it?" she murmured.

"But I'm glad of it, Ysolt. Remember, I know nothing of these people. I wish that you would tell me more about them."

"It is almost three ... let me unfasten your ribbon and brush your hair."

"Be careful when you brush this side. Do you see the wound?"

"I do, mistress. It is a wonder you survived it."

53

"Why do you say the clocks don't strike since the fire, Ysolt?"

"Her ladyship had all the chimes removed, in memory of her mother. The hour has never struck in Castell Marten since the news came that Pen Maen was burnt, and Lady Dyffryn dead. A quiet house, is this. More restful than some with chiming clocks all over them, like Hafod Hall."

She began to brush my hair with long even strokes. "Tell me if I am hurting you, mistress. Beautiful hair, it is..."

"Hafod Hall... who lives there?"

"Why, Lord and Lady Carnaby, mistress, and their two grown children. The Honourable Mathilda is my Lady Castelmarten's goddaughter. You will meet her soon, for she visits my lady very often. Indeed, 'tis said..."

"What do the gossips say, Ysolt?"

"Why, that Miss Mathilda and his lordship have an understanding."

"Then they are to marry?" I exclaimed, recalling the conversation between Mrs. Jones and Dr. Glynn about his friend, who had made my herb pillow.

"'Tis her ladyship's dearest wish, they say. But come, mistress. Let me tie your ribbon, and then I will take you to my lady."

She conducted me out to the gallery, and back towards the stairs. As we reached the stairhead, Ysolt turned to the right and knocked on a great door.

"The Royal Bedchamber, mistress," she whispered.

"Come in," commanded a thin, imperative voice. Ysolt opened the door and stood back for me to enter.

I picked up my skirts and limped forward. A sudden wail made me pause. I could hear another person sobbing steadily. This was a house of mourning, I remembered belatedly. The younger son had died and I, a stranger, must intrude upon the family grief.

With a sinking heart, I entered the room.

Chapter Five

The Royal Bedchamber was as imposing as its name, of princely proportions under a vaulted ceiling. It was dimly lit and seemed at first to be full of shadows, until I realized that there were three ladies present and a maid, all dressed in deepest mourning. One of the women was actually wringing her hands and moaning aloud behind her flowing veil, while the lady's maid sobbed unrestrainedly in the background.

"That will do, Parry," wearily declared the same thin voice which had bade me enter. "You may leave us now."

My eyes, becoming accustomed to the gloom, perceived that the speaker was reclining in a tall wing chair. She leaned forward now, putting back her veil with a long white hand.

"I am Elaine Castelmarten," she announced. "Come here, young woman, and let me look at you."

The maid brushed past me as I hobbled forward. I caught a flash of resentment from her swollen eyes, and then the door closed behind her with more than a suggestion of a slam.

I curtsied, feeling myself flushing almost guiltily as my eyes met those of Lady Castelmarten, deeply set in a proud but ravaged face.

"So you may be my daughter-in-law," she said quietly. "Gerry's widow ... and yet you cannot even tell me how he died?"

I shook my head wordlessly.

"Oh, Elaine, it is too terrible to be borne!" exclaimed the wailing one, dabbing at her eyes behind the veil. "Poor Gerry—the shock! And now this—this terrible ordeal!"

"Be quiet, Esther. Have you no self-command? How I

wish I could persuade you to leave me in peace!"

"Oh, no, Elaine," wailed Miss Esther. "How could you expect us to be so unfeeling as to let you mourn alone? It is at times like these that the family tie is closest . . . we who have endured so much together!"

The other lady spoke. She had a dry, spinsterish voice. "If we did abandon you to your grief, Elaine, I dare say you would soon regret it."

"I could better bear any degree of sorrow in solitude."

"No, dear," said the other lady firmly. "It would not be good for you. Why, you have only to look at Father! Besides, I am older than you: you must allow me to know best."

Lady Castelmarten silenced her sisters with a commanding gesture. She returned her attention to me, still standing awkwardly before her.

"I understand," she said coolly, "that we are to call you Rose?"

"If—if you please, ma'am," I stammered. "Just until I recall my proper name . . ."

"Very well. Enid, allow me to present Miss Rose. Miss Dyffryn, Rose; this is my older sister. And this is my younger sister, Miss Esther. Miss Dyffryn is known more commonly in the family as Miss Enid, which was her style before our oldest sister Gwynneth died."

"How do you do?" I said faintly, curtsying to first one disapproving sister and then the other. Miss Enid stiffly inclined her head. Miss Esther turned away with an involuntary shudder.

"You had better sit down," Lady Castelmarten commanded me. "You do not look well," she informed me objectively. "Is it really true that you remember nothing— nothing that happened before the accident?"

"Alas, no ma'am. Nothing of significance."

"You do recall something then," she said quickly. "Tell me exactly—nothing is too trivial, for what has no significance to you might have some for me. That is one of the reasons I insisted that Lucian should bring you here, under my eye, so that you could inform me instantly if anything comes back to you."

I found I was trembling. My headache had returned, but I strove to ignore it, as I was sure that Lady Castelmarten would have done in my place.

"Very well, ma'am," I said in a low voice. "I can remember a basket of blackberries...someone had dropped it, and the blackberries were lying in the grass." I shivered. I did not like that memory, and did not even wish to know what it portended.

"Yes?" prompted Lady Castelmarten gently. "And what else?"

"An old man's hand...blue-veined, knotted, freckled with brown—" I paused as something else flashed into my mind. "He was holding the round knob of a walking stick—I have just remembered it!"

"Excellent. What more?"

"There was someone...in a mask, I think."

"A mask?" She frowned.

I said quickly, "And I know I like dogs."

"Ah!" A gleam of warmth softened Lady Castelmarten's rigid features. She had been, and perhaps still was, a handsome woman, I perceived.

"Then we have a bond between us, miss. My sisters have an unaccountable preference for cats. But is this really the full sum of your recollections? You have no memory of Gervais?"

"I am sorry..." I swallowed. "The truth is, that I could as well be Mary Ramsey, as Mrs. Marten."

She raised a thinly arched eyebrow. "The illegitimate rag-picker? Somehow, I do not think so."

"But her mother was a lady, and brought her up—"

"I know the story. Lucian told me. We were discussing it last night with the Vaughans. Mr. Vaughan is our vicar, by the way. They kindly called to offer their condolences—but only succeeded in sending Esther into a fit of the hysterics. Gerry was Esther's favourite nephew, you see," she added dryly.

"He was Gwynneth's, too," Miss Esther cried. "She left him Mama's fortune, did she not?"

It was Miss Enid who answered, in her precise manner. "Mama left her fortune to Gwynneth because, as a

57

hunchback, Gwynneth was unlikely to marry. When Gwynneth came to make her will, it was apparent that you and I, dear Esther, were needed here at Castell Marten. I because the household could scarcely run without me; and you because you are the closest to dear Father. Gervais, on the other hand, made no secret of his dislike for this place and needed the legacy to make a home elsewhere. Gwynneth hoped that by the time he attained the age of twenty-five, dear Gerry would have settled down sufficiently to be entrusted with the money—"

"It was very wrong!" cried Miss Esther passionately. "It was last winter that he needed it—when his father died. If he had been independent of Lucian then—"

I had been glancing from one to the other of the sisters. Lady Castelmarten was undoubtedly the best-looking of them, though they had a pronounced family resemblance and shared several similar features, which despite the mourning veils, I could see were in Miss Enid too sharp for beauty, and were in Miss Esther almost lost in the plump roundness of her face.

Lady Castelmarten, who appeared to have ignored her sisters' conversation, now leaned forward and drew my attention to a gold locket pinned to the front of her black gown.

"Would you like to see what Gervais looked like?" she asked, and pressed the spring without waiting for my reply.

Inside was a tiny double miniature, painted on ivory, of two young men. The darker one I recognized as Lord Castelmarten. The other at first glance appeared to be his mirror image except that his hair was a lighter shade. Then I observed that his expression was more carefree, his mouth seeming to tremble on the edge of an easy smile.

"Does that face mean nothing to you?"

"No, my lady. I am sorry..."

She sighed, and straightened in her high-backed chair. She remarked in a distant manner, "We generally have some refreshment at about this hour. Will you join us in a dish of tea?"

"Thank you, ma'am."

"In that case, would you kindly ring the bell?"

My head ached, my hand throbbed, and my ankle was painful to walk upon, but I dared not think of disobeying.

Miss Enid said sharply, "I see you have a limp, Miss Rose. Is that the result of your accident?"

I stood still. "Dr. Glynn informed me that my foot was twisted when I was thrown out of the coach. I am afraid that if I had been born a cripple, I would have no recollection of it."

"Of course not, poor child," said Lady Castelmarten quickly. "I must ask you to forgive my sister. Indeed, we none of us are quite ourselves just now."

"No—no! It is a dreadful situation—and the worse in that I can explain nothing—cannot even tell you of your son's last days—"

I would have done better to have kept silent.

"Oh!" wailed Miss Esther, as a thought occurred to her. "You cannot even tell us where to find his grave!"

Lady Castelmarten said coldly, "The place of interment is mentioned on the burial certificate. Stop making a display of yourself, Esther."

"Oo-ooh! We all know you love Lucian best—and so does Enid! Whenever there was trouble between them, you always took Lucian's part! Why, if it had not been for you, Gerry would never have been banished from this house—"

"That will do, Esther. Miss Rose, you look pale. I think after all, you would be better in your room. I shall have tea sent to you there. Can you find your way?"

I was only too delighted to escape. I curtsied hastily and clumsily to the sisters, and a moment later closed the door upon the sounds of what promised to be a family quarrel of no mean proportions.

I let out my breath and took a few shaky steps along the gallery. When I was obliged to pause I found myself by an open window where I was glad to cool my cheeks for a few minutes in the sharp spring air.

But at least the ordeal of the first meeting was over, I

thought thankfully. And Lady Castelmarten had been ... perhaps kind was too strong a word, but she had not been unkind to me. Indeed, I fancied that perhaps her ladyship had been somewhat relieved to find me as I was ... if her son had led her to expect a vulgar scheming harpy, then her relief was understandable, of course. And I for my part was relieved that she was prepared to wait for the evidence before condemning me, as I felt her sisters had already done. I could not say I felt greatly drawn to either of the Miss Dyffryns. Miss Enid was tart and spinsterish. No doubt she ran the household admirably, with method and discipline, if little imagination. Miss Esther was very different, untidy, and easily moved to emotion—she should have been easier to like, but somehow I suspected it would be wearing to see much of her.

I sighed, and turned my attention to the view. I was overlooking the cobbled yard, on the opposite side of the house from my bedchamber, I discovered. Was it only this morning that I had alighted in that courtyard for the first time? On the far side of the square was the gatehouse and entrance archway, connected to the castle by two battlemented wings to the right and left. Away to the right I could see the upper stories of the island tower, black shapes of birds circling like spiralling leaves about its ruined roof; while some way beyond, the great mountain range rose in blue folds to the clouds.

I turned around. About three feet away from me I was astonished to see a young woman standing motionless. She was plainly but elegantly dressed, and with her pointed chin, tightly confined dark hair, and slightly slanting blue eyes, was striking rather than beautiful.

"Who are you?" I gasped, considerably startled by this sudden apparition.

She dropped a slight curtsy.

"Sarah Vaughan, at your service, Ma'am." She had a trace of the Welsh lilt in her voice, a tendency to dwell on her s's, and her tone was subtly mocking. "You, I assume, are the presumptive Mrs. Marten?"

I found my heart was beating hard, and strove for calm. "I am—to be known as Rose," I said. "As you seem to be aware, I am not yet certain of my identity, but it is more convenient to have a name."

"A rose by any other name smells as sweet? But as it happens, I don't agree with that. I fancy names are more important than we know. Gerry and Lucian, for example—they could never have been the other way about. And I—I am Sarah to most people. But to a special few, I am known as Sal." She seemed to watch me intently as she said this. I looked enquiring, and she shrugged.

"Sarah is the well-brought-up young daughter of the Vicarage," she explained. "Sal—is someone quite other!" She glanced down the gallery. "Shall we go to your room? I came to visit Lady Castelmarten, but I would far rather talk to you."

"I am afraid I am not feeling quite ready for visitors—"

"Then you will certainly need me to assist you." Miss Vaughan gestured towards the passage which led to my door. "The second-best spare bedchamber?" she hazarded. "Come, let us go and sit there. Yours is such an affecting story," she said lightly, slipping her arm through mine and drawing me down the gallery. "I am eager to hear every detail. Besides, you look as if you are in no case to be standing."

When we reached my door, she opened it and stood back with an assumption of humility.

"Do, pray, precede me. For you are the married woman, it appears."

I caught my breath and hobbled past her, with my head held high.

"This is an impressive chamber," Miss Vaughan observed, following me. "I believe I have only had a glimpse of it before—never been inside, unless I did so as a child. There was a time when we ran wild at Castell Marten, Ned and I...What a remarkable bed! I vow I should not sleep a wink in it." She crossed over to the right-hand window. "Ah, you can see our house from here—that ugly square building, hard by the church. You

61

have quite a good view of the village, if you lean out. You can even see something of the old wall, which used to enclose it."

"Much of it seems to have crumbled away," I remarked, after a cursory glance.

"Yes, or been used to build *friddoed*—sheep pens, that is to say."

Miss Vaughan abandoned the window and resumed her scrutiny of my bedchamber. "Is this a door, here in the paneling? Oh, it is! A winding stair! How Gothic! And how gloomy. Castelmarten should have the creepers cleared away from those arrow slits if he does not want his guests to break their ankles."

"I believe the stairway is not used."

Miss Vaughan closed the door. She smiled, and waved me to a chair. All at once, she looked very pretty.

"Do sit down. And may I borrow this stool? You are cross with me for staring at you in the gallery just now—but I am so interested in you. Really, you must forgive me. The fact is, that we seldom meet strangers here, in this lost land."

She sat down, put her hands together and looked at me appealingly over her fingertips. "I am an awkward country girl, Miss—Rose. *Farouche*, is the word my mother uses to describe me. My mother is fond of using a French word, when she can think of one—especially in company. And then the news you brought was so very shocking! I don't mean Gerry's marriage so much—but his death! He was so strong and vital—somehow I can't believe it yet. He was almost like a brother to me, you must know. There was a time when Ned and he and I ran together—I was a dreadful hoyden, my mother tells me." She gave a husky little laugh. "But I don't know why I am rattling on like this. Perhaps it is because you are so silent. Why don't you say something?"

I rallied my thoughts. "I find it hard to talk, somehow," I owned. "You know that I have lost my memory. My world begins therefore in Mrs. Jones's bedchamber at the Castell Marten Arms. You must see that doesn't leave me many subjects of conversation to draw upon."

Miss Vaughan fluttered her eyelashes. They were probably her best feature, being lustrous, long, and dark, an alluring frame for those strange bright eyes. "Then—it is really true?" she murmured. "I mean, we had heard as much—but it is so hard to comprehend. You can remember nothing at all of—of Dunstable, or wherever it was?"

"Nothing of anywhere. It is just as possible that I come from Lichfield, and am not Mrs. Marten at all."

Miss Vaughan stared. "So you really remember nothing?" she repeated insistently. "Like a black curtain in your mind? How terrible that must be!"

"Perhaps it is less like a curtain than a veil—for there are brief tantalizing glimpses that don't mean anything. But I expect more will come as time passes."

"Do you, indeed? But what if you never regain your memory? What then, Miss Rose? Do you intend to stay forever at Castell Marten, neither maid, nor wife, nor widow?"

I shook my head.

Miss Vaughan sprang from her chair. She dropped to her knees beside me. "What a blunderer you must think me! And how unkind! You have a headache, I am sure. But there is a reason for my behaviour, you see. I am—greatly concerned about Gerry—we all are, of course—and last night Castelmarten actually hinted that there was a chance Gerry might not be dead, after all. If only my brother Ned were here! He and Gerry were two of a kind: I am sure he would be able to fathom the mystery. But Ned is—out of touch with us, alas, and in the meantime you seem to be the only person who could know—yet you remember nothing! But I hope you understand and can find it in you to forgive me for probing."

I assured her that she was forgiven, and added that I felt as if my memory might return in the end, if I left it alone.

"You will let me know the instant you begin to recall? Before anyone?"

I stared at her. "I will tell you anything I remember, certainly. But surely the family should be informed . . . ?"

Miss Vaughan stood up and bent to dust down her skirts

before returning to her chair.

"I don't quite know how to explain," she murmured. "How to warn you..."

"Warn me! Against whom, Miss Vaughan?"

She looked down at her hands. "The family, I suppose. Castelmarten was not quite so devoted to his brother Gerry as he may have intimated to you. I think—there are reasons why you cannot expect him to be your friend, I fear. And there are others here, whose interests..." She shook her head. "Perhaps I will confide in you more fully when I know you better." She raised her startling eyes to mine. "What steps are being taken, in the matter of proving your identity?" she asked directly.

"I believe Lord Castelmarten intends to visit Dunstable quite soon. He hopes to find there somone who knew his brother, and who will be able to inform him of the story of the last few weeks. And if any of—of Mrs. Marten's family are there, they will probably be willing to travel here in order to identify me. And that in turn, if I am indeed Mrs. Marten, might prompt my memory."

"Yes," said Miss Vaughan. "I see that it might. But has Castelmarten not suggested that it would be a good deal simpler for you to travel there yourself?"

"You mean—" I strove to steady my voice. "You think it would be best for me to—leave Wales?"

"No!" she cried with passionate sincerity, startling me. It had occurred to me, when she spoke of warning me that it might have been Miss Vaughan who had sent me the unsigned note at the Castell Marten Arms. Now I was sure I was mistaken. "It would not be best," she went on emphatically. "It would be—wretchedly rash! Do not allow yourself to be alone with Castelmarten at any time! And least of all, upon a journey, with its unlimited opportunities—but there, I do not know you well enough to talk to you of Castelmarten! I could tell you tales—but I had better not. Do you ride?" she enquired, with that somewhat disconcerting change of tone and mood.

"I—do not know, of course."

"Of course you do not know—how stupid I am!"

I leaned forward. "Miss Vaughan, you do believe me,

then? That I have lost my memory?"

"To be sure I do! Why, what object would there be... Ah, I think I have it! If you were the other girl, the illegitimate, then it might profit you to step into Mrs. Marten's shoes—and that could be done most convincingly by losing your memory! Is that what Castelmarten thinks!"

I inclined my head.

She smiled sunnily, and put her hand on mine. "To be sure, he would, devil that he is. But I believe you are the young lady from Dunstable! Now, if you used to ride, you will not have forgotten how to do it, I suppose? We must find out. I dare say Lady Castelmarten will lend you a horse, even if her son would not."

"Oh, I dare not ask her," I cried. "I feel I have imposed on her sufficiently. Besides, I am not well enough. But perhaps you can suggest it in a few days, when I am more recovered?"

"I wonder. Her ladyship dislikes me, I fear; but perhaps it can be contrived. I, of course, shall have to be content with riding the miserable cob who pulls our gig. But perhaps if your mount is spirited, we might exchange? I love a good gallop. That is, Sal does... but Sal is rather a wild creature, I fear."

She glanced at the quietly ticking clock and rose to her feet, exclaiming that she must be on her way.

"We are to dine at Hafod Hall this evening, and though that odious Mathilda Carnaby has no looks to speak of, she is rich enough to be able to dress like an angel, so I shall be obliged to give a great deal of thought to my own toilette. Besides, Freddy will be there..."

"Freddy?" I queried, my attention caught by a particular inflection in her voice.

"Mr. Carnaby, that is to say, the son and heir. He and I..." She sighed and glanced away. "But somehow we will find a chance to talk together," she went on more cheerfully. "Papa will be playing chess with Lord Carnaby, Mama will be gossiping with Lady Carnaby—and very likely Mathilda will join the older ladies, for she is a very model chatelaine, always busy about the stillroom, and their conversation will be more agreeable to her than that of her brother and myself, who are comparatively frivolous, I fear. But you are looking very tired, Miss Rose. I had better ring for your maid."

She did so, and bade me a warm farewell. When she had left, I lay back on my pillows reflecting that I had one friend at least in Wales, and was glad indeed to find I had been wrong in suspecting that Miss Vaughan would be jealous of me for my possible relationship with Gervais Marten, for it sounded very much as if she had transferred her affections to the even more eligible Mr. Freddy Carnaby.

Ysolt, when she answered the bell, brought in my supper on a tray, as well as the promised cup of tea, by her ladyship's order. After the tray had been removed I was surprised to receive a visit from Miss Enid.

"My sister suggested I should see that you had settled in quite comfortably," she informed me, as if afraid that I might impute some kind motive to herself. "Everything is quite in order, I trust?" she asked, darting sharp glances about the room, and then at me, daring me to deny it.

Ysolt, who had undressed me, said in her soft voice, "Bruised she is, Miss Enid, and has the headache badly. I was thinking one of your cordials might be the very thing for her, indeed."

Miss Enid warmed towards me slightly, I could feel. "The headache, is it? Well, I shall prepare a little potion for you, child. I have quite a reputation for my draughts. Be sure you drink it, and then I shall have no need to wish you a good night."

She rustled away in her black silk, and Ysolt busied herself collecting my clothes and rolling some of them into a bundle to be washed. "Plenty of rest you will be needing, mistress," she advised me. "Miss Enid's draught will settle you... they used to say the stillroom at Pen Maen was in a witch's charge, and that Miss Enid had her craft from her, when she was yet a child."

"I have no objection," I murmured, for I was ready to take anything for my headache that might cure it; and when the footman presently bore in a steaming brew I drank it to the very dregs, black and bitter though they were.

Afterwards I lay back, watching Ysolt moving in the firelight and wondering when I would start to feel sleepy.

I remembered that I had not said my prayers; but I had scarcely begun them before I felt myself drifting away.

I tried to waken in the night. There was a pressing reason to do so, but I did not know what it was. I struggled to open my eyes, but it was as if the drug sat firmly upon my lids. I moaned, but only the merest breath of sound came from my lips. Then the sense of urgency passed and I spun down again, down into a dark and dreamless sleep.

Chapter Six

I made a slow awakening in the morning. Every time I opened my eyes, they closed again. Ysolt brought me my breakfast in bed and informed me that her ladyship had sent for Dr. Glynn. She drew back my curtains and stood for some while by the window looking out. There was something strange about the intentness of her attitude, but I had not the strength then to ask her any questions.

By the time Dr. Glynn arrived, I was feeling a good deal recovered. He rubbed his hands to warm them at the fire, and then examined me.

"Your wounds are healing famously," he declared. "My friend will be glad to know her salve worked so well. You still have the herb pillow, I am glad to see. How did you sleep?"

"Too heavily," I told him. "I felt as if I would never wake or breathe again."

He glanced at Ysolt, who was standing silently, her face in shadow.

"'Tis true, sir, I had much ado to rouse her this morning. Miss Enid made her a potion last night . . . but I know her draughts and they have not usually this effect."

He clicked his tongue, plainly annoyed. "The patient should not have taken anything without consulting me!"

"But you know Miss Dyffryn's reputation, sir," Ysolt protested. "Famous, she is, for her medicines and such."

"I might have known how it would be," Dr. Glynn exclaimed. "I am not saying a word against Miss Enid, mind, even if she has not quite the skill of—some. It is merely that Miss—Miss Rose, is peculiarly susceptible, it seems. What would be a normal dosage of, for example, laudanum, acts on her with twice the potency. This is partly due to her head wound, no doubt, and makes the taking of such draughts a decision to be reached with caution."

I felt it time to intervene.

"I do feel much better now," I said with truth. "My headache is quite gone...I wanted to ask you, Dr. Glynn, about my memory. Do you think it will return?"

"Ah," he murmured, diverted. "That question is not quite so straightforward as it might appear. Injuries to the brain are not yet fully understood, nor may they ever be. In some cases, another blow upon the head restores the memory completely. In others, it is lost forever. In still further cases, it almost seems as if the patient has some reason against remembering, some problem too great to be borne...and removal of the problem has been known to restore the memory in these persons. Without years of training, miss, years of study and of application, I could not expect you to understand, nor should I attempt to explain, the various humours of the brain, and their delicate balances..."

In a word, I thought, he did not know the answer.

I sighed. "Certainly, another blow upon the head seems a drastic cure—"

"On no account attempt it!" he cried. "A fatal hemorrhage might well result!!"

"No, I believe I can promise to run no risk of it. As for wishing not to remember, I am sure that cannot be the case. I long to know my past, my family. The only thing—"

"What is it?" he said keenly.

I glanced at Ysolt. He understood, and turned to her.

"Go into the passage for a moment, if you please. Miss Rose has a confidence to impart. Leave the door open, of course. Now, Miss Rose, what is it?"

I licked my lips. I was reluctant to divulge what troubled me, but if it might indeed have some bearing on my condition...

"It is true that there might be something more behind my loss of memory," I murmured.

"What? What? This is very interesting, miss. Come

now, don't be afraid. My lips are sealed, you know, and I am only anxious to assist you."

Thus encouraged, I whispered that someone did not want me here in Wales—that I had received a note of warning, bidding me to leave.

"I see," he murmured, stroking his chin. "And you have no notion who might have sent you such a warning? Could it perhaps have been a joke?"

"A wretched joke to play upon a person injured in an accident!"

"True, true, but time, no doubt, will solve the riddle. Well, I must be on my way. And if Miss Enid makes you any more of her potions, I advise you to pour them out of the window . . . though you need not say I told you to do so! Ysolt," he called, "I am ready now to leave. But you look worried, girl," he remarked, scrutinizing her closely. "Is it the weather?"

She replied in a spate of Welsh, and he shook his head, murmuring a few words of consolation, which appeared to fail in their intention.

When he had gone, to report on me to Lady Castelmarten, I also asked Ysolt what was the matter.

For a moment I wondered if she would confide in me. Then, crossing to the window again, she said, "There's snow in the air. I can smell it."

"Snow? So late in the year?"

"It is not very late, for Wales."

"And if it does snow, Ysolt, what of it?"

"Why," she cried out in a ringing voice, "Ty Newydd is sick and so my husband Evans is top man on the mountain for the gathering."

I shook my head, conscious with momentary alarm that this explanation might as well have been in Welsh for all the sense it made to me.

"What gathering?" I asked blankly.

Ysolt stared at me, disconcerted by my ignorance. Then she plainly recalled my disability, and spoke as to a child, "They are gathering the sheep, mistress. Bringing them down off the mountain for the lambing."

"Ah, now I begin to understand. Your husband needs

clear weather so that he can find the sheep."

"More than that, mistress. Many dangers are there on the mountain. 'Tis not sheep alone, but men who will be lost if it comes on to snow, or if the *niwl* comes down—the mist. But what if Evans was lost up there on the mountain, that is what I ask myself and the children. Most of my wages go to paying Sionedd Jones to look after them, you see, but a cottage needs a man about it. You can't be asking a woman like Sionedd to be putting slates on the roof..."

"Surely the Martens would look after you?" I suggested.

Ysolt tossed her head. "Indeed they would. But I don't care for charity, thank you very much."

Dr. Glynn had agreed I might get up, and Ysolt helped to dress me in my warmest clothes, for I wanted to walk in the Dutch gardens below my window. I was thoughtful as I limped down the gallery, and reflected that it had been good for me to realize that I was not alone in having problems. Compared with Ysolt, indeed, perhaps I was fortunate; I had no one else to worry over and, for the present at least, I was being looked after without having to work for my bread. If no one loved me in the world, and if my future was uncertain in the extreme, I still had much for which to be thankful.

I went down the great newel stairway and paused at the foot of it to look into the Banqueting Hall, a vast mediaeval chamber with red painted walls hung with ancient weapons, and a heavily beamed ceiling. A passage divided it from the kitchen quarters, a flagstoned passage worn by the tread of countless feet. At the far end a door set in a pointed archway led out into the garden.

The wind was cold, so cold it brought tears to my eyes. I huddled the cloak round myself and stepped out into the wintry day.

I found myself standing between a neatly arranged Dutch garden to my right and an avenue of yew trees to my left leading to a tumble of ruins set in a wilderness. It did not take me long to explore the Dutch garden, with its straggle of wilting spring flowers protected from the worst of the wind by clipped box hedges set about a silent fountain; and presently I began to limp down the gloomy

71

avenue, already feeling somewhat better for the air and exercise.

Suddenly a magnificent peacock crossed my path at a run. Others followed, some younger cocks and a few drab peahens. A moment later I realized Lord Castelmarten was standing in a sort of antechamber bounded by a high yew hedge, throwing handfuls of corn to the birds. As I stared, he turned, throwing the last handful and dusting his hands together. His brows rose as he saw me there, and his expression hardened.

"Good morning, Miss Rose. I trust you are feeling rested—fit to meet our family lawyer."

Why did he always speak as though I angered him, I wondered; and as if he wished to anger me?

"I am quite willing to meet your lawyer, of course," I returned softly. "Though I am afraid I can have very little to tell him."

"You can show him those papers that were in the reticule. You are not wearing it, I see?"

"No, sir, I find I have not the habit of carrying it," I confessed. His eyes narrowed and I continued quickly, "A rag-picker would not have much use for such an article—but neither would a girl living in the depths of the country, I suppose, accustomed to run out into the gardens several times a day. It would only be used when visiting, shopping, or travelling... I have it in my room."

"Very well. You can fetch it presently; and make sure the certificates are in it. I want Prys-Roberts to take charge of them for the time being, in order to make certain comparisons of handwriting at his convenience."

I found myself strongly against any such suggestion. I had felt the same reluctance at parting with the family ring, I recalled. I wondered if I was naturally possessive, or if it was merely that I had so little, if anything, to call my own.

"Do you suspect forgery, sir?" I asked, my voice trembling a little, despite myself.

"All possibilities must be explored, Miss Rose. Surely you agree?"

His suggestion was reasonable, certainly. I was

72

surprised to hear myself asking tartly, "What if I will not let you have them?"

"How can you prevent it?" he countered indifferently. I was illogically enraged to realize that he expected me to be disobliging, and was ready for it.

"It is not as if that reticule had been found in your possession," he continued. "You have as yet no positive claim to it, nor to its contents; whereas I believe I must have some legal title to documents bearing my brother's name and signature."

"But they are in my possession now," I cried. "And there is a very good chance that they may be mine. A woman should always keep her marriage lines..."

Where had I heard that piece of wisdom? I did not know, yet I could remember the voice that had uttered it: a strong sour voice, belonging to a woman who was certain of being in the right—a woman who had power over me, whom I feared and distrusted, a woman who had once punished me sadistically, and beaten me... but then the memory eluded me, and even the echo of that antagonistic voice was gone.

"Miss Rose," said Lord Castelmarten sternly. I blinked, returning to the present. He was looking unduly annoyed, I observed, and it occurred to me that any unfavourable expression seemed to transform his face to hard Welsh rock, perhaps lending his displeasure more weight than he actually felt. It should have been a comforting reflection, but the fact remained that I still found his anger overpowering.

"I hesitate to remind you," he was saying in a crushing tone, "that the only reason you are enjoying our hospitality here is because you have some claim to be my brother's widow. Mrs. Gervais Marten, one supposes, would be only too anxious to have the legality of her status proved. Any obstruction on your part would seem to suggest that you have some reason to doubt your right to be at Castell Marten."

"Doubt it?" I exclaimed. "Of course I doubt it—I don't know who I am, therefore I must doubt everything."

"In that case," he suggested coolly, "you will surely be

happy to oblige me in this. You are shivering," he went on, "allow me to take your arm." He began to march me towards the ruins at the far end of the garden. "The burial certificate in particular is needed," he informed me. "I require it in order to apply for permission to exhume my brother's body. You will understand that my mother is extremely anxious to have it transported here, to lie among his ancestors."

I felt ashamed of myself, as no doubt he had intended. Why had I felt so defensive about those papers? It was not as if the earl would dare to destroy them, for after all, others had seen them at the time of the accident.

"Of course you can have them," I said quickly. "I am sorry, I did not understand. I suppose I was afraid to lose sight of those papers."

"It is quite natural," he said quickly, surprising me with his look of sympathy. "You have so little, I can understand the possession of the papers must be inexpressibly valuable to you."

Then, as if he despised himself for having betrayed a momentary weakness, he added harshly, "Immensely valuable—like my brother's ring."

I said carefully, "Am I to suppose you think it is the material value I am considering?"

His voice sounded sneering, though he kept his grip upon my arm. "Is it not a reasonable supposition?"

"It is an unwarrantable one! The implication is, that if I am indeed your brother's widow, then I must have married him for gain."

"Are you telling me that you were madly in love with him, ma'am?"

"You know I can't remember him; but you might give me the benefit of the doubt. How do you know that I am not an heiress, in my own right, for instance?"

He looked me up and down. "The clothes that were found on the stagecoach, Miss Rose, were not those of an heiress, I assure you."

"No... I must allow that they were not."

"And though Gervais had seldom a feather to fly with," Lord Castelmarten continued, "it was pretty generally

74

known that he had inherited a fortune from his aunt, the unrestricted use of which he would be free to enjoy from his next birthday—his five-and-twentieth which is not far off."

I shook my head. "I suppose if I say I am sure that would not have weighed with me, you will not believe me. Besides, since he is dead, he may have left his fortune to anyone, for all I know."

"Precisely so, Miss Rose. And that is why I have sent for Prys-Roberts, my lawyer: to discover, if I can, whether my brother left a will, and what will happen to that fortune now."

I shivered. "Well, I don't want your aunt's fortune, I assure you."

And I didn't, either—and yet, it would be very pleasant to be independent of the Martens, I reflected.

"I shall go to Northamptonshire so soon as my mother is over the worst of the shock," Lord Castelmarten went on. "It would be best, of course, for you to accompany me—"

I stiffened, casting him a frightened glance.

"But Dr. Glynn has informed me you will not be fit to travel so far for some time," he continued smoothly, so that I could not tell how much of a disappointment to his plans this might have been.

"However, no doubt your—the family of Mrs. Marten will be able to tell me all I need to know."

"My family!" I murmured wonderingly.

"Unless you are Mary Ramsey," he reminded me unkindly, turning me back towards the house.

I caught my breath. "I seem to keep forgetting that possibility," I admitted. "I believe I do begin to think I must be—your brother's wife."

"And I am beginning to be positive that that is the one person you cannot be!"

I blinked. "Why . . . do you say that, sir?"

"Because you are so sensitive," he snapped, "and Gerry liked his women bold and hard!"

"But—for a wife?"

He glared at me. "Gerry did what he felt like doing—never what was wise," he said.

75

I bit my lip. The last few minutes had brought home to me the fact that, little as the Castelmartens had made me welcome, yet I was terrified of the alternative: terrified of finding I was Mary Ramsey after all, bound by law to Mother Cliffe; my only chance of escape from her the post of slave to Mrs. Thomas, who would treat me, no doubt, as a shameful bastard, a blot on her respectability.

"Your brother sounds so impetuous," I stammered, "that it seems he might even choose a wife who would not suit him!"

"It is useless to discuss it," the earl informed me sternly. "Your future does not depend on any whim of mine, so it is no use to turn those pleading eyes upon me. It depends upon the truth—upon your actual past. Brrr! It is too cold to be walking here. Let us go inside. Now, what have I done to alarm you?" he demanded in exasperation.

"Not you—a snowflake!" I stared up into the lowering sky. "I thought a snowflake touched my cheek. I was thinking of the gathering..."

Lord Castelmarten stared.

"What a strange person you are! What do you know or care about the gathering?" Then he grasped my arm. "Come, let us go in, for it's madness to linger out here on such a day—" It had indeed begun to snow in earnest, and he hurried me towards the door. "Don't be afraid for Evan Evans, Miss Rose. He may be small, but he's wiry—and he knows every crevice in those rocks."

"I would like to send Ysolt home, if I may, to stay with her children."

"Very well, if you can manage without her. I'll have a word with Hughes and he can speak to Mrs. Meredith about it."

He struggled with the pointed door, and flung it open, hurrying me inside.

"You'd best get upstairs, and into something dry—"

"But how could I have got damp in so short a time?"

He frowned. "You defy me even in the smallest trifles, do you not? You will at least wish to take off your cloak. After that, I would be obliged if you would come straight down to the library, in the southwest wing beyond the

Armoury. And be sure to bring those papers with you."

I inclined my head stiffly, and swept away with as much dignity as I could manage with a limping foot.

When I reached my chamber, it was to find the little maid gathering up her mop and duster, while Ysolt was tidying my clothes. I sent Ysolt upon her way home at once—she did not stay to argue with me, but swiftly looked and spoke her gratitude before hastening from the room. I took off my cloak, and tidied my hair. Then I went to the shelf where my reticule lay.

Even as I lifted it down, I knew something was amiss.

My fingers were shaking as I pulled out the drawstring. Clumsily I fumbled within the bag. The stiffly folded certificates were gone. In their place was a tiny twist of paper. I opened it out and read the unevenly printed message on it.

"GO! DANGER! GO!"

Chapter Seven

I searched the reticule frantically, but apart from the note it seemed to contain only a purse and scissors. I probed further into the base, reluctant to accept the evidence of my eyes and fingers—and found the hard lump in the bottom of the reticule which I now remembered having noticed at the inn. Something bracket-shaped had been carefully sewn into the bottom of the lining, something with curves about the diameter of a cup ... what could it be?

I pulled vainly at the stitching, but it had been too neatly done to tear. I took up the scissors, ripped out the lining, and held up my trophy to the light.

It was a bracelet of solid gold, made of two hinging halves with an ornate catch, and it was chased with a fine design of fleurs-de-lis.

As I stared at it, lying there on the palm of my hand, I was filled with an inexplicable horror and loathing for the object, itself an ornament of beauty and considerable value. I realized it must have some deep and horrible significance for me, and I wondered fearfully where I had seen it before. The conviction grew on me that if only I could remember that, then the whole dark mystery of Mr. Gervais Marten's marriage and death, to say nothing of my own identity, would be solved at once. As it was, I wondered if the fact that this bracelet was so familiar to me, and that it had been hidden in Miss Merridew's reticule, might prove to connect me with that young lady rather than the other one.

But before I could satisfactorily follow this train of thought, a knock fell upon the door.

I started almost guiltily. Pausing only to wrap myself in

my warmest shawl, I hurried to answer it. The footman who stood outside was a dark fellow with a disapproving look. He spoke in Welsh, and motioned towards the gallery. It was not difficult for me to deduce that his lordship was growing tired of waiting for me, and I caught the name Prys-Roberts also. I pulled on my left glove rather hastily, therefore, and slipped the strings of the reticule over my wrist, for I was resolved not to be parted from the bracelet even though I could not bring myself to wear it. Then I stepped out into the passage with some of the pride, determination, and stark terror of one approaching the guillotine.

Lord Castelmarten was waiting for me in the hall. He hailed me with impatience.

"Where have you been? You have not even changed your gown!"

"No..." I swallowed. "I was looking for those papers."

I halted before him, clasped my hands behind my back, and baldly announced, "I could not find them!"

Quite involuntarily, I closed my eyes; but when the expected explosion did not come, I was obliged to open them again.

Lord Castelmarten looked very stern and...yes, contemptuous was the word, I decided.

"It is not my fault!" I cried. "They were in the reticule. Ysolt put it away in the wardrobe, on the shelf. I found it exactly where I expected—but the papers were not in it—"

He looked as if he wanted to shake me, and I took a step backwards.

"Have you asked Ysolt about it?" he demanded.

"No...she had left before I discovered they were gone. But in any event, it would be useless."

"I am sure it would be," he unexpectedly agreed.

I stared at him, and realized with horror that he thought I had hidden them myself.

"Someone deliberately removed them," I began.

"Of course, Miss Rose. I had come to the same conclusion."

"The papers were not in my bag—but a note had been left there for me to find," I cried.

He raised an eyebrow. "Indeed?"

"Yes, sir. I have it here." I trust it towards him.

He took it, and smoothed it out.

"Well, well," he murmured. "And who do you suppose was responsible for this?"

I was surprised the note had not had more effect upon him.

"Why," I stammered, "anyone who did not want to think of your brother having married! Any member of your family, my lord—even you!" Perhaps it was madness to taunt him, but there was a heady pleasure in it.

"I have a different suggestion, Miss Rose," he said coldly. "Mine is that you wrote it yourself."

For a moment I stared at him, speechless.

"But—but I had another such note," I said at last. "While I was at the Castell Marten Arms... I showed it to Mrs. Jones."

"Indeed? And why should you not have written that one also?"

"You know I cannot write, with this wound in my hand!"

"True, but it is very badly printed. It looks as if it could well have been penned by the wrong hand. Your left hand is uninjured, Miss Rose, I think?"

"Yes, but—why in the world should I have written a warning to myself?"

He looked at me consideringly. "You also suffered a blow upon the head," he murmured.

I felt indignant colour surge into my cheeks. With an effort I controlled my anger.

"I am sorry that you cannot bring yourself to trust my word. Nevertheless, I did receive these notes, sir, and I have no idea who wrote them." I remembered something. "I did think it might have been Miss Vaughan, if she resented my connection with your brother, but she was quite insistent that she at least did not want me leaving Wales."

"You have spoken to Miss Vaughan about it?" he asked, surprised.

I recalled that there was some enmity between his lordship and Miss Vaughan.

"Certainly I have," I informed him proudly. "Miss Vaughan is my only real friend in Wales."

He stared at me, yet I had the impression his thoughts were far away.

"Interesting..." he murmured.

I was making up my mind to overcome my reluctance to show him the bracelet when a light sound caused us both to turn our heads. A little wrinkled man approached us, stepping with a curiously jaunty gait, almost upon his toes. He wore a full suit of mourning and a curled unpowdered but grizzled wig, like a ghost from a past century.

"Ah, Prys-Roberts," said Lord Castelmarten. "This is Miss Rose, who is sorry to have kept us waiting. It appears she has mislaid the papers of which I spoke to you. But let us continue our conversation in the library."

We walked down the gloomy lower gallery to the accompaniment of little gasps and cries from the attorney.

"Tut, tut! Dear me, 'tis most unfortunate! I wonder, now...such a curious case. There is the register, to be sure. A search...time-consuming and expensive, yet inevitable, I fear. Dear, dear. Yes, inevitable."

He paused and absently produced a snuffbox which he offered to the earl, who curtly refused it. Mr. Prys-Roberts then pinched up some snuff himself, with a deprecating murmur, sneezed, dusted himself down with a large plain handkerchief, and hopped into the library after us almost as if he expected a portcullis to drop down and exclude him from our company.

Lord Castelmarten motioned us to be seated. He himself took the place at the writing table and got out a sheet of paper. He dipped a pen in the ink and began to write, frowning, and with frequent pauses.

"I am attempting to reproduce the missing documents, as well as I am able," he murmured. "It is not so easy as one might suppose, to recall the wording with accuracy."

Mr. Prys-Roberts cocked his head. "Did anyone else set

eyes upon them beside yourself, my lord? Did you, Miss Rose?"

"Yes," I owned. "But I glanced at them only briefly, I fear. Reading them meant little to me, beyond that Gervais Marten had married Clarissa—no, Victoria Clarissa Merridew. I cannot even recall the date . . . As for the death certificate—"

"Certificate of burial," corrected Lord Castelmarten.

"Yes . . . it said he died of—no, following, an inflammation of the lungs, I think—"

"Of an inflammation of the lungs, following influenza."

"Yes, that was it. And both took place in the Parish of Michael's, Upper Buzzard. I remember they were both signed."

"Yes," said the earl coldly. "If we had them still, we could compare your signature with that of Miss Merridew's. I have only been waiting for your hand to mend."

That then was why he suspected me of destroying them, I realized. He thought I knew very well I was not Miss Merridew, and that I feared the comparison of handwriting.

I found myself upon the verge of tears. "Even if—even if I had taken the marriage certificate—which I did not, of course—but I would never have destroyed the certificate of burial, after what you said this morning—" I paused, afraid that I was only making matters worse.

"I will look everywhere for them," I went on desperately. "Someone took them while I was asleep, I expect. I was heavily drugged last night. Your aunt made me a sleeping potion . . . If they are in this house, I will find them!"

Lord Castelmarten was silent a moment. Then he roused himself. "I doubt it," he said at last. "There are a thousand hiding places . . . and anyone who wanted the papers not to be found would obviously destroy them."

Mr. Prys-Roberts put his fingertips together. "These papers were, presumably, only copies," he said soothingly. "The originals will be in the parish register. A tracing can be made there of the signature, for purposes of comparison."

"Yes," said the earl grimly. "That is another reason why I feel I must go myself to Dunstable. Here," he added, holding out his jottings to the lawyer. "What do you make of these?"

Mr. Prys-Roberts carefully took out a pair of spectacles and polished them on his handkerchief before balancing them upon his nose.

"Yes," he pronounced at length. "These seem to be in the customary form. You do not recall the name of this witness to the wedding?"

"It was somewhat illegible—some name like Farren, Farmer, or Fanner. The occupation was given as maidservant. The signature of the clergyman was also indistinct, but I took it to be 'Edmund Fremantle.'"

"The wedding took place at the Church Cottage," the lawyer observed. "One presumes that was the home of Miss Merridew. Mr. Gervais was buried in the same Parish of St. Michael's, according to your recollection of the document, my lord. Your search, then, should not prove too hard, with the evidence at your command. Tracings of the original certificates, a statement from the relatives... To make all certain, of course, it would be best to persuade somebody who knows Miss Merridew to return with you in order to identify this lady, since, as you say, she is as yet unfit to travel herself." He bowed in my direction, obviously preferring to safeguard his future interest with me by giving me the benefit of the doubt; there would be time enough to spurn me later, if Miss Merridew's connections disowned me.

"That done," Mr. Prys-Roberts continued smoothly, "we will be able to proceed to probate."

"Ah!" Lord Castelmarten exclaimed. "Then my brother left a will?"

"Yes, my lord. He made it shortly before he left for the last time. I had advised him to do so ever since Miss Dyffryn's will was proved, under the terms of which he was named her residuary legatee. A considerable amount of capital is involved, though at the time of his death Mr. Marten did not have control of the principal. Our firm, as you know, was administering the fortune under the terms of the late Miss Dyffryn's will—a matter merely of sound investment, and the quarterly disbursement of a fractional interest."

"But Gerry's will?" Lord Castelmarten sounded impatient, and Mr. Prys-Roberts raised his brows. "Are you at liberty to divulge the terms of that?"

"I see no reason why I should not do so," the lawyer decided, after a moment's hesitation. "The document, by Mr. Gervais's own request, was simple in the extreme. On the event of his decease, his estate was to go to his wife, in its entirety. No mention was made of any issue. 'Time enough for that,' Mr. Marten told me. 'First I have to find my wife, and then we may discuss the matter.' 'And if you die a bachelor?' I asked him. He laughed. 'Oh, then my brother may inherit,' he declared. 'Surely he will find a worthy use for it, if it is only to keep Aunt Gwynnie's sisters comfortable in their old age. But I think it will not come to that.'"

Mr. Prys-Roberts untied a folder and drew out a single sheet of paper. "You may see for yourself, my lord; for I have here a copy of the will. It is very short and plain. Mr. Gervais would have it so."

Lord Castelmarten frowned at the document. I felt quite faint, reflecting that if Mr. Marten had not married, Lord Castelmarten would have been considerably the richer. No wonder he was so anxious to prove that his brother's widow was no longer alive!

I said tentatively, "The other young woman who might have been Mrs. Marten died in the accident. It seems unlikely that she made a will, and I doubt if I have ever done so. Do you think that now I should?" It had occurred to me that I might protect myself by making it known that any possible estate of mine would be left well away from the Martens—to Mrs. Jones at the Arms, for instance.

But Mr. Prys-Roberts pursed his lips and shook his head. "You can scarcely make a will, madam, until your own identity is proved," he pointed out. "Once it is, and assuming you are Mr. Marten's widow, and his beneficiary, then I would indeed advise you to make a testamentary disposition without further loss of time."

84

He placed his fingertips together and looked at me over the tops of his spectacles. "I would like to take this opportunity of assuring you, ma'am, of my happiness to serve you if at any time you should find yourself in need of advice in legal matters."

"Thank you," I murmured. "Of course, if I am Mary Ramsey, the question will not arise."

"It is an interesting situation," the lawyer remarked primly. "It would certainly be convenient if your memory were to return."

Lord Castelmarten leaned back in his chair. He hooked a thumb into the armhole of his waistcoat and looked at me with an eyebrow raised as if he dared me to defy him.

"And how is your memory, Miss Rose?" he demanded challengingly.

I raised my chin. "It does improve a little, sir. This morning when I awoke, I was rather confused, and thought the hangings of my bed a tent. I remembered then lying in a tent while some woman—my mother, I suppose—leaned over me."

"A tent," repeated the earl reflectively.

"And a little later this morning, when I had dressed and was looking out of the window, suddenly another window came into my mind... mullioned also, but very dark... dusty and cobwebbed, high up, and seeming to look out at bricks only a few inches away..."

"Very interesting as architectural memoirs, no doubt," Lord Castelmarten observed sardonically, "but of very little use to us, I fear."

I sighed a little, and looked away.

"Any improvement is surely encouraging," Mr. Prys-Roberts suggested kindly. He glanced diffidently at Lord Castelmarten. "If I might enquire, my lord, when do you propose to visit Dunstable?"

"I mean to set off tomorrow, if the weather permits, and if my mother is no worse."

"Tomorrow!" I exclaimed.

The earl stared at me, and I felt myself colouring at his inimical expression.

"I do not wonder at your apprehension, miss," he

85

drawled, his dark eyes narrowed. "But rest assured, I detest hackneyed situations and shall wait until the snow is melted before I turn you from my doors."

Mr. Prys-Roberts was overcome with a fit of coughing. "Ahem!" he cried, in some distress. "Pray do not let us make hasty assumptions, my lord! First, let us satisfy ourselves as to the truth."

"The truth," said Lord Castelmarten grimly, "is exactly what I intend to discover. I should be entering upon the task with rather more enthusiasm, however, if I could be sure that it had not been tampered with."

"What do you mean, sir?" I demanded, sensitive to the accusation in his tone.

"Why, I have the feeling that the truth has been deliberately perverted here, Miss Rose. The situation is so extraordinary that it occurs to me that it has been manipulated. I have been considering many possibilities to explain the facts, and one of the most reasonable explanations seems that either you tricked my brother into marriage, or forged a marriage certificate after his death, knowing full well that his widow stood to inherit a fortune. If this is indeed the case, then it is not impossible that you have an accomplice acting for you—"

Mr. Prys-Roberts sprang to his feet, scattering papers as he rose.

"Pray be careful, my lord," he cried agitatedly. "The laws of slander—"

"On the other hand," the earl continued imperturbably, "it is also possible that Miss Rose is an innocent victim of circumstance, and that she is herself being manipulated. I am endeavouring," he added with a mocking look, "to preserve an open mind."

The snow stopped soon after midday, the sun shone fitfully, and Ysolt returned to her duties. I questioned her about the reticule, of course, and she assured me, with her expressionless look, that though it had been she who placed it on the shelf, she had not presumed to look inside it. I hoped I was able to persuade her that I believed her, which was true because I was convinced that the papers had been stolen by the same mysterious figure who had stared in at me through the slits of a mask, from the window of my chamber at the Castell Marten Arms. It seemed so unlikely that there could be more than one sinister figure meddling in my life that I felt myself justified in believing that he must also be the author of the warning notes. If Mrs. Jones had not been watching by my bed that night at the inn, no doubt the certificates would have been stolen then, before ever I came to the castle.

But who, I wondered, would profit from the removal of certificates which after all were only copies of events recorded in a parish register?

Some person, I answered myself, either stupid, or illogical, who hated the idea of either Mr. Marten's marriage, or his death—and that must absolve Lord Castelmarten who, if prejudiced, was far from stupid and in whose interest it was to have the burial proved, if not the marriage. On the other hand, I reflected, if the thief was literally working in the dark, he would have had to have abstracted both the documents even if his intention was to destroy one and return the other. And everything pointed to it having been a member of the household . . .

I sat down abruptly on the window seat. It had just occurred to me that since it would be pointless to steal the copies while the originals existed, the thief had either seen to it that the originals had been destroyed, or was about to do so. And Lord Castelmarten proposed to set out for Dunstable upon the morrow! If something did not happen to prevent him, then in two or three days' time all proof of Gervais Marten's marriage and burial might well have disappeared.

Then I forced myself to think more calmly. Neither a marriage nor a burial could be kept entirely secret. There must have been witnesses, a minister . . . to say nothing of the family of Miss Merridew. And there could not be many new graves in a country churchyard; nor probably, would Mr. Marten's body yet be beyond the possibility of identification.

Yet from some dark corner of my mind came the thought that Lord Castelmarten was very powerful, that witnesses could be bought; the truth, as he had said himself, could be manipulated.

On impulse, I rang for Ysolt and asked for writing materials. When she brought the desk, I took the pen in my left hand, and very awkwardly wrote a short note to the attorney.

"Can you see that this letter is delivered to Mr. Prys-Roberts, who was here this morning?" I asked, when I had sanded and sealed it.

"Why, yes, mistress. My cousin Emrys will send a groom with it to his chambers."

"Emrys?"

"Yes. He is the head groom here."

"I see. Mr. Prys-Roberts said that I could communicate with him, if I so wished . . . only, I do not particularly want it known that I have done so."

Ysolt looked inscrutable.

"In that case, mistress, I will ask Emrys to deliver it himself."

"Thank you, Ysolt."

She curtsied and took the note. "I will give it to him at once, mistress."

Dinner was served in the Caroline dining room on informal occasions, as I discovered when I went downstairs that evening. It was a gloomy apartment in one of the courtyard wings on the ground floor, panelled and furnished in dark oak. Lady Castelmarten was dining in her room, and Miss Esther had at the last moment decided to share her sister's early retirement. Only Miss Enid was left, rising grimly to her duty of chaperoning the cuckoo in the nest, as I was sure she regarded me.

In fact, I was grateful for her disapproving presence which saved me the embarrassment of a tête-à-tête with his lordship. He looked tired and somber and drank several glasses of wine, which did not seem to affect him unduly, except perhaps to inhibit his powers of conversation. Miss Enid, however, had been brought up in a stricter school, and did not allow us to relapse entirely into silence. She introduced a variety of topics, which I endeavoured to enlarge upon, but the only one in which Lord Castelmarten showed any real interest was that concerning sheep until, in a sort of desperation, I impulsively announced my discovery of the hidden bracelet. Then indeed he glanced at me with close attention, and brusquely demanded a description of the ornament.

I withdrew the bracelet from the reticule, watching Miss Enid's face as well as his. Both stared at it, Miss Enid blankly, the earl, I thought, with a slightly startled look.

"Fleurs-de-lis," he murmured. "Put it on."

I resented his autocratic tone, but supposed he hoped to jog his memory by seeing the bracelet worn. I obeyed him, therefore, with extreme reluctance. It was extraordinary how the ornament affected me, so much so that actual contact with it was distasteful to me. It did look very pretty, however, shining against my black glove as I twisted my arm this way and that in the soft light of the wax candles.

"Is it real gold?" Miss Enid asked sharply.

"Why, yes, I think so. It is heavy enough. Have you ever seen one like it, ma'am?"

"Never," she said firmly. "How could I have done so, if you brought it from Dunstable and kept it hidden? It is an unusual piece—belonged to some French emigrée, no doubt."

"But did she bring it from Dunstable, I wonder?" The earl raised his wine glass, staring at me as he drank. "That reticule is obviously Mrs. Marten's—or perhaps I should say Victoria Merridew's—but there is nothing to tell us that it belongs to Miss Rose."

I narrowed my eyes until the bracelet was a shimmering blur. "Now there is . . ." I said. "I know this bracelet— though I cannot recall where I saw it before."

Lord Castelmarten reflected for a moment. "If you know it, and if it was found in Mrs. Marten's reticule, that still does not prove that you are she. Assuming for the sake of argument that you are Mary Ramsey, is it not possible that, striking up an acquaintance with Mrs. Marten in the coach, you might have sold the bracelet to her? Or, since I agree that it is more likely to have belonged to Mrs. Marten than to a ragpicker, might she not have shown it to you before she hid it? You might even have helped her to buy it, perhaps, at some earlier stage of the journey—or she might have asked you to sew it into place for her, wanting to hide it for reasons of security."

After that, no doubt satisfied that he had depressed my pretensions for the time being, the earl relapsed into silence. I pressed the tiny knob which released the catch, and hinged open the bracelet. I offered it to him, but he shook his head, and since Miss Enid made no comment, I slid it back into my reticule.

I could hardly remember later what I had eaten, beyond the mutton which I was learning was almost inevitable at a Welshman's table; but I retained the impression that the food was carefully prepared and well-served, without being lavish in any way. I do not know quite what I had expected—footmen behind every chair, and gold plate, perhaps; but the reality was more austere. Miss Enid and the housekeeper, Mrs. Meredith, whom I had only briefly glimpsed, managed the running of the house between them, very capably, I judged, but without great expenditure. Then I wondered what training in my past had led to my having any opinion on the subject.

In the upstairs Parlour I observed that the books were shabby, the curtains faded, and the upholstery neatly darned. No doubt living in a castle must strain even a large fortune, I reflected.

Miss Enid asked me to play the pianoforte, while we waited for Lord Castelmarten to join us.

"You don't seem to have great powers of conversation," she observed candidly, "and we have little enough in common if you can't even recall my nephew. It would hardly be seemly to play cards in a house so recently bereaved, so there is nothing for it but a little music. Esther plays sometimes. I believe you will find the instrument to be in tune."

I did not dare protest, although I had not the least notion whether I had ever learned to play.

I walked reluctantly towards the piano, and turned

back the lid. I sat down and looked at the keys. They were shadowy, for the candles in the holders had not been lit. I laid my fingers on the ivory, and closed my eyes. It seemed a miracle when music began to ripple out under my fingers, a light lilting tune.

"Very nice," said Miss Enid when I paused. "But pray go on."

"I can't," I owned unhappily. "It—stopped. I mean, I can't remember any more."

"I had forgotten your affliction, for the moment. Try the music, child."

I held up a book of music to the lamp. "I don't believe I know how to read music."

I laid down the book and dropped my hands again upon the keys. A chord rang out, and another tune began to follow, stumblingly at first, then gaining in power and accuracy. When I had finished, I felt so cold and drained I determined not to play again until my memory returned.

"Bravo," murmured Lord Castelmarten. I had not even heard him enter. He moved forward to stand beside me. He looked ruffled, I noticed, as if he had been running his hands through his hair.

"I was in the stableyard this afternoon," he said abruptly. "Ysolt brought out a note and gave it to Emrys to deliver to Prys-Roberts. As I was going there myself, I took the liberty of delivering your letter to him, and as soon as he had read it, Prys-Roberts showed it to me."

I was silent, my fingers tightly clasped upon my lap.

"I can understand that you don't trust me," he said angrily, "but I cannot understand why you sent that note to him." He gave a sudden laugh. "The irony of it is, that I had ridden there to discuss the very same suggestion with Prys-Roberts with the result that he has offered to lend me his clerk to travel with me as a witness. It is a damnable nuisance, of course, for Williams will slow me down considerably, but it seems to us all to be a wise precaution."

I took a breath. "I wonder if the suggestion came first from Mr. Prys-Roberts, or from you, my lord?"

I could see his fist clench. Then he said, "Why, I believe

the first hint came from him, this morning after you had left us... it is not hard to understand why such a careful legal mind should think of such a precaution. Your having done so, however, leads me to suppose either that you have prepared the ground at Dunstable very carefully indeed; or, what I find hard to believe, that I have misjudged you."

"And why," I said in a small voice, "do you find it so hard to believe I am exactly as I seem?"

He stared. "First, because it has all worked out so conveniently for you—"

"Conveniently?" I cried, quite forgetful of Miss Enid. "You call it convenient to have been involved in a terrible accident, and barely to have survived it? Convenient to have lost my memory of all the past, of any family or friends I may have had? Convenient to find myself here exiled in a foreign land, at the mercy of—of a hostile tyrant?"

He folded his arms and leaned back against the panelled wall.

"Is that how it appears to you? You are a pretty little actress, that I grant you."

I longed to hit him, a sensation that I was sure was quite foreign to my nature.

"Why do you not try to give me the benefit of the doubt?" I demanded. "Why not allow yourself to believe what is true, that I awoke at the Castell Marten Arms without the least notion of whom I was? I assure you that I do not know any more of the circumstances of my marriage than do you, or if indeed I am the girl your brother married. But one thing I do know, and that is that I would never have married him for gain alone!"

"No?" murmured the earl, raising a sceptical eyebrow.

"No," I cried passionately. "Why, supposing that your lordship were so obliging as to offer for me, do you imagine for one moment that I would accept, eligible as you are?"

"Not if you were trying to prove yourself my brother's wife," he said dryly. "Our relationship, if there is one, is within the forbidden degree. But just supposing—though I

92

know better—that you are at the same time high principled and my sister-in-law, what explanation could justify such a hasty, hole-in-corner marriage, to a man whom you could have barely known—"

"What makes you so sure of that?" I demanded. "We might have been childhood sweethearts, for all you know!"

"I think not. I never heard of Gerry setting foot in Dunstable before this."

"You would not have heard of it even now, if I—or the other girl—had not brought the news to you," I pointed out. "No doubt there are other whole areas of your brother's life equally unsuspected by you!"

His eyes narrowed. "Are you forgetting that we were only ? year apart in age?" he demanded. "Gervais was at school with me until I was eighteen. He followed me to Oxford a year later. Some eighteen months after that, when it was plain enough he had no turn for the academic life, he persuaded Father to buy him a pair of colours. He was with his regiment, first in Sussex, and then in Ireland until last autumn when at his request, I bought him out. After that he stayed here at Castel Marten, hunting, shooting, and quarrelling with his neighbors, making a nuisance of himself, until in desperation I packed him off to London to stay with a strict and admirable uncle of ours—where needless to say, he never arrived."

"Well, what does that prove? I might have met him in Ireland for all I know. Who is to say? Certainly not you!"

"If you did meet him earlier, it would certainly explain why he should feel compelled to make a will in favour of his wife," said the earl unkindly.

"Allow me to inform your lordship that you are prejudiced beyond belief! How do you know I did not persuade him to make a later will, leaving everything to charity—or even to you?"

"You have a devious mind, Miss Rose—and that does not encourage me to suspect you the less. No, you have not convinced me of your innocence, I fear. You see, you yourself have provided me with proof enough that you are capable of lying and deceit."

Even Miss Enid, who had been watching and listening in silence, allowed a startled exclamation to escape her at this accusation.

Lord Castelmarten brought out two pieces of paper from his waistcoat pocket.

"You have no need to study these, Miss Rose, since I believe you wrote them—but perhaps you can explain why both your letters to Prys-Roberts and the unsigned warning to leave Wales should appear to be in the same hand?"

I stared uncomprehendingly for a moment. Then I realized that the note which I had found in my reticule did bear a strange resemblance to the ill-written one which I had penned with my left hand to the lawyer.

I found it hard to speak. "I did not write them both," I managed to say at last. "But the handwriting in both does appear to be disguised..." I raised my bandaged right hand, but before I could say more, Miss Enid had stood up.

"I will not listen to any more of this ridiculous conversation," she said coldly. "Miss Rose, I apologize for my graceless nephew, who appears to have taken leave of his senses. I can only beg you to remember that, like the rest of us in this house, he has suffered grievous loss, and is still feeling the effects of shock and hurt."

I quickly rose. "I too have said more than I should have done." I forced myself to meet Lord Castelmarten's sardonic gaze. "Forgive me, sir, for any impoliteness."

He bowed slightly. "For your impoliteness, I forgive you, Miss Rose. For the rest—we shall see, when I return from Dunstable."

With that he turned on his heel, and left the room.

Miss Enid and I stared at each other.

"Well, indeed!" she said. "I don't know what has got into that young man, I am sure! I have never seen him behave so badly!" Then she appeared to recollect to whom she was speaking, and drew herself up stiffly.

"Come, Miss Rose," she said severely, "It is time you were abed."

Chapter Eight

The following day was clear and bright. I looked out at the high pastures, barely salted with white, and decided there could have been nothing to prevent Lord Castelmarten from embarking on his journey. It would be a relief to be free of his disturbing presence for a while, I reflected, yet immediately I found myself suspecting that the castle might be rather dull without him.

"Today looks better for the gathering," I said to Ysolt. "How long does it take to bring in the sheep?"

"Many days... many men. And when one gathering is finished, there is another waiting. Other farmers help us out, and we must help them in our turn. Will you be eating breakfast in the Morning Room today, mistress?"

Feeling much better, I agreed to do so; I wished that I had stayed in my room, however, when I was confronted by the sight of Miss Esther, with a cup of coffee to her lips.

But to my surprise, I soon saw that Miss Esther had made a remarkable recovery. She was not at all the wailing woman of our first meeting, though still clad in deepest mourning. No longer hysterical over her beloved nephew's death, she appeared quite cheerful, and suprisingly friendly towards me.

"Do sit down, here by me," she cried. "We have so much to talk about... Can you recall anything yet of dear Gervais?"

"No, ma'am, I am afraid I still cannot remember."

"Oh, what a pity! But still, if he loved you, that should be enough for me."

"Thank you, Miss Esther. But we don't yet know that I am—his widow."

"In a week or so, we shall be sure of it. I feel it, my dear.

95

I am intuitive, you know. I sense meanings of things that escape other people. Lucian is terribly insensitive, I fear. He can only believe the evidence of his eyes. He pretends to disbelieve your claim, but as soon as I realized how deeply he disliked and—yes, feared you—I understood that he must really be persuaded that you are indeed the woman Gerry married."

I spread a piece of bread with sweet Welsh butter, and began to eat it thoughtfully.

"I suppose Lord Castelmarten's antipathy towards me is very obvious," I mused.

"Oh, to be sure, Lucian does not trouble to hide his feelings! Gerry's choice could never be a favourite with him."

"It seems—unfair."

"Certainly it does. Lucian was always unfair to Gerry."

"So, no matter who I was, if Lord Castelmarten thought his brother liked me, he would have been my enemy?"

"Of course. Just as he is mine, and poor Sarah Vaughan's. Oh, not openly, I grant you. In my case—his mother sees to that! But he is quite impatient with me sometimes. Only last night when we were talking about that bracelet you found—but never mind that!" She laid a finger to her lips and looked mysterious.

"Has Lord Castelmarten left?" I asked, pouring my coffee.

"Oh, yes. He rode away at dawn. The place feels quite different without him."

"It seems unfortunate that you are obliged to live under the same roof," I ventured.

"My dear, if you knew how I longed to set up my own establishment! I even have a friend, another artist, Miss Williams, Pen-y-Bont, whose ambition is to share a cottage with me. But though she possesses an ample independence, I, alas, could contribute nothing, and I would not join her on such terms." She sighed gustily. "Even a room of my own would be a luxury almost beyond imagining."

"But this is a castle! Surely you could have a room to yourself, if you desired it?"

She sighed again. "If only I dared propose it! But Enid

would be so hurt. She and I, you know, have always shared a room." Miss Esther brought out a mourning fan and fluttered it. Her eyes met mine in a swift glance over the black scalloped edge. "She is your enemy too, you know. She is afraid that if you are recognized as Mrs. Marten, you will usurp her authority. She is the real housekeeper here at Castell Marten—Mrs. Meredith is but her tool—and she intends to remain . . . queen of the castle."

"Does she, Miss Esther?"

I had the feeling of sailing in forbidden waters; but I found Miss Esther's indiscretions extremely interesting, and told myself it was important to know all I could discover of the undercurrents at Castell Marten, if I were to keep myself afloat.

"Oh, yes, Enid must always be queen . . . the only person she really respects is dear Elaine. I suppose if Lucian marries, Enid will not care to compete with Mathilda, and might then remove with Elaine to the Dower House, but there would not be room for the three of us, I think." She leaned forward to whisper confidentially, "Unlike our sister Elaine, Enid and I would prefer Lucian *not* to marry Miss Carnaby. It would be very uncomfortable for us all if he did! I see no reason why she should not make a love match with Dr. Glynn, since no one would offer for her in London—but I dare say her parents would not agree with me in that!"

She patted my hand and winked as if we were conspirators. Sipping my coffee, I pondered on her change of attitude towards me. It must be, I belatedly realized, that in me she had suddenly seen a possible hope of financial assistance, if I were indeed her niece. And if I did inherit, I too would be free, I reflected. Everything depended on the news Lord Castelmarten would bring from Dunstable, which would alter my whole position and my future. I might even have a home to go to of my own! Church Cottage, Upper Buzzard—it sounded cozy, if humble; and presumably I would be bound to love my own family. Considerably cheered by this reflection, I concluded my breakfast with a good appetite.

"Perhaps you would like to see my paintings?" Miss

Esther suggested, and gave me her arm up the stairs while entertaining me with a dissertation on the difficulty of obtaining paints, or even the materials with which to make her own, here in the heart of Wales.

The chamber into which she ushered me was larger than mine and very mixed in character. I could not repress a smile as I saw how rigidly it was divided down the middle. One side was untidy, with bright lengths of material flung carelessly over chairs, dried flowers and peacock feathers bursting from richly ornamented jars, and the bed half-hidden by a lacquer screen on which a variety of fans had been pinned in striking display. Miss Enid's side of the room appeared by contrast to be monkishly ascetic, embellished only with a few severe engravings, and a large writing table, bare of all but standish, pen tray, and sandbox. The only things common to both seemed to be the carpet and three cats, two of whom fled at our approach. The third, who looked complacently expectant, continued to knead the pillow on Miss Enid's bed.

"I won't keep you waiting a moment," said Miss Esther, bursting towards a small door at the far end of the room. "I keep my paintings in the powder closet," she explained, her voice muffled as she entered it. "Enid appreciates them, of course, but she finds them—somewhat distracting at close quarters."

She reappeared with her arms full of mounts and frames, and a pile of odd pieces of paper, which she cast lavishly upon the bed.

"Sit there," she cried, waving me to Miss Enid's straightbacked chair. "Let me just...there! And now—" She busied herself with propping up her works of art on chairs and on the floor against the wall, and on any other surface she could find.

I stared at them. I could sympathize with Miss Enid's sentiments regarding them, for they were indeed peculiarly distracting. Though executed in watercolours, they yet contrived to be very bright and strange, with a good deal of insistence on the primary colours. On closer examination, I distinguished in one painting red dragons emerging from blue forests, breathing yellow fire; in another a gaunt hand, tortured with purple shadows, emerged from a snowdrift brandishing a sword; and in the largest, a group of persons, gloomy but gaudily clad, lounged about a table, feasting but depressed—possibly because they were aware of how badly their garments clashed.

"All allegorical, as you see," explained Miss Esther proudly.

I searched desperately for some sensible, yet encouraging comment.

"You are very fond of red dragons," I observed lamely.

"The red dragon of Wales! Our heraldic beast! And here, Excalibur, King Arthur's sword, rising from the mere..."

"And these people?" Surely it could not be the Last Supper?

"The knights of the Round Table—it is very hard to draw a circle, you know. And in any case, it would appear more of an ellipse, I thought. And this red hand is that of Owain ab Gruffyd, Lord of Glyndyfrdwy—he whom you English call Glyn Dwyer, of course."

"Extremely interesting. Do they take long to execute?"

"Oh no, I dash them off in no time."

She sat down on the crimson bed, an incongruous figure in her dark mourning among the violently coloured paintings. "I need bright colours, you see," she explained superfluously. "It is like a hunger in me...it is very hard for me to be condemned to wearing black."

"I don't like it either," I assured her. I had a fleeting vision of all the black-clad women moving somberly about the old stone castle. "Even white would be greatly preferable—"

"Anything would be preferable to that horrid gown," Miss Esther agreed frankly. "But your wardrobe is sadly limited, Ysolt tells me—scarcely what one might expect of Gerry's wife. But then he was kept so short...I don't know why Gwynneth left her money so tied up that he could only enjoy a portion of the interest until he was twenty-five. I have a notion Lucian persuaded Prys-

Roberts to insist upon it. I have heard him say that Gerry would only have gambled the rest away, if he could have laid his hands upon it. I believe Lucian was wrong, and that Gerry was irresponsible precisely because he was treated as a child. We will never know, alas. But I do hope you, and not Lucian, are the one to inherit poor Gwynneth's fortune."

She stood up, and I began to help her restore the paintings to their hiding place. "I suppose, since it was originally your mother's money, ma'am, the fortune should properly be divided between Miss Enid and yourself."

"No, my dear," she replied, to my surprise. "Gwynneth would have left it to us if she thought we needed it. She knew, you see, that if we were financially independent Lucian would feel himself at liberty to push us out into the world; and though that would suit me well enough, between ourselves, I do not know what would become of Enid. I take after Father, and Enid and I would never survive cottage life together. She and Elaine, perhaps . . . but I do not know how Elaine would feel about leaving the castle. Besides, Gerry had a right to leave his money to his wife, and there's an end of it—though if she felt like helping us out from time to time, I for one would not be too proud to accept an occasional present."

She pushed the last of the paintings into the back of the powder closet, and flung a shawl over them. "There! That's better. Enid thinks me dreadfully untidy, I'm afraid, and she is certainly wretchedly unhappy unless everything is in its proper place, which I think very dull. She says sometimes that she quite despairs of me—thank you, dear," as I handed her a painting we had overlooked, which she then tossed vaguely towards the others. "Now, where was I?" she added, shutting the closet door. "Ah, yes. Enid thinks I am not quite right, you know. Of course, it is true that I take after Father and that he is very odd sometimes, but I don't think that need mean—in any case, and I am sure Elaine agrees with me in this, it is poor Enid, if anyone, who is a little . . . But Father is not by any means senile, you know. He won't let Enid or myself come near him, alas, but he sits up there in his tower watching from his window and he knows—well, Gervais used to say that he knew everything, piecing it together from what he saw. Gervais was very close to his grandfather—dear Gerry!"

A slight sound startled her and she clutched my arm. "Sh!" she whispered, like a schoolgirl. "It's Enid! Not a word!"

She hurried me across the room as Miss Enid entered it, and almost pushed me out onto the gallery. As the door closed behind me I could hear Miss Enid scolding her sister in her cool, dry voice, to a background of Miss Esther's breathless protests.

I paused by a window on the gallery to stare across the courtyard to the Keep where old Lord Dyffryn lived in solitude. If he knew everything, and if he had been very close to Gerry, was it not possible that the eccentric old hermit might be able to furnish me with some of the answers I required? Had I the courage to find my own way to the Keep in order to question Lord Dyffryn while I had the chance to speak to him alone? If Lord Castelmarten had been at home, I knew I should not have dared attempt it; but as matters stood, I had hardly conceived the thought before I determined to act upon it.

I hurried to my room to put on my outdoor clothes. Ysolt had mentioned that the way to the Keep lay through the bookcase in the Parlour, and presently I was crossing the threadbare carpet of that room, and running my hands over the bookshelves nearest to the fireplace. It did not take me long to discover that the whole bookcase could be pulled open like a door, hinged to the next case, revealing a dark hole beyond.

I hesitated, wondering if I should go back for a lamp, and the pause gave me time to reconsider. Was I mad to think of launching myself down those dark stairs without a guide? And even supposing that I did not break my neck, and that I was able to manipulate the drawbridge, which was extremely doubtful—how was I going to explain my uninvited presence to the recluse within? I did not know if it would constitute an act of trespass, but even if not, it seemed the height of bad manners to force my unwanted

101

company upon the hermit. Besides, for all I knew, he might be dangerous—he sounded very odd indeed.

But Miss Esther had said that he knew everything, and that Gervais had been very close to him ... I had to take this opportunity of attempting to discover what he knew. And in addition, I did not want to admit myself a coward, so I screwed my resolution to the sticking point and walked into the darkness.

I pulled the door shut behind me, after discovering that it was weighted so as to take no more than a push to open it from within. I stood in the dark until it gradually lightened, glad that I had brought my cloak, for it was cold. A wet river smell was all about me, and draughts stirred my hair under the black bonnet.

I took a cautious step, and then another, and found I was at the top of a winding stair. I began to make my way down, clinging to the central column of crumbling stone, because there seemed to be no rail on the outer wall, where the steps were wider. A final twist of the stair enabled me to see the vaulted room below, with narrow slitted windows letting in a greenish light. I stopped and looked about me carefully. The wall opposite the stairs had a central panel which seemed to be made of some dark wood, old and splintered, with some broken boards in it and loops of rusty chains hanging on either side of it. That would be the drawbridge, I supposed. The wall to the right of it supported an antique arrangement of wheels and cogs, and cables of twisted metal led in various directions, some disappearing through the wall itself. I approached the mechanism doubtfully, forced myself to grasp the largest wheel, and began reluctantly to turn it.

There came a series of protesting creaks from the wooden panel, and then it began slowly to drop outward from the top, revealing first the middle and then the lower portions of the ruined tower, a good deal closer than I had expected it to be. At length, with many pauses for me to regain my breath and rest my aching arms, the far end of the drawbridge dropped into place, linking the castle with the Keep.

I stepped nervously onto the splintered oaken boards,

only to be presented with a new difficulty. Below me the river moat swirled brownish-green and I found myself sick and shaken with unreasoning terror. I was afraid of water—terribly afraid!

But having come so far, I could not allow myself to turn back now. I told myself firmly that my fear was quite ridiculous—perhaps I had been nearly drowned in the Afon Ystwyth not long ago, but I was safe enough upon the bridge as long as I kept off the broken boards, and fixing my eyes on the cavernous opening yawning before me in the Keep, I stepped slowly at first, and then more rapidly, towards it.

Relieved though I was to have left the moat behind me, I could find little to reassure me in the gloomy chamber in which I found myself. The room was dank and echoing, with slimy trails of moisture dripping down its green-stained walls.

I noticed a twin mechanism on the wall and felt that I should raise the drawbridge lest it attract attention; but my efforts had tired me and I decided it was better to conserve my strength. Besides, I might need a quick way of escape...

I made my way to the stairs and began to climb them. The air was damp and unpleasant, and the stone stairs treacherous underfoot, but I tried to hearten myself with the reflection that the company of Lord Dyffryn must be attractive indeed to have persuaded his visitors to overcome such hazards in approaching him.

I was not physically in good condition. I found myself breathing heavily and my muscles aching as I neared the top. Something flapped across my face and I caught my breath upon a shriek. A moment later I stumbled against a door, and pulling the bobbin, burst it open. Light flooded about me, showing me that what I had feared must be at least a bat was nothing more alarming than a frond of a luxuriant fern.

"What's this? What's this?" cried a tetchy voice from within the room. "Company, eh? Will they never learn that I detest company?"

I believe I might have turned and run at that, had not the

hermit pulled the door roughly from my grasp, and stood confronting me with an intolerant glare, which slowly faded.

"Oh, a young lady, is it," he remarked in a different tone. "I suppose you'll be wanting to come in and stare at the poor old man? Well, what do you think of him, eh? Have a good look while you're about it."

It was impossible not to take him at his word, and I stared my fill.

Lord Dyffryn was a small man of shabby appearance. He was even, it must be confessed, rather dirty. His long beard was more yellow than white, his nails wrinkled and overgrown. Fortunately he had the good sense not to attempt wearing linen, but was dressed in a biblical robe of practical brown wool with a plaited belt and sturdy boots, not sandals, on his little feet. Bent over with age as he was, his head scarcely reached my shoulder.

He peered up at me, his head cocked to one side. "And who might you be, miss?" he demanded.

This simple question naturally struck me dumb, but the hermit answered it himself.

"Gerry's widow, it is, indeed to goodness? Elaine was over here yesterday with some tale about young Gerry—I've forgotten the half of it now, and did not believe a quarter of it at the time. But she seemed pretty certain young Gerry was dead, and I'm not surprised at it. Reckless young scapegrace that he was, cared for nothing but his own way, though he did play a fair game of chess, since I taught him myself. Well, so you are his wife, are you? *Diw*, but I'm sorry for any wife of his, that I can tell you. How did he die, eh?"

"I have lost my memory," I said desperately. "I was in an accident . . . I fear I can't recall your grandson. I do not even know if I was his wife."

"Well, you may be fortunate, when all's said. But you don't seem to have much claim to be here, do you?" he demanded, his face darkening. "And no call, as far as I can see, to come disturbing my chosen solitude. In fact, miss," he cried, working himself into a passion, "you'd better leave, if you know what's good for you. Ay, go—and leave

104

the castle, too, for I can tell you are a worry and a trouble to my daughter." He flapped his tiny hands at me. "We want no strangers here—out, miss!"

I stood my ground. "Was it you, sir, who sent me warnings to leave Wales?" I cried impetuously.

"I? Why should I do such a thing? But if you have been warned, then you had best be off, I say."

"I won't stay long to plague you, sir," I promised him. "The reason for my coming to see you here was because Miss Esther told me—"

"Esther! Can't abide the woman, comes fussing over me like a mother hen and cries at so much as an angry word. I told her I'd throw her down the stairs if she came clacking after me again."

"She said that you know everything, Lord Dyffryn. That you watched from your window here—"

"Ay, that I do—and see more than they bargain for, I'll warrant!"

"And that you were close to—to Gervais, sir."

"Well, well—he'd come to see me, scamp that he was, bring me wine—not that I would ever touch such poison, except to keep him company—and play, as I say—ay, we'd play chess together. He wouldn't take offense, like Esther, nor try to bully me like Enid. Besides, he'd make me laugh with that quick wit of his, and tell me all the gossip in exchange for mine."

"Do you know where he went from here?" I asked, hands clasped together.

He shot me a quick glance. "He was up to no good, I'll tell you that. But you look pale, miss. You'd best sit down." He gestured me towards a chair. "And what am I supposed to call you, if you have no name? Rose, eh? Well, that's pretty enough. Not Welsh, alas, but I dare say that can't be helped. Are you interested in poetry, miss?"

"I—yes, I believe I—"

"Ach, I thought you would be!" And he began to declaim with great intensity in what I assumed to be Welsh, though it might as well have been Greek for all I understood of it. The poem, if such it was, gave me plenty of time to study both Lord Dyffryn and the miserable conditions in which he chose to live. The room was small and the rough walls had been whitewashed at one time; but now dust lay along the ledges and in every crack, and cobwebs festooned the corners. There was a fireplace full of grey ashes stirring in the draught, and two windows set in the thick walls with wide seats, on one of which several books had been thrown down haphazardly, and on the other a jackdaw solemnly paced, looking at me sideways. There was an oaken settle, sadly in need of polish, and two hard chairs pulled up to a gatelegged table covered with papers and open books. One wall was shelved and overflowing with more books, piled upon each other and bristling with paper markers. Against the fourth wall stood a tent bed heaped with animal skins, or worn-out furs. There was a good thick rug on the floor, but it was grey with dust and covered with yet more heaps of papers and books. A basket stood in one corner, containing dirty dishes; and a cracked pottery bowl of exceedingly wrinkled apples completed the decoration of this singular apartment.

"Well, young woman," demanded Lord Dyffryn, "what do you think of it, eh?"

With a start I realized he was referring to the poem, which he had apparently concluded.

"Very beautiful," I said politely. "I did not understand it, of course, but the—the cadences are—are very sonorous and satisfying."

"Nonsense!" he returned briskly. "How can you possibly know anything about it if you do not speak Welsh? But never mind that. Pretty young ladies are not expected to be bluestockings, and you are certainly pretty enough...Gerry would not have had it otherwise, of course. What are you looking at, miss? My chessboard?"

"Yes..." I moved over to the table, and stood fingering the ivory knight, my thoughts far away.

"You don't play, by any chance? No, no, that is too much to hope for—"

"Yes, I do," I began eagerly, but then I stood appalled, wondering what in the world had possessed me, to lay claim to a skill so easily tested.

106

"Excellent! Excellent!" he cried, rubbing his hands together, the papery skin making a horrid whispering sound. "You'll not deny an old man the pleasure of a game, I trust? Come, help me set out the board, there's a good girl."

"Oh no," I cried, "I must not stay . . ."

"To be sure, you must. First we'll clear the table. Now, to find the pieces. Some of them are in the bed," he added testily, while I stared at him uncomprehendingly.

"In the bed, sir?"

"Yes, yes. I was testing out a theory . . . a knotty problem, and I wondered if sleeping with my head upon the pieces involved might resolve it in a dream."

"And did it?" I asked, diverted by this original approach.

"Well—partly, yes. I did begin to dream I was playing chess, and with those very pieces, but then they began to sprout and grow, and before I knew it they had all turned to yews—we had just such topiary work at Pen Maen once—and then I was obliged to dig them up and replant them every time I moved one. I found it very tiring and woke up in quite a perspiration. But I was some way towards solving the problem, I believe. Come, child, surely you have found them by this time?"

"Yes, I have found some; but I don't know what to do with all the papers on this chair."

"Put them on the floor, of course." He turned up his eyes with an exasperated look. "That is precisely why I am obliged to live here in retreat. Women are so hidebound, so conventional, even Esther, who at least understands that art must come before order. I detest women on the whole—managing women, that is—I find their petty ways enough to aggravate one to violence—and I am opposed to violence, miss. I gave Fox my support, you know, in this iniquitous war against the French. Let them treat their monarchs how they will, I told him. 'Tis no affair of ours, and I doubt if the French will trouble to invade us so long as we have not declared war on them. If they were to do so, of course, 'twould put a different complexion on the matter. Well, Fox listened to me at the time, but—tush! He

107

is an unstable fellow, brilliant if you like, but no match for young Pitt. I washed my hands of it in the end—ay, and everything else. If they will not choose to listen to me, why should I throw my pearls before such swine, eh? Tell me that!"

"They used to listen to you, sir, so I am told, and they would still, perhaps, if you chose to encourage them—"

"If I were not so rude to them, you mean, do you not? Why do you hesitate? Have you yet to learn an honest man appreciates an honest criticism, eh? What I can't abide is mealy-mouthed platitudes, dithering and dallying—let me have oak and stone and skins about me, bones to gnaw, and good honest bread—none of your made-up flummery!"

"No, sir. There, I think that's right," I added, staring at the chessboard.

"Of course it's right. Now, come, Miss Rose, you take that chair, and let us begin. Or—" He peered at me suspiciously, as I hesitated. "Or are you afraid of me, eh? Afraid to play?"

"Well, I am a little afraid of you, sir," I truthfully declared. "I never met your like before—I think. But as I told you, I am suffering from loss of memory. I am not even sure, now that I reflect upon it, that I can play chess."

He was not angry, to my relief. "Well, well," he said mildly enough, "let us try it, at all events. I have been wearying for a game this many a day."

I pulled a handkerchief from my reticule and dusted the chair before sitting down. "I understand the Vicar, Mr. Vaughan, is a notable chess player," I ventured.

"True, true, and a poet also. We were at Oxford together—but his wife won't let him visit me, odious woman, just because I am a Deist, and she doesn't approve."

"A Deist?" I repeated blankly.

"Ay, ay. We reject formal religion, you understand, while still acknowledging the existence of God. Madame Vaughan, who is as mighty a potentate within the limits of her domain as ever Nero was, chooses to take my private beliefs as a personal slight, and Gwylim, poor fellow, dares not oppose her by seeking out my company. Young Ned Vaughan used to play with me from time to time, but I haven't set eyes on him for months. He took up with playactors, the young fool, and ran away from home—no one seems to know where he is living now. London, most likely . . . You have the white, miss," he snapped suddenly. "Am I to wait all day or are you to make your move?"

I murmured an apology and moved the king's pawn.

"Correct, if unadventurous," remarked Lord Dyffryn, advancing his own. "It wouldn't surprise me, however, to hear Ned had made his name as an actor, though it's no profession for a gentleman. He had a real talent for mimicry, as I recall—have you heard that there's some discussion about allowing the pawns to advance two squares in their first move, by the by? To my mind, such a change would in certain circumstances give too great an advantage . . . you have moved your knight. I, my queen's pawn, then. Yes, young Ned Vaughan was an amusing fellow, though one could hardly admire him. But he used to come in here with Gerry sometimes and tell me of his doings—would imitate old Carnaby nodding in church, the old man, I mean, not the fellow who has the title now; and his mother acting the *grande dame*, as she'd call it—ay, and that minx of a sister of his, Miss Sarah. I've seen her once or twice," he added, with a sharp look at me. "Elaine tells me that Freddy Carnaby affects her—but of course his parents will not hear of such a match. His mother was a Williams-Wynn, you know, as starchy as can be, and with a greater fortune than is good for her, no doubt."

I moved my bishop to queen's knight five, to check his king, reflecting that it seemed not improbable the rich and powerful Carnabys might have to resign themselves to two mismatches in the family before very long . . . and who then would Lord Castelmarten marry?

Lord Dyffryn raised his eyebrows and advanced his bishop's pawn. I saw then what a weak move mine had been, and brought out my queen's knight to protect the bishop. Lord Dyffryn took it; I took his pawn and he brought up his castle's pawn, sighing in exasperation and forcing me to retreat. Presently he had moved up his king's pawn and had my knight and bishop in exchange for two pawns of his, and had forced me to move my king, thus ruining my hopes of castling. Too late I realized I could have moved my queen instead . . . and I was not surprised when Lord Dyffryn soon cornered my king and shouted "*Shah mat*" or, as he told me with ill-concealed triumph, "The king is defeated." He told me where I had erred, but I could not pay attention. I found I had a headache and was shivering with cold. Indeed, I thought it remarkable enough that I had known the moves.

"Pray excuse me, sir," I said, pulling my cloak more tightly round me. "I believe I may give you a better game when I am more myself. My mind is distracted at the moment. I must find out, if I can, where Gervais went and what he did, after he left the castle. Can you help me?"

The old man chuckled. "Ay, perhaps—and perhaps not. He did not confide in me directly, look you, but I could tell you a good deal about him that might surprise you, about him and the young Vaughans. Ay, and my own daughters, too: I know what Esther dreams of, and what Enid fears. And I know a thing or two about the Carnabys . . . the young ones rode into the courtyard a few minutes ago, by the by. And I am tired of company and you look cold, so we had better continue our conversation at another time. I'll send for you, perhaps . . . be off, child. They'll be waiting for you in the Banqueting Hall, I dare say."

He flapped his hands at me and I bade him a hasty farewell, to which he replied in Welsh. I hurried from the room and made my way down the treacherous stairs as quickly as I dared, thankful that I had left the drawbridge down, for if visitors had arrived it was likely that I had already been sent for, and I did not want the Dyffryn sisters to know where I had been. I intended to tell them in my own time that I had been. I intended to tell them in my own time that I had spoken to their father, on some occasion when I could search each face to discover which, if any, of them was dismayed to learn I had conversed with the person who knew more than most of the secrets of Castell Marten.

Chapter Nine

Lady Castelmarten was receiving her visitors in the Banqueting Hall, as Lord Dyffryn had predicted. Wooden screens had been drawn up to make a division of the room before the great fire blazing in the ox-wide fireplace. Lady Castelmarten and a sandy-haired young lady were engaged in the homely occupation of winding wool. Beyond the fireplace a young man lounged uncomfortably upon a settle, his boots almost in the flames. He sprang to his feet when I appeared, obviously happy to be diverted.

"This is—Miss Rose," said Lady Castelmarten. "I have explained that she is possibly my daughter-in-law. Miss Carnaby, Miss Rose; and this is Mr. Carnaby, Miss Rose."

I curtsied politely. Miss Carnaby stared at me, and I at her, with interest. She was quite plain, with freckled, pale skin, and though her blue eyes were wide, they too were pale and slightly bulbous; but she was young, looked intelligent, had a neat figure, and her riding dress had been cut by a master hand. She would not disgrace Lord Castelmarten as the mistress of his house, I thought—but I could see what Miss Esther had meant when she said it would be uncomfortable if he married her.

Miss Carnaby returned my greeting, but made no further remark, though she continued to observe me frankly with those disturbing eyes. Her brother was more sociable. He too had sandy hair and a freckled skin, but he had better features and a more friendly manner. Like his sister, he was appropriately dressed in clothes whose very simplicity proclaimed them to be expensive.

"I am very glad to make your acquaintance, Miss Rose," he cried. "You are quite famous in these parts—the talk of the *cantref*, you must know."

"Hush, Freddy," said Miss Carnaby solemnly. "You will be making Miss Rose uncomfortable, telling her she is an object of speculation."

"I am sure she knows that after a long winter we have little enough to talk about; she has done us a great service, arriving so mysteriously in our midst."

"She brought terrible tidings," Mis Carnaby reminded him, those wide eyes still unblinking, as if she sought to draw out all my secrets by their power. "How are you, Miss Rose?" she added. "Your wounds are healing? And your memory . . . ?"

"I have not regained it, ma'am." It would be tactless, I decided, to thank Miss Carnaby for her efforts on my behalf.

Mr. Carnaby shook his head. "It is very hard to think of Gerry leaving no impression on you, if you were really married to him." I glanced at him, wondering if I had imagined the implication in his voice, that Gervais Marten had not been a favourite of his.

"We are not sure yet that Miss Rose was married to him," remarked Miss Enid, who had been sitting quietly concealed in a high wing chair.

Miss Carnaby turned her gaze on Lady Castelmarten. "How long does Lucian intend to be away from home?" she asked.

"The journey will take two or three days, I suppose, depending on the condition of the roads—perhaps longer. Then one must allow another three days for his researches, I think. I believe we must not look for him for ten days at least."

Miss Carnaby looked down at her hands. "So tiresome," she sighed; but I thought I had seen a look of—what? relief? lighten her face. "He will miss the last of the hunting . . ."

"Is there hunting here?" I asked. "I should have supposed these slopes to be too steep, the terrain too treacherous."

Mr. Carnaby answered eagerly, "Oh, we contrive to hunt—even if we are obliged to go on foot. But the days we meet in the valley, then we ride—and often find ourselves in trouble, for the foxes make for the heights if they can. Sir Caerleon ap Owen is our master here. Do you ride, Miss—Miss Rose?"

I gathered my courage. "Miss Vaughan and I are hoping to find out whether I can ride, sir. When I am feeling a little stronger, Lady Castelmarten, I wonder if I might borrow a mount from the stables here?"

"Oh, do you think—" Miss Carnaby exclaimed, and then, colouring, relapsed into silence. Lady Castelmarten replied graciously enough that she would give Emrys orders to saddle something suitable, if Dr. Glynn thought it advisable.

"Then...I have your permission to ride with Miss Vaughan, ma'am?"

"Certainly, if you have an escort."

"Allow me to offer my services, ma'am," suggested Mr. Carnaby quickly. He looked at me with an air almost of pleading. "Shall you feel ready for it by tomorrow, Miss Rose?"

"Oh no—I am sorry, sir, but I fear I would not be able to go as soon as that."

"I will call in at the Vicarage on the way home, in any case," said Mr. Carnaby, "and inform Miss Vaughan what is in the wind. I dare say she would like me to provide a mount for her, also. Perhaps she could ride your mare, Matty?"

"I am afraid I shall be riding Jewel myself," said Miss Carnaby, still unsmiling. "Miss Vaughan has a horse of her own."

"But such a sad hack! Come, Matty, we have a dozen horses you could ride—or I would lend you Dragon, if you prefer."

"That beast! You know I can't control him. Miss Vaughan may ride him if she likes. And why should I ride one of the other horses, when I am very well satisfied with my own?"

"Very well, ride Jewel if you are set on joining the party. Miss Vaughan has asked me before if she could ride Dragon. I only hope she can master him."

"She certainly has daring enough to try."

113

"Now, Matty, why cannot you two be friends?"

Miss Carnaby turned her shoulder on him. "Here is your wool, dear Aunt. Is that the last of it? Do you want me to bring you some more? I have been spinning industriously these last weeks."

"Did you try out the new dyes you mentioned?" asked Miss Enid.

"Oh yes, I meant to bring you some samples. Indeed, I believe I have them in my pocket..." She pulled out a handful of variously coloured wools, and the ladies exclaimed admiringly. Miss Carnaby was not only eligible, but practical and industrious, it seemed.

Hughes appeared in the doorway. "Dr. Glynn," he announced.

I stared at Miss Esther. She smiled, and glanced towards Miss Carnaby. Following her gaze, I saw that Miss Carnaby's colour had risen, though she did not pause in her conversation with Miss Enid.

The doctor entered. He bowed very low, and addressed himself to Lady Castelmarten.

"I trust I am not intruding, ma'am. I called to see how my patient did."

"You had better ask her, Dr. Glynn. And she had better ask you whether she is fit to go riding one of these days."

"Ah, is that proposed? And how do you feel about it yourself, Miss Rose?"

"I am anxious to try it—if I find I have never sat a horse before, then I will abandon the scheme, of course."

"How did you sleep last night? May I take your pulse?" We moved away a little, and he pulled out his watch. "Miss Carnaby is to accompany you, you say? Then you will be in excellent hands. And yet, it is rather foolhardy, perhaps. Supposing if you were to have a fall?"

"I might strike my head, and recover my memory, sir."

"You might suffer a hemorrhage to the brain. You had better make sure your mount is a quiet one."

"Yes, indeed. I shall leave the heroics to Miss Vaughan."

He looked up sharply, his eyes very bright beneath his shaggy brows. "Miss Vaughan is to be of the party?"

"Mr. Carnaby hopes so, at all events. Yes, sir, it was Miss

Vaughan who suggested riding with me."

He seemed troubled. "Lady Carnaby will be displeased," he murmured, in response to my enquiring look, feeling, no doubt, that if the Carnaby heir threw himself away on the Vicar's daughter, his own chances of marrying into the aristocratic family would be sadly lessened.

"Dr. Glynn, it was Miss Carnaby, was it not, who made up the lotions for me, and that excellent herb pillow?"

"Oh! Ahem! Now, what in the world made you imagine—was I so indiscreet as to have mentioned it? No one is supposed to know—"

He looked quite distressed, and I hastened to reassure him.

"I will not speak of it," I promised. He pressed my hand in gratitude, and over his shoulder I saw Miss Carnaby's eyes narrow as she observed it. I felt the color flame in my cheeks, as I realized that she was jealous of me. Perhaps if I encouraged it, it might help her come to a decision, I reflected; and leaning towards the doctor I asked him how I was, in a low tone and with a languishing look which fortunately he did not see.

"No significant outward signs, ma'am; the wound on your head has healed up well; that on your thumb is a trifle infected still, but you have no fever..."

Miss Carnaby had approached us. Now she spoke. "I think it would be foolish for Miss Rose to risk herself on horseback so soon after her accident, doctor. Do you not agree?"

"Ahem! I did not see you there, Miss Carnaby. I was—yes, I was just telling Miss Rose that though she has no fever, her hand is still infected. In another three or four days, perhaps—but in the meanwhile, no, I believe I should forbid it. Let us see how you are on Monday, Miss Rose, and then we can discuss it again."

He bustled away to inform Lady Castelmarten of the change of plan. I faced Miss Carnaby with a feeling of indignation not entirely assumed.

"Dr. Glynn would have allowed me to ride as soon as I felt able. Why did you persuade him otherwise?"

She smiled faintly. "You should be grateful to me, Miss Rose. I am interested in your health, you see."

"And is not Dr. Glynn, and is not he better qualified to judge it?"

"Perhaps, but he thinks too well of people, and I, on the contrary, see them as they are."

"Now you speak in riddles, ma'am. I beg you to explain yourself."

"Very well. I think you would be rash to have any connection with Miss Vaughan. She is a strange, headstrong creature. She was very fond of Gerry, and will be jealous of you. Perhaps even—madly jealous."

I stared at her. "I don't think so. Miss Vaughan seems anxious to be friends."

Miss Carnaby shrugged. "As you please. For myself, I think you would be wiser to remove yourself from Wales before she has a chance to harm you."

When all three visitors had taken their leave shortly after, Miss Esther whispered to me, "Did you see how cleverly Dr. Glynn found an excuse to accompany the Carnabys on their way? It is quite a case between him and Miss Carnaby if I am any judge! And she, of course, is jealous of her brother's interest in Miss Vaughan. It is quite a tangle!"

Miss Enid, meanwhile, was speaking to Lady Castelmarten. "Do you really mean Lucian to marry that oddity of a girl?" she demanded. I found myself straining to hear the answer.

"Mathilda is my goddaughter, and a good child. She would run the castle very competently—which I am aware is her chief defect in your eyes—and I am sure Lucian would not allow her to dictate to him unduly. Do you not wish to see him married?"

"Of course I do," Miss Enid was obliged to protest. "Only I cannot like Mathilda Carnaby, for all her virtues."

"Then propose someone else for him."

"You should encourage him to visit London for the season. He would find plenty of eligible young ladies to choose from there."

"They would bore him to extinction. Besides, he detests

116

dancing, and he has no conversation. Very likely, he would find no one to accept him."

"Elaine! How can you say that, when you consider the advantages he has to offer?"

"What are they? An old but empty title, and a ruined castle in Wales?"

"He is a young man, intelligent, healthy, and well-built."

"He can be abominably rude, and most girls find him alarming, I believe."

"The title alone renders him supremely eligible."

"And do you think he wants to be married for his title alone? At least he knows Matty is very fond of him, even if she cannot love him yet. But this conversation is scarcely edifying for Miss Rose. I believe I hear Hughes—can it be the dinner hour already?"

Miss Esther took my arm as we walked to the dining room.

"I wish you could marry Lucian," she whispered unexpectedly. "I am sure you must be in love with him and he certainly cannot take his eyes off you."

"Miss Esther! I—indeed, indeed, you are mistaken."

"Oh, never fear—I know it cannot be. You are quite ineligible, for either you are his sister; or you are that other one, the poor bastard ragpicker. It is just a pity, when it is obvious you suit so well."

"We do not suit, Miss Esther," I replied with spirit. "Lord Castelmarten despises me. If I am not a fortune hunter, in his opinion I am an adventuress."

"That is how he defends himself against you, perhaps. And what do you think of him?"

"I? Why, Miss Esther, I am obliged to own that his lordship annoys me very much. Indeed, I fear I cannot like him." That I dared not trust him either, I was able to prevent myself from saying.

We reached the dining room and sat down to mutton broth, removed with a fine jugged hare. Conversation was not lively, but when it turned to architecture, I remembered something that had puzzled me.

"Why does the entrance to the Keep begin in the

117

Parlour, and not on the ground floor?" I asked, helping myself to red currant jelly.

Miss Enid gazed at me severely. "In my day," she said repressively, "well-brought-up girls were not expected nor required to introduce subjects of conversation. The rule was that they did not speak unless spoken to."

"But perhaps Miss Rose is a married woman," suggested Miss Esther rather pertly.

Lady Castelmarten observed that I was to be treated as a member of the family, and that she believed we need not stand on ceremony. "The reason the entrance to the Keep is so situated, Miss Rose," she continued, "is that in those troubled times when this castle was designed, the family had to beware of treachery from within, as well as from without. The Keep was the family's final stronghold, capable of being held against great forces. The entrance to it had to be more readily accessible to the family than to others, so that it would be possible to retire into its fastness at a moment's notice—as was done, as we are told, on at least two occasions, when the castle itself fell into alien hands. But how did you know where to find the entrance to the Keep, may I ask?"

I took an encouraging sip of wine. "I was exploring this morning," I announced. "I found my way over to the Keep and met Lord Dyffryn. We talked, and played chess. He was most interesting."

I glanced from one face to another. They seemed startled, disconcerted, and in Miss Enid's case, quite outraged.

"You found your way to the Keep?" she repeated incredulously. "Do you mean to tell us, Miss Rose, that you had the effrontery to introduce yourself to Father without so much as consulting us?"

"If only you had told me you wished to see him, I would have taken you myself," cried Miss Esther reproachfully.

Lady Castelmarten sighed. "The harm, if any, has been done," she pointed out. "Fortunately, I had already told Father of Miss Rose's presence here, and that she might be Gerry's widow. You know he likes to be kept informed of our affairs, however remote he might hold himself from them." She glanced at me. "You played chess, Miss Rose?"

"When he asked me if I could play, I said I could—and then I wondered if I would in fact be able to do so. When we sat down to the board, however, the moves seemed to come back to me, though I did not give him a good game, I fear."

"You could hardly be expected to do so," said Miss Enid proudly, "since Lord Dyffryn is one of the foremost players in the country."

"What did our ancestors do without the game?" Lady Castelmarten wondered. "Since it was introduced into England it has become immensely popular with those who have the understanding for it."

"One would not expect to find a chess player among ragpickers, I think," suggested Miss Esther. "The cost of a set of chessmen alone would tend to limit the pastime to the more privileged classes."

"Your point is well taken," Lady Castelmarten conceded. "One must also take into account the time it takes to play a game of chess." She stared at me frankly. "It really does seem very likely, Miss Rose, that you are not—Mary Ramsey."

I felt a glad rush of relief. And yet—did I want to be Gervais Marten's widow? Yes, I told myself, of course my lot as the Honourable Mrs. Marten would be preferable to that of an illegitimate ragpicker... but I wondered why I sensed this instinctive reluctance to step into Victoria Merridew's shoes. Then, as always when I thought too intently about my situation, my head began to ache.

Miss Enid was asking her sister if she did not think it premature to be arriving at conclusions before Lord Castelmarten returned from Dunstable. Lady Castelmarten replied that she had merely expressed an opinion.

"In any case," said Miss Enid severely, "I think this is neither the time nor the place for such discussion."

"The footmen don't understand English," said Miss Esther, as one bent to remove her plate. "Even those among them who can speak a few words of it. Well,

119

Elaine, I for one am glad to hear your acknowledging the likelihood of what has been quite obvious to me almost from the first."

Miss Enid stared at Lady Castelmarten. "I must say, sister, that your opinion does not seem to be affording you a great deal of pleasure," she observed.

Lady Castelmarten raised an eyebrow, looking absurdly like her elder son. "We do not yet know to what kind of family the alliance has connected us," she replied coolly. "More important, we do not know what this young lady's motives for the marriage were."

Miss Enid looked as if she had no doubts on that score. She contented herself with saying acidly that, whoever I might be, it was plain to see I had not had the advantage of a strict upbringing.

"Miss Rose has beautiful table manners," Miss Esther declared.

I felt unhappy, and lonely, despite Miss Esther's support. I was glad when the time came to retire, though I felt I would not be able to sleep. When the house had settled down, I opened my door again and stood looking down the gallery, a small lamp in my hand. Ever since I had lost my papers and found the note of warning in my reticule, I had wondered from time to time if someone who wished me harm might be actually hiding here in the house. All at once it occurred to me that tonight would be an excellent opportunity to search that upper floor, no longer inhabited since Gervais had departed.

I pulled my wrapper firmly about my shoulders and, carrying the lamp, began to glide swiftly down the gallery towards the stairway at the farther end that led up to the next storey, and away from the sisters' rooms.

The stair, when I found it, was narrow and badly polished. My kid slippers made scarcely a sound as I climbed it slowly, for I still could not trust all my weight to my right ankle. Every now and then I paused to listen, but there was utter silence in this castle where no clocks were allowed to chime, and where the servants were abed in their own attics, above the dining room in the other wing.

The stair ended on a second and narrower gallery, dark and silent. I was beginning to feel rather foolish, but I had committed myself to the search and flung open the first door with resolution.

I stared into a large dusty chamber, dominated by a great four-poster. The dark curtains hung still and lifeless, the fireplace yawned cold and empty. There were sporting prints upon the walls, silver-backed brushes on the dressing table. I held my lamp high as I crossed the room. I could see my reflection in the window, and wondered if some lonely shepherd would think Gervais had come home. I picked up one of the brushes. A monogram was chased upon the back, and as I had expected, among the initials there intertwined, a *G* was prominent.

I set down the lamp and looked about me. So this was indeed his room—the room belonging to a man who might have been my husband!

I opened a drawer, but there was nothing in it beyond a small pile of cravats and handkerchiefs. Another revealed shirts; a third, nightshirts. I pulled out a small drawer in the dressing table. A promising litter met my eye. This drawer was obviously forbidden to the servants. Buttons, scraps of paper, coins, bills from posting inns—I picked one up and held it to the light. It was headed, "Neat four-wheel post chaises" and underneath an engraving of a rose was printed, "Sam Forlon, CAMBRIDGE." Below was the account, elegantly written but curiously spelled:

	s.	d.
Loin Mutton in Stakes	3.	6
Clarett	10.	0
Dish Veal Cuttlets	3.	0
Collyflowerd	.	10
Cheese	.	6
Pickles	.	4
Tarts etc.	2.	6
Cod & Shrimp Sauce	4.	6
Madeira	3.	0
Bread & Best Ale	2.	9
	£1. 10.	11 d.

Beside the total a careless hand had written, "Inn Bill—I paid half. (15/5½d)"

I laid it down and took up another scrap of paper. "IOU Sir Caerleon ap Owen 2 gns for his lady being brought to bed of a daughter, not a son, as I wagered Feb. 3rd, 1802."

A third was of more interest. In a feminine hand it said, "Gerry—I'll be by the great oak at eleven o'clock—your Sal."

Sarah Vaughan, I thought. She had certainly been upon intimate terms with Gervais Marten.

I stirred the contents of the drawer. There were two other notes apparently of assignation though both were in Welsh, one from "Fanwy," the other 'Nell.'

There were some other bills, for boots and tailoring, an IOU from Freddy Carnaby—nothing in the least revealing, and certainly no mention of Victoria Merridew.

I sighed and closed the drawer. Then I stood quite still, for it seemed that another sigh had echoed mine. In that moment I knew what it was to have one's blood run cold.

But nothing moved—all was still. Only there was a slight change in the air—a breath of scent, perhaps, too faint to identify. I breathed it in, my nostrils flaring like a startled horse. Scent—or snuff? But it was gone, if it had ever been.

Softly, I tiptoed to the door—and flung it open.

No one was there—but a board creaked down the passage, and a door was open there that surely had been closed before.

The shadows trembled before me as the lamp shook in my hand. Biting my lip, I fearfully approached that door. As I pushed it wider I held up the lamp, my eyes straining to look everywhere at once.

The room was completely empty of furniture—no one could be hiding there. But plain in the lamplight I could read a message written in the dust on the once-polished floor.

"Get out! Go back to Lichfield."

I turned and ran for the shelter of my room, disregarding the aching of my ankle, the slopping of the oil in the lamp, and the leaping of the flame, my one thought to find sanctuary and escape from whoever lurked up there in empty rooms, knowing, or pretending to know, that my name was Mary Ramsey, and that I had no right at Castell Marten.

Chapter Ten

By morning, of course, I had persuaded myself that the message might well have been written days before—that I had no proof I had not been alone up on the second floor. And it was true that no one had pursued me to my room, nor interrupted my restless dreams that night.

The next days passed uneventfully, each one seeing an improvement in my health and strength. Fragments of memory began to return, too, but early memories that any child might have had; memories of fears, and a comforting mother figure; of struggling to learn my letters; of being lost in a crowd, and a gentleman putting me up upon his shoulders; of standing in a field of wheat, the green stalks tall above my head, the poppies flaming in the sun.

Outside, the weather turned to heavy rain which, cold though it was, melted the last of the snows off the lower slopes of the mountain. The sheep came steadily down, some to the meadows and some to the *friddoed*, and Ysolt reported that the younger ewes had begun to lamb. Within, Lady Castelmarten gave me two black silk mourning gowns and ordered her maid Parry to alter them for me, which she did so resentfully that I almost persuaded myself that it was she who was my enemy. But Parry could not speak a word of English, I remembered, and could not therefore have been the author of those messages warning me to leave Wales.

When the first gown was ready, Lady Castelmarten took me calling. Our visit to Hafod Hall was interesting, if socially uncomfortable. The house was approached in the grand manner, through a rolling park agreeably laid out, complete with stands of ancient oaks and herds of grazing deer. The Hall was a large house of grey stone, executed in the classical form. If one had not suspected it before, from the moment of entering the marble pillared hall it was apparent that the Carnabys must be extremely rich. Lady Castelmarten had told me that fortunes in coal and slate supported them. Now I was able to see the evidence of it for myself, in the works of art upon the walls, the numerous well-trained servants, in the quality of the hangings, the furniture, the decoration. Alas, the owners of all this magnificence could not be said to be happy in their enjoyment of it; they had not spoken to each other for ten years, but exchanged terse notes when positively obliged to do so.

Lord Carnaby, a narrow, fox-faced man, did look in on us as we sat making conversation with his wife in the great drawing room; he even volunteered a few remarks, but his wife was noticeably excluded from them. She on the other hand was plump and looked placid, but had little tricks of fidgeting with her rings and hair that pointed to an inner nervousness. It was from her that Mathilda inherited her bulging eyes, but Lady Carnaby's hair was fair and still had some gold lights in it; probably it once had been her crowning beauty.

From her conversation with Lady Castelmarten I realized that Lady Carnaby considered the match between her daughter and Lord Castelmarten as good as settled, which I had felt was far from being the case. Miss Mathilda seemed quite impervious to the undercurrents I felt so keenly; she stared solemnly at me with her round blue eyes and told me of a scheme she had for starting up a charity school. She and her mother were both obstinate women, accustomed to having their own way, and I wondered what would happen if it came to an open disagreement between them.

On another occasion, Lady Castelmarten took me to the Vicarage. I had seen the house on my way to church, and felt quite apprehensive as we drove between the yews and pulled up by the gothic arch of the front door. A neat but sour-looking manservant showed us in, and I had time to remember that Mrs. Vaughan had the reputation of being something of a martinet and to expect her to be tall and commanding, before I was presented with the reality, a little woman with a plump figure, and a somewhat overflattering manner towards Lady Castelmarten.

We were shown into a small tidy parlour which had the air of being seldom used, where Miss Vaughan was waiting for us with her father. He was a scholarly-looking man, and after a very few minutes excused himself rather vaguely and drifted away to be seen a moment later passing the window in the direction of the church.

"I am afraid my husband does not care for company," explained Mrs. Vaughan, making no effort to hide her annoyance. "It is extraordinary in a Christian, who should love his fellow man, as I have frequen·'y reminded him. But there he is, only happy in the church, or locked away in his study with some musty tome—*tout à fait ennuyant*."

"My husband was quite the reverse," said Lady Castelmarten, smiling faintly. "He, as you remember, ma'am, was hospitable to a fault—delighted to see friends at any hour of day or night. How often had my heart sunk to hear him offering dinner and a night's lodging to some chance-met stranger on the least pretext! However, the house seems sadly quiet now he has gone, and what used to irritate me most in him is now what I would give almost anything to recover—or so I think. But there is no pleasing us females, I fear..."

Mrs. Vaughan looked as if she would not go so far as to agree with that. Instead, having seated us on her rather uncomfortable chairs, overstuffed and prickly, she turned to me and addressed me with unexpected condescension.

"My daughter tells me you and the Carnabys have planned to ride together when the weather improves. You must have been disappointed in the rain. Such a wretched spring!"

"At least it melted the snow, ma'am," I replied, thinking of the gathering. Miss Vaughan glanced at the window. "It seems to be clearing now. What do you think, Miss Rose? Shall we hope to ride tomorrow?"

"Well—perhaps." I found myself rather nervous at the prospect and wondered if I was even yet ready for the test.

"Oh, but you cannot disappoint us! Mr. Carnaby said he would bring round the horses at eleven, on the first fine day." Miss Vaughan looked at me with pleading in her bright eyes, and I reminded myself I was standing in the way of their meeting, so long as I procrastinated.

"Very well then—if it is fine," I agreed, winning smiles of approval not only from Miss Vaughan, but from her mother also.

"And where are you planning to ride, *chérie*? Not up the mountain, I trust."

"No, *Maman*. We thought it better to stay in the valley, as Miss Rose does not know how much experience she has had with horses. We will go to Plas Celli, I think, and down by Melin Llyd. It is a pretty ride, and there is a gallop through the woods."

"Yes, and the old mill is very picturesque," Mrs. Vaughan agreed.

Lady Castelmarten smiled at me. "It is a favourite spot with artists, Miss Rose." She turned to Mrs. Vaughan. "Whatever became of that old clergyman at Plas Celli? The one who knits? Am I right in thinking that he met with some accident?"

Mrs. Vaughan looked astonished. "My dear ma'am!" she exclaimed. "Surely you remember, he drowned in the millpond last Christmastide. A bad business—but then he would walk about with his knitting, like some old farm woman, never heeding where he went—"

"Yes, I remember now. It was so soon after my husband's death, I believe I did not take it in properly at the time. He was a character, Evans Plas Celli: I am sure I should miss him, if I ever have cause to pass that way."

"What did he knit?" I asked, imagining a long shapeless garment flowing off the needles and over his shoulder, trailing on the ground for yards behind him.

"Stockings," said Miss Vaughan unexpectedly. "Army agents commissioned them from him. I believe they were his only source of income, once ill health had obliged him to give up his parish."

Her mother stared at her. "Sarah! How in the world do you know that?"

"I—I—" stammered Miss Vaughan, reduced at once to incoherence.

"Well?" her mother persisted sharply.

Miss Vaughan bit her lip. "It was—my brother who told me," she muttered. "Ned was fond of the old man."

"Oh," said Mrs. Vaughan, changing colour. "I see. Very well. Will you take a dish of tea, your ladyship? And some *bara brith*, perhaps. Sarah, ring the bell."

A tray of tea was brought, and Miss Vaughan carried round the cups. When she had passed the bread and butter, she seated herself beside me.

"Well, Miss Rose, is there any word from his lordship yet?"

"No, Miss Vaughan. There has hardly been time, I suppose."

"At least you had the good sense to take my advice."

"Your advice, ma'am?"

"Yes. You did not travel with him."

"Oh! No, it was agreed I was not well enough to do so."

"And how do you enjoy the society of my lady's sisters up there at castle?"

I glanced at Lady Castelmarten, but she was talking to Mrs. Vaughan and I felt there was small chance of her overhearing us.

"Miss Esther has been very kind to me."

Miss Vaughan leaned forward, her blue eyes glinting. "Do not trust her, Miss Rose!"

"Really, Miss Vaughan, what can you mean?"

"Is it not plain that none of them would want Gerry to have married? Do you think they want to see their sister's fortune go to an outsider? Would it not be easier for them to rid themselves of you before your memory returns?"

I stared at her in horror. "To rid themselves... you cannot mean...?"

She sat up and shrugged. "Who knows what they are capable of, those two? Miss Enid is able to plan; and I believe Miss Esther could act—if she felt her happiness depended on it."

I remembered Miss Esther talking of the cottage she longed to share with a friend.

"No..." I whispered. "No!"

But I remembered also the sleeping potion Miss Enid had mixed for me the night my papers were stolen. Could it, after all, have been she and not Miss Carnaby who wanted me away from Wales? And if I persisted in staying, was it possible that the sisters would go further in the hope of getting rid of me? "Oh no," I whispered again. "How can you think such things?"

"Those Dyffryns are very strange," Miss Vaughan murmured, picking up a framed miniature of herself and pretending to discuss it with me. "The spinsters were jealous when their sister married so well. I have even heard it suggested that it was no accident that burned Pen Maen and caused them all to settle more comfortably at Castell Marten..."

My eyes felt almost as if they were falling out of my head. Lady Dyffryn had died in that fire, I recalled.

Miss Vaughan seemed to read my thought. "Everything did not go according to plan on that occasion, perhaps... but the main purpose was achieved. You don't thank me for this warning, I can see, nor do I expect it. If I have put you a little on your guard, then I shall be satisfied."

I reflected that my drink had been drugged and my papers stolen most probably by a member of the household at Castell Marten; I recalled the warning notes I had received, and my persistent conviction that I had not been alone in the upper storey of the southeast wing. How easy it would have been for one or both of the Miss Dyffryns to have accounted for all this!

"What are you whispering about over there, *ma petite*?" demanded Mrs. Vaughan suspiciously. Lady Castelmarten at once stood up to make her farewells, and, successfully diverted, Mrs. Vaughan thanked her fulsomely for having condescended to visit the Vicarage.

Miss Vaughan caught my hand as I was taking leave of her. "I shall be looking forward to our ride tomorrow—even if it is not absolutely fine," she said insistently, with a dancing look.

The manservant showed us out and a few moments later the door of the chaise was closed upon us.

"What a relief to be going home," exclaimed Lady Castelmarten. "It is almost worth visiting the Vicarage because it is so delightful when the ordeal is over. Tedious woman! I only recognize her because I am sorry for her husband and daughter, whom no doubt she would blame if I cut the connection. Harriet Carnaby feels the same. Really, one can hardly blame poor Ned for leaving home."

"I had heard that Miss Vaughan had a brother," I ventured. "It was an awkward moment when she was obliged to mention his name."

"I hope she is not punished for it! Ned's name has been expunged from the family record. His mother doted on him to an extraordinary degree, would barely let him think or speak for himself, and tried to supervise his every movement, which is no doubt why he left."

"What do you think became of him, ma'am?"

Lady Castelmarten seemed quite disposed to gossip with me while the chaise slowly climbed the hill. "Why, I believe he must have joined a company of strolling players, for Ned could think of nothing but acting, to his mother's disgust. The trouble started when he visited Dunstable some years ago. They infected him there with the disease of playacting, and since he was remarkably clever at it, his interest in it did not lessen with the years but rather increased until last winter he informed his mother that he was taking to the boards. The battle raged, and in the midst of it, he ran away. The Vaughans cut him off from that moment, and forbade his name to be mentioned."

I reflected on this. "It seems quite surprising that Mrs. Vaughan allowed her daughter to visit the Morton-Johns after that."

"Yes, so I thought, until I learned the reason for it. Mrs. Vaughan is an extremely ambitious woman, and was hoping her late sister's successor would give Sarah an entrée into society; but the second Mrs. Morton-Johns, of course, is no relation to her and could not see any reason why she should put herself to the trouble of bringing out Miss Vaughan—who would undoubtedly put her own insipid stepdaughter in the shade."

"No doubt Miss Vaughan will make a match here, in Wales," I suggested.

Lady Castelmarten shook her head. "It is very difficult for persons of that middling sort, if the mother has ideas above her station, as in this case. Those who would offer for the girl, Mrs. Vaughan would never accept, and those she imagines suitable, would not demean themselves. Absurd, isn't it? I can see you think it so. Most young people would agree with you. Fortunately they are not in charge of their own affairs, for the fact of the matter is, that it is a greater risk to marry out of your class, than it would be to marry out of your country."

She caught herself up there, and cried with sudden warmth, "Oh, my dear! I hope you will not think I had you in mind when I spoke of mismatches. Not that I take back a word of it, but I would not hurt you for the world."

I assured her that she had not hurt me. "For, knowing nothing of my antecedents, I prefer to suppose myself a princess *incognita*," I suggested, smiling.

For the first time since we met, Lady Castelmarten put back her veil and looked at me with complete candour. "I feel it more likely that you were an innocent girl with no prospects, easily dazzled by Gerry's charm, and his more obvious advantages," she said frankly. "What I find harder to understand is why ... why he married you."

Despite myself, I was conscious of indignation. "Why should it not have been a love match between us, ma'am?" I demanded, as the carriage came to a halt in the courtyard at Castell Marten.

She did not look away, but dropped the veil. The fine black net blotted out her features and her voice too was quiet and without emphasis as she murmured, "Because, alas, I do not believe Gervais was capable of love."

Lady Castelmarten had directed her maid Parry to alter one of her riding habits for me, and when Ysolt buttoned me into the black-ribbed silk the following morning, I was glad to find it was a perfect fit.

"There's elegant you look, mistress," exclaimed Ysolt, setting the velvet hat, garnished with ostrich plumes, upon my hair. "See you by here, in the looking glass."

I stared at my reflection, and the thought occurred to

131

me that this morning, at least, I looked like a widow of some consequence. Now that I had more colour in my cheeks the deep black became me, and the skillful cut of the riding habit flattered my figure. I tossed my head to set the shimmering plumes nodding, and smiled at Ysolt.

"Between you and Parry, you have transformed me," I declared.

Ysolt pursed her thin lips and said seriously, "Clothes do make a deal of difference, no use denying it."

One of the footmen knocked, and spoke in Welsh.

"It seems they are waiting for you in the courtyard, mistress," Ysolt explained.

I picked up my soft black leather gloves. "Very well, I am ready to go down. And please thank Parry, Ysolt, for her excellent work."

I rustled along the gallery, enjoying the sweep of the long heavy skirts on the polished boards behind me, but as I began to descend the stairs, a feeling of apprehension rushed over me and I forgot about my appearance. What if I could not ride, and looked ridiculous trying to balance on a horse? What if my mount threw me, sending me back into that vile limbo?

As soon as I entered the courtyard, however, and saw the horses waiting, I knew with a thrilling certainty that whether I could ride or not, I was no stranger to horses, and had loved them in the past.

"Greetings!" cried Miss Vaughan in her lively manner. "You look very fine today, Miss Rose."

I swept her a curtsy and confessed that I was decked in borrowed plumes. I greeted the other two members of the party, noticing that Mr. Carnaby was riding a heavy brown horse which looked as if it might pull, but would never tire; his sister was on a quiet bay. Despite the elegance of her blue habit, Miss Carnaby did not look well on horseback. Miss Vaughan, on the other hand, appeared a diamond of the first water. Her striking colouring, the neatness of her figure, the suggestion of wildness about her, together with the magnificence of the black horse she was riding, served to show her at her best and render insignificant those minor faults of feature or expression that at other times might prevent one from considering her to be a beauty.

The head groom, Emrys, was holding a neat chestnut mare, with a star and a long blaze down her nose. Her nostrils flared as I approached her. She was pure Arab, I thought, and felt again that superstitious thrill of which I was always conscious when some gleam penetrated the murky waters of my past. At least, if I had been neither rich nor noble, I had known about horses once, I told myself, and gathering up the reins in my left hand, allowed Emrys to raise me into the saddle.

There I was surprised to find I did not feel quite so much at home as I would have wished. But the mare arched her neck in response to my signal, and began to walk in the direction I indicated to her.

"So you can ride, I see!" Mr. Carnaby exclaimed. "Capital! But don't press too close to Dragon's heels. I'm afraid he kicks."

I turned the chestnut, Juniper, and rode out under the gatehouse arch. The cobbles of the bridge rang hollow under the mare's hoofs, and she danced a little. I settled in the saddle, and found I was smiling as I brought her under control.

Miss Carnaby, jogging at my side, stared at me, and said nothing. Miss Vaughan looked over her shoulder and raised her dark eyebrows.

"This is certainly not the first time you have been upon a horse, Miss Rose," she remarked.

"No," I agreed. "I feel as if I must have ridden all my life."

"By Jove!" cried Freddy Carnaby "Then you can't be that other girl, can you—the ragpicker?"

I bit my lip on a surge of excitement. "Mary Ramsey? No . . . I doubt if she could have had much opportunity to ride."

"D'ye hear that, Matty? It seems we have proved Miss Rose to be—Mrs. Marten, after all."

Miss Carnaby answered her brother coolly. "I think you are confusing proof with probability, perhaps."

"The proof is to come, when Lord Castelmarten

133

returns," I agreed. "But I must confess, I do begin to feel as if I must be Victoria Marten."

Miss Vaughan looked at me with amusement. "Then you weren't sure of it?" she asked, above the clatter of hoofs echoing back from the villagers' houses.

"No, how could I have been? I found it hard to believe I was married . . . at least, I thought it would feel different. But then, I had no way of knowing how I felt before. I am explaining very badly, I know, but it is extraordinarily difficult to put such matters into words. I can tell you I do not feel at all like a ragpicker—but then, who knows how ragpickers feel?"

"However they feel, I am sure they do not ride," Mr. Carnaby declared.

Sarah Vaughan spurred her mount to a ringing trot, and Mr. Carnaby hurried his stallion after her. She threw some laughing remark over her shoulder to him, and they turned the corner together.

"Come on, Jewel," said Miss Carnaby, in a despairing tone. I saw that she was trying to urge her bay to a faster pace, without success.

"Shall we trot?" I suggested. She nodded sulkily. As I had hoped, her mount followed mine quite meekly. Miss Carnaby bounced unhappily. She had obviously only joined us in the hope of preventing her brother from finding himself alone with Miss Vaughan, and already she had been foiled in her intention.

Since Miss Carnaby did not seem disposed to converse, and indeed had all she could do to keep her seat, I took the opportunity to look about me. I could hear the clack of looms on every side, and as the day was fine and many doors were open, I was able to catch occasional glimpses of the weavers at their work, and of their wives spinning their wheels, often with children playing at their feet. Each cottage stood in its own garden, and it was apparent that spring was on the way. A haze of young green showed where leaves would soon be bursting, and bulbs thrust their spears up in all the flowerbeds. In the sloping meadows beyond the village, lambs were skipping and sheep grazing, or lying about with a placid air of contentment. There was a good deal of activity in the arable fields, too, where men were ploughing and harrowing, some sowing oats and others dunging potatoes.

"There is Dr. Glynn," said Miss Carnaby breathlessly, as if the words had been jerked out of her.

The doctor was standing outside a small apothecary's shop. He was just taking his horse's reins from the hand of a small boy, preparatory to climbing into his gig. When he saw us approaching, he swept off his hat and greeted us with a beaming smile.

Miss Carnaby murmured, "Good day," and relapsed into silence. It was left to me to make conversation.

"What a lovely day, Dr. Glynn, is it not? And I, as you see, am now quite well, and fit to ride."

"I see you *can* ride, ma'am, which must be a pleasant discovery."

"Yes! I feel a liberated spirit. Of course, this mare is a beautiful creature, excellently trained. I would have to be an ingrate indeed not to enjoy riding her."

"And you are not an ingrate, ma'am. I have been meaning to thank you for the charming note you sent me..."

I glanced towards Miss Carnaby. She was staring at me with a very disapproving look.

"I—I had to thank the doctor for his care," I explained hurriedly to her.

"Indeed? Extremely civil of you—except I thought your injuries prevented you from writing."

"My injury is much improved. I held the pen a little differently. It was not a very neat missive, I fear..."

"We must be on our way," said Miss Carnaby, rather abruptly. "We must not let the others get too far ahead."

"Ah," cried Dr. Glynn with a knowing look. "You are playing the unenviable role of chaperone this morning, Miss Carnaby!"

She threw a withering glance in his direction, which no doubt she would soon regret, and bade him a curt farewell before jogging off after the others.

Dr. Glynn looked at me apologetically. "Miss Carnaby

does not like riding, alas. She does not seem quite herself this morning," he added.

I took a breath. "Miss Carnaby is very fond of you, Dr. Glynn," I said boldly. "I will wish you a very good morning!"

Chapter Eleven

I soon overtook Miss Carnaby, and we turned out of the village by the old inn to find her brother and Miss Vaughan had drawn up their horses and were engaged in animated conversation. Miss Vaughan tossed her head when she saw us. She clapped her heel to her horses's side, turning him off the road into a field with a wide grass track leading to the wood beyond. She spurred Dragon to a gallop, and Mr. Carnaby thundered after her, uttering a loud halloo. His sister was struggling to hold back her mare, which had become mildly excited, and I abandoned the prospect of a gallop with regret, staying beside Miss Carnaby until the others pulled up by the wood to wait for us, while we cantered sedately towards them.

The wood was just breaking into leaf, and as we entered it the air was full of birdsong. A little rushing sound became stronger as we rode. I realized it was a waterfall and found that I was shivering. I could remember nothing now of falling from the coach, but Mrs. Jones had told me I had been found below the waterfall, and my body, at all events, seemed to remember it.

"Capital day, isn't it?" Freddy Carnaby demanded. "Capital!"

The way through the wood was carpeted with leaves so our passage was almost silent except for the creaking of leather and the grunts of the horses. The path narrowed, and Mr. Carnaby fell back to allow Miss Vaughan and myself to ride ahead.

"Come on," said Miss Vaughan. "If we cannot gallop, we can trot. I can't bear to waste the paces of such a horse as this!"

In a way, I agreed with her. The silence of the wood was

137

lovely, but the exhilaration of riding at speed was something my youth craved; and my body felt as if it had been too long confined. Our trot increased to a canter; twigs and humus flew out beneath our horses' hoofs, and we rounded a great oak side by side, with the other immediately behind.

There was a muffled shout, a flurry of unexpected movement, and the horses plunged to a halt. I realized with dismay that we had almost knocked down an old woman with a large bundle of firewood on her head, tied up in an apron. She had a pipe in her mouth, and shook her stick at us, before pulling out the pipe and screeching at us in her native tongue.

Mr. Carnaby flung her a coin, which effectively silenced her, and we rode on more sedately.

"Did you understand what that old woman said?" asked impulsively.

"I was wondering if I had heard her aright," said Mr. Carnaby. "Do you know her, Miss Vaughan?"

"I believe she used to keep house for old Evans Plas Celli," Miss Vaughan replied. She turned to me. "I could swear she called you 'Mrs. Marten.' Have you ever seen her before?"

"No, not that I am aware of. So the words do mean the same in Welsh?" I strove to control my rising excitement. "Could we go back and question her, and discover what she knows about me?"

"It would do you no good, I am afraid," Miss Vaughan said sympathetically. "The reason that she knows your name is probably because you have been pointed out to her, in church, perhaps."

"Of course, that must be it," Miss Carnaby agreed. She looked at me solemnly with those round blue eyes that so successfully disguised her intelligence. "For a moment wondered... but mysteries usually have quite simple explanations. Let us go on, Miss Rose."

As we trotted on, I found myself wondering what Miss Vaughan would feel if, in fact, that old woman had some genuine knowledge that I was Mrs. Marten. Would Miss Vaughan be happy for me, glad that her friend Gervas had known the satisfaction of a successful courtship before he died—or would she be angry at his deceit, and jealous of me, a stranger who might in innocence have usurped what she believed to be her rights? For in spite of her complaint of being constantly watched over, to say nothing of her interest in Mr. Carnaby, I could not forget that on at least one occasion, Miss Vaughan had planned to meet Gervais by assignation under an oak tree in the night.

We passed two men on the outskirts of the wood, loading branches on a sledge. They stood back for us respectfully enough, but did not return my greeting. I was somehow aware then that I too knew what it was to stand aside when riders passed by heedlessly. There were walkers and riders in the world . . . perhaps after all I had not been in the way of riding so regularly as I had supposed. Perhaps my knowledge of horses had been gained in blissful stolen moments . . . and even as this thought occurred to me, the edge of a memory came—an unlikely memory, yet it had all the insistence of reality. I could remember riding astride, without a saddle. I could recall the feel of the horse's sun-warmed body between my knees . . . and yet I had obviously at some time been taught to ride sidesaddle like any other young lady.

The memory was gone, and Miss Vaughan was now some way ahead, clear of the trees. With a surge of delight, I sent the mare into a gallop. There was never anything to equal this, I thought, as the wind tore at my face, drying my mouth, loosening my hair beneath the hat. This was glorious, this burst of speed and knowledge of power barely controlled; but it had to end, and I pulled up beside Miss Vaughan to await the Carnabys.

"That is Melin Llyd." Miss Vaughan gestured towards an old building, half-hidden by trees and overlooking a dark pool. "You can see why artists love to paint it. And there is the miller with his cart. He is a villainous old winebibber, stone deaf, and surly at the best of times, and there are those who say it was he who drowned old Evans Plas Celli, the clergyman."

Miss Carnaby pulled us beside us.

"I don't like the millpond," she remarked, staring at it

with her wide gaze. "It looks so deep and dark."

"It is bottomless, they say. Follow me over the packbridge, Miss Rose, for this is where we cross the river."

"By Jove, yes," said Mr. Carnaby. "Let me go first, just to see if it is quite safe, you know. There is no parapet, Miss Rose. Be very careful."

Miss Carnaby followed her brother onto the bridge, Miss Vaughan went next, and I came last. The horses snorted and pawed at the stones. It was a little alarming, but I was not really frightened until Miss Vaughan stopped abruptly, and my mare got too close to Dragon, who immediately lashed out. The mare reared up, and for a moment I thought she was going over into the millpond, but I struck her smartly between the ears and she dropped to her feet. Miss Vaughan had ridden on, and only turned when she had reached the other side.

"Thank God you are such a good horsewoman," she said in a low voice as I came up to her. "It was Mathilda's fault. She stopped suddenly, and I had to rein back."

"What happened?" cried Miss Carnaby. "I heard your horses prancing, but dared not look back. Is everyone all right?"

"We were too close," I told her. "Miss Vaughan had to stop, and then Dragon kicked out at Juniper."

"Come, Miss Vaughan," said Mr. Carnaby, who appeared to have noticed nothing out of the way, "let us see if anyone seems to have taken Plas Celli for the summer."

Miss Carnaby watched them ride off together. Then she said quietly, "Wales is dangerous for you, Miss Rose. I believe you should lose no time in making plans to leave."

"I am doing no harm to anyone," I cried. "I stand in no one's way—certainly not yours!"

Her colour rose. "I did not say you did. I merely warned you—that you might be sorry if you stayed."

"Have you written me any notes on the subject?" I demanded.

She only stared at me, her blue eyes round and blank. "I don't know what you mean," she declared eventually, and urned to ride after the others. I stared after her, thinking that it was a pity so elegant a habit should be worn by someone who looked so ill upon a horse.

Then I found myself wondering if it was only because of my association with Dr. Glynn that Miss Carnaby wished to be rid of me. It was not as if she were planning to marry the doctor, after all. To all appearances, it was Lord Castelmarten to whom she was virtually betrothed, and she had certainly no cause to be jealous of me there. Not only did the earl plainly dislike me, but it seemed that he was barred from me by the laws of consanguinity. Well, one must set her down as no more than a dog in the manger, I thought, and clapped my heel impatiently to Juniper's sleek side.

Plas Celli had no garden. It was a square stone building, with regular rows of windows and a modest porch, like a child's drawing. If it had been situated anywhere else, it would have appeared innocuous in the extreme, but as it was in the middle of the wood, with branches tapping at the very windows, it seemed curiously sinister.

"I heard some talk of a retired naval captain renting it," Mr. Carnaby remarked. "But there seem to be no signs of life."

"I heard that two ladies were to take it over and make an arboretum here," Miss Vaughan said, smiling. "But they say in the village that the house is haunted, so probably no one would care to take it on."

"Haunted," I murmured, "by an old man knitting up his beard, and trailing weeds from the millpond..."

"Don't," said Miss Carnaby quite sharply. "Let us go home. The sun has gone in, the wind is cold, and a rainstorm is sweeping up the valley."

"Matty is right," agreed her brother. "What a botheration! We'll ride out again another day, however. Let us go, Miss Vaughan."

"Certainly," she answered, but she was staring at the house as if it fascinated her.

"Have you ever been inside, Miss Vaughan?" I asked.

"Yes," she replied with a flutter of her lashes and an

audible sigh. "The last time I saw my brother Ned was in this house last winter. It seems years since we met then, to say farewell."

"It was only a few months ago," observed Mr. Carnaby, in his literal way. "Poor old Ned, I wonder what became of him. Well, he always seemed to come out of any scrape he was in—I dare say he is contriving well enough. But I really think we should be going, ladies, before it rains."

"Yes." Miss Vaughan agreed. "You are quite right, Mr. Carnaby. Let us go. I am shivering—and the past is dead."

I found myself riding beside Freddy Carnaby. "Strange girl, Miss Vaughan," he murmured. "Fascinating, don't you think?"

I owned to recognizing the fascination of Miss Vaughan.

"She and Ned were very close. Must have been wretched for her when he went. You've had the pleasure of meeting her mama, I collect?"

"We took tea at the Vicarage yesterday."

"Feel sorry for old Vaughan," Freddy mused. "He was the finest student of his year at Oxford, m'father says—and look at him now. That's what marriage to a dissatisfied woman does for a fellow . . . and she won't leave the poor dev—hmm!—man, alone. I mean to say, my parents don't agree, but at least they have agreed to differ, as it were. Better a civilized correspondence by letter than trying to knock holes in a chap all the time, don't you agree?"

"Neither sounds ideal," I replied diplomatically. "Do you suppose married people are ever happy?"

"Oh, I don't know. I expect they are at first. And I can think of some who rub along well enough. Why, the Castelmartens did not agree in everything, but they were devoted to each other."

"When did he die—the late earl?"

"Some time last winter—late autumn it was. Yes, in November."

"Then the present Lord Castelmarten is still in mourning?"

He did not answer, and I mused aloud, "And so

was . . . Gervais. It seems strange . . ."

Mr. Carnaby glanced at me. "Ay. That's why there was a scandal when he left. Or do you mean it was strange that he should marry while he was in mourning?"

"Strange that he left, I suppose. Why did he go?"

Mr. Carnaby looked curiously uncomfortable.

"Some say Lucian exiled him, because he was such a trial to their mother. Myself, I think Gerry found life so plaguy dull here without Ned, there was no holding him."

"Perhaps he planned to find his friend—perhaps he knew where Ned was living."

"Ay, 'tis possible; but they wouldn't have had a groat between them—and Gerry needed money, if ever a man did, for his fortune was all tied up until his next birthday. Lucian controlled it—only think of the humiliation of having your brother holding the purse strings when the money's properly your own!"

"Quite odious, I imagine."

"Lucian kept him short, or so he told us. Said Gerry would have to behave himself in London if his pockets were to let." Mr. Carnaby let out a sigh. "I must own, it's been devilish dull since Gerry left. There's so few fellows of my age about."

"There is Lord Castelmarten."

"Oh, Lucian. Well, d'ye know, he's a trifle too deep for me. Looks at a fellow, and then says something there's no understanding. He thinks more than he says, you know. Makes a fellow uncomfortable. Yoiks! There's a fallen tree!" He set his horse at the trunk of a considerable elm, and cleared it, while my mare snatched at the bit and followed eagerly. I could feel her gather herself for the leap, and for one glorious moment we seemed to be flying. But then came the descent, and it was suddenly horribly apparent to me that I had not been accustomed to jumping on horseback, however familiar I might have been with the animals. I lost my stirrup, felt myself falling, grabbed at the black mane, and with a great effort pulled myself back into the saddle. I was in place, though rather flushed and breathless, by the time I caught up with the others.

It was as well summer was coming, I thought: I must not accept any invitation to go hunting until I had a better understanding of my limitations.

When we rode into the village, Mr. Carnaby cried out to the landlord of the inn, who was supervising the whitewashing of a wall, to know if he had any news as to whether Plas Celli had been let or sold.

The landlord shook his head, calling back in Welsh. Mr. Carnaby turned up his collar against the icy drizzle that had begun to fall.

"The Hudson business fell through, alas," he informed us. "And there were two sons and three daughters in the family!"

Miss Vaughan fluttered her long lashes at him. "Then we will have to make do with the company available to us, will we not?" she suggested sweetly.

Mr. Carnaby blushed. "You must not suppose it was the daughters I was thinking of," he said in embarrassment. "It was the sons...if a fellow wants to go to a cockfight, you know, or some such thing, he needs a companion, don't you see?"

"I suppose so—but I could always put on an old pair of Ned's breeches, and ride with you," Miss Vaughan daringly suggested.

Mr. Carnaby was plainly shocked. Rather hastily, Miss Vaughan assured him she had not meant it. But I was left with the impression that she was perfectly capable of such a wild start; anxious though she seemed for the time being to mould herself into the more conventional shape that Mr. Carnaby desired.

A few drops of rain had fallen, but as we rode over the bridge across the moat a shaft of sunlight slanted through the swiftly moving clouds.

"The weather is improving," cried Miss Vaughan, reining in. "I feel like a final canter on this charming Dragon. Would you care to ride a little further, Miss Rose? I would like to show you Glasffynonban—it is a fairy pool, they say."

"It sounds delightful. Very well, Miss Vaughan. What do you say, Miss Carnaby?"

She looked disgusted. "I have had quite enough of riding for one day," she declared. "If you mean to go up the mountain, I shall ask to be driven home directly."

"Just as you please," Miss Vaughan said sweetly. "Will you escort us, Mr. Carnaby—or shall we go alone?"

"I must come with you, of course—but do you think it wise?"

"Oh, pooh to wisdom!" she replied pertly. "We mean to enjoy ourselves and we won't be long, in any event. Besides, the wind is blowing!"

"It can always drop," Mr. Carnaby began, but she had wheeled her mount and was trotting off without a backward glance, over the bridge and away to the right.

Mr. Carnaby and I exchanged rueful glances before following. I thought of Lord Dyffryn and glanced up towards the Keep. As I had expected, the white blur of his face was visible at one of the high windows, watching us.

We came up with Miss Vaughan as she was opening the gate which led onto the moor. The short-bitten turf track wound between gorse bushes already sprinkled with yellow flowers, to disappear some way above behind a shoulder of rock. A little way below us to the left, a pleasant grey stone house nestled in a wooded valley.

"The Dower House," Miss Vaughan remarked, observing my interest. "The Castell Marten steward, Hughes, lives there at the moment, just to keep it aired."

"No doubt the Dyffryns will remove to it, when Castelmarten weds my sister," Mr. Carnaby remarked. Miss Vaughan smiled, and it was plain that she, at least, would give the marriage her blessing. No doubt she felt, with Dr. Glynn, that while the Carnabys would consider two mésalliances in the family quite unthinkable, if one of their children married well, they might be brought to overlook a mismatch in the other.

"Glasffynonban means 'high blue spring,'" Miss Vaughan remarked as the path steepened and the horses slowed their pace. "It is a well in a pretty fern-filled place

145

among the rocks where the sheep come to drink. It is reputed to be a wishing well."

"Then I must certainly see it." I glanced about me. "I did not realize we were to ride so high up the mountain. The sky is a queer colour, is it not?"

"The wind has dropped," said Mr. Carnaby. "I believe we should turn back."

"Oh no," cried Miss Vaughan. "We have just come to a level patch, and I am challenging you, Mr. Carnaby, to race me to that pile of rocks!"

They spurred away together and I followed at a canter. As Juniper's smooth stride lengthened under me, I found my vague apprehensions vanishing as if I had been transported to a happy, simpler world. The fresh mountain air, scented with new grass and buttery gorse blossoms, seemed to waft away my fears. The freedom of movement lifted my heart, and the drumming of hoofbeats throbbed like an echo from forgotten halcyon days.

I drew rein reluctantly when I heard the others calling me from somewhere over to my right. The mare halted, snorting, and I stared in surprise at the strangely enlarged but fading shapes of my companions beyond the bracken-filled corrie which lay between us. Mr. Carnaby began to urge his horse towards me, but even as I watched, veils of mist swirled about him and thickening, soon removed him altogether from my sight.

I began to trot the mare towards where I had last seen him, down into the rocky corrie, but soon I too was in the mist and forced to drop back to a walk. I heard Miss Vaughan calling, and turned in that direction, higher and to the left. Then Mr. Carnaby shouted from my right. I called back, changing direction again to go downhill, concentrating my efforts now on finding him. From time to time I could hear both him and Miss Vaughan calling to me, but it became harder to determine from what direction their voices proceeded, and it did not seem that we were getting any closer to each other.

I told myself not to be frightened: I had only to keep going downhill and even if I did not find the others I would surely soon be below the mountain mist. But I was shivering and my mouth was dry, when suddenly Miss Vaughan loomed up before me.

"Thank God!" she cried, echoing my own relief. "Follow me closely—"

But Juniper had taken alarm at the unexpected apparition. She was rapidly backing away, despite my soothing words. I could understand her feelings, for the effect of the mist was to make Miss Vaughan on the black stallion seem unnaturally gargantuan. I had Juniper pretty well under control, however, when a sheep ran up almost beneath her hoofs, nearly startling me out of the saddle and sending the mare into a blind gallop downhill across the moor.

I had been almost unseated and clung to the pommel until I regained my balance. Then I took a firmer grip on the reins and tried to stop the mare, by now swerving between great heaps of rock. At last I was able to take advantage of one such swerve, by leaning over and bringing the mare round in a circle so tight that she was forced to halt.

I patted her damp neck, and spoke to her continually until I could feel her trembling cease. When she was sufficiently calm to try to snatch at a tuft of grass I urged her forward, riding with a loose rein and hoping that Juniper knew the way, for by now a wall of wet cloud seemed to enclose us and I found it impossible to guess in what direction we might be travelling. The mare stumbled on, however, turning this way and that, snorting occasionally, and sometimes mouthing at sprays of gorse. I felt hopelessly lost.

Suddenly Juniper stopped. She stood absolutely still as if afraid to move, and began to shake all over.

"What is it?" I whispered.

The mare waved her head from side to side. I left the reins slack, and Juniper took a backward step. Her feet came out of the wet ground slowly, with a sucking sound. I remembered then having heard of moorland bogs which could swallow man and beast, leaving no trace. I scarcely breathed while the mare backed out of the quagmire, and when her shod hoof rang against a rock and told me we were for the moment safe, I found I, too, was trembling uncontrollably.

Juniper made a quarter turn and plodded steadily on for a while. Then, rounding a pile of rocks, a horse and rider loomed before us, and she shied again, almost unseating me.

"Mr. Carnaby!" I cried to the wavering shape before me. "Sarah! Is that you?"

There was silence in the mist. And then the soft whinny told me that I had not imagined the shape I had seen.

"Help me," I cried. "Don't go—"

But with a creak of leather and the jingle of a bit, the horseman had gone, swallowed up like a phantom in the cloud.

Chapter Twelve

It could have been only a few minutes later when the mare halted again, throwing up her head and staring with pricked ears into the mist. A voice cried out in Welsh, and I answered quickly.

"*Diw*, mistress, is it you?" came the welcome response, and a man on foot appeared before me, a shepherd's crook in his hand. He caught at the reins. "Is it the young lady from the Castell?"

"Yes—yes. How did you know me?"

"My wife, Ysolt, is maiding you, mistress," he said slowly, choosing his words carefully in the unfamiliar English. "She told me about you—and there are not many ladies hereabouts who would think to ride alone on the mountain and in the *niwl*."

"You are Mr. Evans, then. Thank God you found me, for I was quite lost."

"Our cottage is quite close," he said. "Let me take you there to warm you by the fire."

"Oh, thank you—but perhaps Miss Vaughan and Mr. Carnaby are lost. We were riding together when the mist came down—so suddenly."

"Ach yes, it does that, the *niwl*. One moment, you are in sunlight and the sky is clear. The next, you are lost indeed. But Miss Vaughan can look after herself, for she has ridden these moors since she was a child."

"I thought I saw her just now, near the bog. But it may have been a man. Did you meet another rider on the path?"

"No, mistress." I wondered if I had imagined that he did not want to meet my eyes. At all events, Mr. Evans turned away and began to lead the mare downhill. "I will take you to the cottage, and then borrow your horse to ride to the Castell, lest they have missed you. If Miss Vaughan has not returned, we can get men there, to search for her. You will be quite safe in my home for Sionedd Jones is there with the children. Humble it is, but there will be *bara brith* to spare for you, and a place by the hearth."

I was wet and cold, and the thought of a warm fire was irresistible. I was immeasurably thankful when Evans halted by a wicket gate in a rough stone wall, and I realized we were already there. I kicked my foot out of the stirrup and slid down from the saddle. My legs threatened to give way beneath me, and I clung to the mare, while the shepherd tethered her to the gatepost.

"Let me just slip ahead to warn them," he murmured. "Wait you there . . ."

He was gone, a shadow in the mist; a moment later I saw a rectangle of yellow light as a door opened. The lamplight streamed down the path, a symbol of warmth and welcome. Then it was blocked by the returning shepherd.

"Come in now, mistress," he said, "and then I'll be off at once."

Miss Sionedd Jones reminded me strongly of her brother, Mr. Jones, host of the Castell Marten Arms. She was no beauty, but like him she had an air of warmth as welcoming as the lamplight had been. She could speak no English, but threw her arms about me as I stood shivering upon her threshold, and pulled me in towards the fire.

Several children were tumbling about the floor, playing with some kittens; and on the other side of the hearth sat an old man with one leg stiffly thrust out before him. Sionedd spoke to him eagerly, and he sat up and turned his weather-beaten face in my direction. He did not meet my eyes, and I realized he was blind.

"Mr. Samson," Sionedd explained to me. She made pinching movements with her fingers and then pointed to my head and the old man's leg, so that I readily understood he was the harper who had been in the accident with me.

I leaned forward and laid my hand on his, bidding him good afternoon. He smiled and nodded, saying something in his native tongue.

Then Sionedd seated me close to the fire, and the damp began to steam out of Lady Castelmarten's fine riding habit. Sionedd murmured something and began to prepare a simple meal. She was one of those women who sing as they work, and she had a lovely voice. From time to time the children would join in the tune, only to fall mute and staring again when I smiled at them. Then the biggest boy brought in a harp and handed it to the blind man on the hearth.

Samson ran his fingers along the strings, and the room fell silent, apart from the crackling of the fire, and the slight sounds Sionedd made with her knife as she buttered the bread.

The beauty of the music that rippled out from the blind harper's fingers brought tears to my eyes. He played on while we ate the *bara brith* and sipped elderberry wine, and I listened entranced until I became aware that one of the children had left the room and now returned. Coming to stand between myself and Sionedd, he held out a crumpled paper to her, and jerked his head at me.

Sionedd glanced at the paper. Then her expression changed. She spoke sharply to the child, who looked sulky and answered back, again gesturing towards me.

"What is it, Miss Jones?" I asked. "Is that paper for me?"

She stammered something, paused, and then with a slight shrug offered me the paper.

It was, I saw, a letter addressed to Mrs. Jones, of the Castell Marten Arms, but another hand had struck out the superscription and written instead, "To Miss Rose, by Ysolt Evans."

Unfolding it, I saw that it was signed with the name Rose. Then I remembered that Mrs. Jones had promised to write to her niece in Dunstable for news of any untoward doings in those parts. I thanked the boy and put the letter in my pocket. Sionedd smiled suddenly, looking years younger. She drew the boy towards her, said something quickly to him, and kissed him lightly.

I became conscious of a little draught. Looking over my shoulder I saw a man had entered the room and was standing just inside the doorway, a man tall and dark, his eyes seeming to burn with the intensity of his thoughts as he stared at me.

"Lord Castelmarten," I faltered, and the music died.

Sionedd turned with a gasp, and fell to a curtsy. The children scampered into an inner room, and Mr. Samson tenderly laid down his harp.

The earl exchanged a few words with Sionedd in rapid Welsh, and then crossed the room in two strides to take the harper by the hand. Some moments later, he turned to me.

"When did you get back, sir?" I demanded, before he could speak. I was thinking of the horseman in the mist. Surely it had been a man?

"Not long after you had set off for your ride, Miss Rose."

"Have you found Miss Vaughan?" I asked, before he could censure me.

"Miss Vaughan was safe enough with Freddy Carnaby," he said grimly. "They looked for you on the mountain for a while, and when they failed to find you, they rode down to the castle to raise the alarm. We were in the courtyard just preparing to go in search of you, when Evans came to say you were safe in his cottage."

He sounded angry, and I saw that he looked extremely tired, as well he might if he had ridden far and fast in the last few days.

"I am glad the others were not lost," I said quietly. I went to Mr. Samson and thanked him for his music, even though I knew he could not understand me. He spoke, and I glanced enquiringly at Lord Castelmarten.

"Samson says that he recalls your voice," he informed me. "It seems you shared a pie with him on the Llangollen coach." He turned back to the old man and asked him something.

Mr. Samson reflected, his head shaking slightly. Then he spoke again.

"He says," the earl translated slowly, "that he asked you on the journey whence you came and whither you were bound, by way of making conversation. He asked in Welsh, and you replied in English—there was a farmer who translated between you—"

"Please go on," I cried.

He stared at me, his dark eyes inscrutable. "The farmer told him you said you had come out of darkness, and were travelling into darkness. He says that from the sound of your voice, you were lost indeed. Come now," he added brusquely, "I must get you home, and out of that wet habit."

I pulled my wits together, and bade farewell to Sionedd and the children. Then we went outside, into the fog.

By the gate a horse loomed; it seemed as large as an elephant. Evans was holding the rein.

"Only one horse?" I exclaimed.

"You will ride pillion," said Lord Castelmarten, taking the horse from Evans and mounting. "Now, put your foot upon my boot and bring yourself up behind me."

I did so, glad that he had not brought his high-spirited chestnut but a broad-backed and sober animal. I thanked Evans rather breathlessly, and the horse moved forward. Once started, I found that it was quite an agreeable method of conveyance. Lord Castelmarten's body sheltered me from the worst of the chill and the damp, and curiously enough his presence was a comfort in the fog.

But then he spoke, and the comfort was dispelled.

"What possessed you," he abruptly demanded, "to go riding on the mountain?"

"Miss Vaughan wanted it," I cried, "and Miss Carnaby said nothing to dissuade us. It was sunny when we set out." I recalled that Mr. Carnaby had expressed some doubt. "Miss Vaughan saw no harm in our taking the mountain path," I assured him, hoping he would not realize the implication in my words.

"She should know how suddenly the *niwl* can come down . . ."

"I am sure the fog was as great a surprise to Miss Vaughan as it was to me," I retorted. "She was certainly most distressed when we lost sight of each other."

"She did seem upset when I saw her," the earl allowed. "However, you are not to go riding on the mountain again—or anywhere else, for that matter," he added sternly.

153

"No, sir," I said meekly. "Do you want me to dismount?"

"You are a minx, Miss Rose," he added gravely. "Has it not yet occurred to you that your life may be in danger? Once your memory returns—but how is it, by the way? Have you remembered anything?"

"Nothing to signify, alas. But pray don't keep me in suspense. What news, sir, do you bring from Dunstable?"

His back straightened. "I will tell you at once," he said in a hard voice. "I could find no proof that my brother was ever in that area—"

"What!" I cried. "Then the—the certificates—"

"Must certainly have been forged. There is no record at St. Michael's Church of Gerry's marriage, or of his death or burial. In a word, I do not think he was ever there."

I sat silent, feeling quite stupid and numb. The horse plodded on steadily, and Lord Castelmarten stared straight before him.

"If you could find no news of your brother," I said at last in a voice so low that he had to turn his head to hear me, "what then of 'Victoria Merridew'? Is there such a person?"

I felt him shrug. "She does exist," he said evenly, "or at least she did. But I was able to discover remarkably little about her. She lived with her grandfather, who died recently. I traced her as far as the stage for Lichfield, which she took three days before—before your accident."

"But, but—" I struggled to control my stammering. "Surely, when you made enquiries at her home—"

"Her home is gone," he said bluntly. "It is nothing but a heap of rubble and charred timbers—burnt to the ground."

"The neighbours?" I asked. My voice sounded dry and husky, as light as dead leaves stirring.

"There are none. The place is singularly isolated. By the time I arrived, everybody knew there had been a fire at Church Cottage. But I could find only one person who could tell me when it happened, and he was caring for his sick wife when he saw the glow beyond the trees, and could not leave her. If his information is correct, the

154

cottage burned down the night Miss Merridew left it."

"Church Cottage," I murmured, after I had assimilated this. "That was the name on the certificate. Is it not near the church?"

"Ay, near the church. But there is no other house near there. The rector lives half a mile away."

"There must have been servants," I persisted. "In the country, everybody knows the other's business. It is hard to believe you could discover no more than that."

"The Merridews kept very much to themselves, it appears. I found a woman who used to work for them, a Mrs. Farren. I remembered the signature on the marriage certificate was something similar, and thought at first I had found the witness. But she denies all knowledge of such a marriage, and I do not think she was lying."

The fog pressed close about us, and my throat felt raw. "So your brother might not only have been unmarried," I exclaimed, "but he might be still alive!"

"I somehow feel he is not alive," said the earl in a grim tone. "I felt it very strongly there. Odd, is it not?"

"Everything is odd," I agreed with a shiver. "What did this woman, Farren, have to say about the Merridews?"

"Very little. She said their furniture was old, the carpets worn, but that there were many objects of value, and curiosities from foreign parts. She thought it possible the place had been burned to hide evidence of a burglary."

"And Miss Merridew herself? What did the woman say of her?"

Again I felt him shrug. "Farren had been dismissed, shortly before. It was plain she bore some resentment to Miss Merridew for this. Plain, also, that she liked the girl in spite of it."

"How did she describe her?" I asked breathlessly.

"As a pretty young lady with brown hair. She was good and kind, though sometimes dreaming, according to Mrs. Farren. She was something of a bluestocking and seemed not to miss the young company she lacked. She nursed the old man devotedly. I must own that she does not sound at all the sort of young woman who would appeal to Gerry!" he concluded.

"You think Miss Merridew sounds dull," I said defensively. "But perhaps Mrs. Farren did not know her well."

"It is true that the woman had not worked there long."

"What did she say about being dismissed?"

"Why, that Miss Merridew took her grandfather's illness very hard, and that she said she needed the house quiet, paid her what was owing, and told her not to come again. Mrs. Farren did not even know the girl had left until a week after she had gone—the same time that she learned about the fire."

"Miss Merridew was coming north," I said. "She had the certificates with her. Surely she must have been coming to Castell Marten?"

"There were some papers, certainly—but they must have been forgeries."

I forced my numbed brain to think. "The parish register, sir, no pages had been torn out?"

"None. And there are no graves in the churchyard that cannot be accounted for."

"Then—in spite of your personal feelings—surely it is not impossible that Gerry is alive, after all. Do you think he could have planned this, sir? Could he have pretended to have died, in order to be free of—to live his own life?"

"To be free of me, you mean? Would he have forfeited his fortune for that, when only a few more months would have brought him both freedom and money?"

"Perhaps that is where the marriage came in," I suggested unhappily. "Perhaps he intended his supposed widow to claim the fortune, and bring it to him."

"No," declared Castelmarten. "That would be too hard a part to play, though my mother thought that if Gerry had done something wrong, if he felt the need to disappear, then he might possibly have planned it so. But for my part, I am persuaded that Gerry was murdered, and that someone else used the girl as a tool, and sent her to Wales to take possession of the money."

"He would have to have been very sure of the girl," I said in a small voice.

"Miss Esther suggested that Miss Merridew might have been the murderer's wife and not Gerry's, after all. The murderer, if there is one, would have had to know a good deal about Gerry's family and his fortune, of course, but then Gerry was not precisely reticent. Still, we are agreed that it would seem more likely to be someone who knew him well." He continued musingly, "Somebody—desperate. And someone, of course, who also knew Miss Merridew." I thought I heard him sigh. "It is all conjecture," he went on. "But if we are to think of someone with connections in both Wales and Dunstable, then Ned Vaughan must come to mind. He is certainly ingenious enough—and yet I would have thought him far too squeamish for murder. He did not object to tormenting with words, but anything like physical cruelty I believe to be quite alien to his nature—but I may be wrong, of course."

There was a little silence while the big horse plodded on. "Are we lost?" I asked at length.

"By no means. I am taking you the long way home because I know it best. Well, what do you think of all I have disclosed?"

My face close against his back, I asked, "Do you think I am Miss Merridew?"

He shrugged, and I sat up straight. "You may be Mrs. Edward Vaughan, for all I know, or Mrs. Gervais Marten, for that matter," he said coldly. "But if you want to be considered an innocent, then you had better place your hopes on being Mary Ramsey."

"I am innocent, I believe; so I had best prepare to take my place with the Thomases of Holyhead."

"The Thomases?" he cried. "Good God, I had forgotten that wretched fellow. No, you cannot go to him."

"Why not?" I asked, driven by a demon of perversity. "No doubt domestic work is not beyond my capabilities."

"You have soft hands, as I remember."

"They would soon harden. Indeed, I am sure I have worked extremely hard upon occasion. I seem to remember scrubbing a floor with a bucket beside me.

157

There were bloodstains in the wood..."

Lord Castelmarten reined in abruptly. "Go on," he commanded.

I shivered. "I—I can't remember more. But I believe it was not long ago."

He turned in the saddle, his face but inches from mine. "Bloodstains," he repeated. "Could that have been my brother's blood?"

"How do I know? But it was very important to remove them, I am nearly sure."

In a hard voice he said, "Does this not prove how right I was to warn you? Your situation is far more serious than you seem to understand. When villainy has been done, and when it is in your power to betray the villain, you should be on your guard lest he attempt to dispose of you."

I caught my breath. In a small voice I said, "Is it your opinion, sir, that I should leave Wales?"

He turned and urged on his horse.

"Of course you should leave," he said roughly. "I would give a great deal to send you away—as far as possible from here. But we would never get to the bottom of the mystery then, would never know who was the traitor in our midst. No, Miss Rose, whoever you are, you have a part to play at Castell Marten, and play it you must for all our sakes. I have told my mother we must seem to accept you now as Mrs. Gervais Marten, at least until you recover your memory, in the hope that some accomplice may attempt to get in touch with you."

"Oh," I said blankly. "You t-told your mother?"

"Naturally, when I returned. Don't be afraid," he added brusquely. "She is only too glad to be able to hope, however vainly, that Gervais might be still alive. She agreed to accept you as his widow while we are waiting. Only you need not run foolish risks while you are at it, for what would it profit us if you were to lose your life?"

"I dare say it would come as a great relief to you," I suggested.

The earl either did not hear me, or pretended not to. "Hold on to me," he cried over his shoulder, and spurred the horse into a canter. How easy it would be for him to kill

158

me now, I thought. Here in the mist, he could throw me down upon the rocks, and say that I had fallen. He could dash my head against the stones, and no one would suspect him. But he did not stop, and I was obliged to cling to him as if I trusted him because there was no one else to whom I could turn.

The mist began to glow. It was dispersing, thinning—and then we burst out of the grey veils into the mellow evening light, and saw the castle lying not far below us.

"How beautiful it is!" I cried.

"Yes. Beautiful and hungry."

"Hungry, sir?" I repeated as he trotted down towards the Keep.

"Hungry for gold. It is the sheep which feed and clothe us, the sheep which keep the roof over our heads. And now new rams must be brought to improve our stock, and new rams are expensive. The gutters in the castle need replacing, and the walls need pointing. There are many things which cannot be put off for much longer; but it looks as if I shall have to stand by and see my home and my flocks go down to ruin."

"Are you blaming me for laying claim to your brother's fortune?" I cried out. "Do you think Gervais would have put it into the estate, if he had not married?"

"I know he would not have done anything so farsighted. I am blaming no one—except perhaps Aunt Gwynneth, who had a soft heart and was easily won over."

As we rode over the bridge towards the gatehouse, I was wondering if I could suggest that I would make over the money to the estate if it should come to me. But then I glanced at the Keep, and remembering that Lord Dyffryn had seen us leave to ride up the mountain, the thought occurred to me that he might have told Lord Castelmarten where to find us, before the search party had been got together. Was it not possible that Lord Castelmarten had ridden after us, into the mist, and that he found me and lost me again before he could accomplish whatever he had set out to do? But before I could ask the earl if he had seen his grandfather since his return, a bird flew past, swooping low into the courtyard and startling the horse which bore us. I reflected that in past times the incident might have been regarded as an omen, a warning perhaps not to trust Lord Castelmarten with either my problematical fortune or my thoughts; and I found my eyes following the bird as it soared over the gatehouse and up, beyond the empty upper storeys of the castle.

A shadow blurred one of the high windows.

"Look!" I cried.

The earl looked up. I felt his muscles stiffen under my hands.

"What is it?" he demanded.

"I saw—there was a man—up there—in that window."

"It must be your imagination," said Lord Castelmarten flatly. "There is no one there."

"No," I agreed. "There is not now, for he has gone..."

But a man had been there, and I was almost certain that the earl had seen him too. Why, then, should he deny it?

Chapter Thirteen

It was not until I was changing that I remembered the letter from Mrs. Jones's niece. I took it out of the pocket of the riding habit when Ysolt was not looking, and slipped it under my pillow, wondering a little at my instinct to keep it secret from her. Later, when she had carried away the habit to dry and brush it, I sat down and smoothed out the crumpled paper.

"Dearest Auntie," it began, and was signed across the margin, "Yrs ever affect, Rose." It was after this niece, I recalled, that Mrs. Jones had named me in the Castell Marten Arms.

I skimmed through the letter. The first part was full of family news. Then the tone of the letter changed.

"You ask if anything out of the way has come to pass down here, and if any Strange Young Gentleman has been seen about the village. I wonder if you mean our Highwaymen! Very bold, they was, while it lasted; but of course that is all over now. Old Jack Coachman, he that drives for the Mayor of Dunstable, swears his guard winged one of them, but be that as it may, the fact is they have not been seen again. A gang of footpads set on a waggoner a sennight agone—but they was not Gentlemen, to be sure. A new young Clergyman was seen hereabouts a time or two, and Sukey at the Sugar Loaf says as he was mighty civil and handsome, but he left for London two or three weeks ago, I believe. Our own Vicar has a nephew lodging with him, to improve his Latin before going to University at Cambridge, he is afflicted with the Spots, and is about eighteen. Then Dr. Rothwell has taken on a new assistant. He is certainly quite Gentlemanly in his dress, his cravats so high he can scarcely turn his head, and his coat so tight, 'tis a wonder he can use his arms. 'Tis fortunate our plague of influenza is upon the wane, for I believe it would have finished him. We have had some floods since all the rain, the rug I made last summer is quite ruined..." My eyes passed on over the next few lines, to stop at a name I knew. "Colonel Morton-Johns has been burgled, these times is lawless indeed. Nothing gone from the house, but some costumes used in their theatricals, for as you know they are a family as takes playacting very seriously indeed, so you may imagine the fussification that was made when they found their costume hampers rifled. But the Constable could find out nothing, and no suspicious characters have been seen about, except the ones I mentioned. But there are always those will steal when they get the chance, and even mummers' clothing has a price. Trusting I have told you all you wish to know, and hoping this finds you, dear Aunt, in good health as it leaves me, Yrs ever affect, Rose."

I was about to reread the letter with more attention when Ysolt returned to tell me that Lady Castelmarten was requesting my presence in her Parlour, at my earliest convenience. I pushed the letter into my reticule, therefore, and hastened to obey the summons.

I found the ladies of the house conversing excitedly together. Even Lady Castelmarten seemed more animated than I had yet seen her, either because her eldest son had safely returned, or because she now believed there was some hope that the youngest one still lived.

They fell silent as I entered, and I realized what I had feared: that the fact of the papers in the reticule being forged had damned me in their eyes. But then they seemed to make a conscious effort to look welcoming, with the exception of Lord Castelmarten, who rose as I entered, and handed me to a chair. He looked dark and severe in his mourning clothes, his face in shadow. I knew that he must be extremely weary after his journey, to say nothing of having had to turn out to rescue me at the end of it, but that did not seem to account for the peculiar intensity of his enigmatic stare.

"I was just saying that it was fortunate Mrs. Farren

162

could identify you," Miss Esther cried impulsively, "when you are well enough to travel so far."

"Or perhaps Mrs. Farren could be persuaded to visit Castell Marten," Miss Enid suggested.

"I invited her to do so," said the earl, "but she refused. Her health is failing, and her eyesight also. She said she might come all this way and still not be able to be sure, so I decided to wait a little while before exerting further pressure on her."

"What else did you do in Northamptonshire, Lucian?" asked Miss Esther. "Did you visit those people, the cousins of the Vaughans?"

"Certainly, but Colonel Morton-Johns was only able to tell me they had not set eyes on Ned for months, and were very sorry for it. I also put a notice in the local newspaper, advertising for Gerry as a missing person, and offering a substantial reward for news of him. William arranged for the answers to be looked into by some local attorney, who agreed to send on anything promising to me. Something may come of that."

"It is an impossible situation," said Lady Castelmarten wearily. "To be able neither to mourn, nor to rejoice. And what is Miss Rose's position to be here, now that we know some villainy is afoot?"

He stared at me mercilessly. "Uncomfortable, I suspect."

I flushed. "I will not stay!" I cried.

"You will stay, ma'am," he coolly contradicted me. "And you will stay as Mrs. Gervais Marten."

"Lucian, are you serious in this?" his mother exclaimed.

"I know it will bear hard on you," he said, laying his hand briefly on her arm. "But as I have explained already the fact is that only by appearing to accept her at her face value, have we any hope of disentangling the mystery. If all appears to be going according to plan, the villain will make his next move. If we seem suspicious, he will merely disappear. If we cast out this girl, we will never see nor hear from any of them again. Perhaps you are content to remain in ignorance of what occurred during the last days of Gerry's life, but I beg to inform you that I am not."

163

"You are very sure that he is dead," she murmured sadly.

"I am, and I am also certain the girl masquerading as his widow could tell us everything we want to know, if she could but remember it." He stared at me. "I wonder if that is why you lost your memory, because you could not bear to think of what you knew?"

Dr. Glynn had suggested something similar, I recalled. "Are—are you accusing *me* of murder?" I heard myself asking, in a whisper.

He shrugged again. "Of being an accessory, perhaps." He stood up slowly, feeling in his pocket. "Here, Mrs. Marten. You had better put this on." He dropped a small object into my lap, and I stared at it with complicated feelings.

It was his brother's ring.

As my fingers closed over the ring, Lord Castelmarten gave me a searching look. I bowed my head, trying to hold back the tears.

With a rustle of silk, Lady Castelmarten hurried to my side. "It is very hard for you," she murmured, putting her arms about me. "For us all, alas! I must beg you to make allowances for Lucian."

"I am sure I could never have been a party to—to murder—or to any wicked plot, indeed!"

She sighed. "I have only known you a few weeks. I would call you innocent, but how can one be certain? To yourself, I am sure, you must seem innocent, since you can remember nothing. And perhaps you are a new person now. Perhaps you have made a fresh start in life. At all events, for the time being will you not put on the ring? I am—we all are—prepared to accept you as Gerry's widow, until something else is proved."

She had put the matter somewhat differently from his lordship, but I did not remind her of it. They all wanted me to stay at Castell Marten, if only as the bait to catch a murderer; and I certainly had nowhere else to go. I slipped the ring onto my finger, where it hung, uncomfortably large.

"Here," cried Miss Esther, darting towards me. "I have some wool, the very thing." She showed me how to wind the wool about my finger, to make the ring a better fit. "There! Now you are Mrs. Marten!" She threw one of her sly glances at me. "I vow it will be quite amusing, like acting in a play. And nothing will happen," she added in a comforting tone. "For either you are Gerry's widow or he is still alive—and you could certainly be in no kind of danger from him. I am persuaded that there is some simple explanation for the whole."

I wished I could agree with her. But there was too much that seemed inexplicable at present to be easily shrugged away: the missing certificates, both copies and originals; the burnt-down cottage; the warning messages. Even the accident to the Holyhead coach now began to seem such a singular coincidence that I was almost tempted to suspect that, too, might have been contrived.

Hughes, the steward, appeared in the doorway.

"Mrs. and Miss Vaughan have called, your ladyship," he announced.

Lady Castelmarten glanced at me. "I was half-expecting them," she murmured. "Are you able to receive them—as Mrs. Marten?"

I inclined my head. She appeared to brace herself. "Pray show them in."

Mrs. Vaughan bustled in, rather flushed from climbing the stairs. Behind her, Miss Vaughan had an air of suppressed excitement. Her eyes were very bright and she glanced quickly about her with a look almost of defiance.

"My dear Lady Castelmarten," cried Mr. Vaughan. "I trust we don't intrude upon you. Only my daughter told me that his lordship had returned and *mon mari* sent me to discover what news he brought. We also wanted to assure ourselves that Miss Rose was quite recovered from her mishap."

"Extremely civil," murmured Lady Castelmarten, while Miss Enid cleared her throat in a faintly derisive manner.

"No, I can see you think it an imposition, ma'am," continued Mrs. Vaughan, no whit abashed. "But the fact of

165

the matter is that Mr. Vaughan has prepared a memorial service for poor Gervais, and he is anxious to know when it should be held. It is a question of fitting it in ... the Bishop is visiting us next week, as you know."

Lady Castelmarten bowed her head. There was a heavy silence. I suddenly realized I was holding my breath, and let it out carefully.

"I would prefer to postpone such a service," she said at last. "As long as his widow cannot remember Gerry, it would seem something of a mockery and an ordeal for her, who must be expected to be the principal mourner. Pray tell Mr. Vaughan that I think it better to hold the ceremony next year, on the anniversary of ... Gerry's death."

Mrs. Vaughan stared at me with unconcealed interest. "Then—then you are now satisfied that this young lady is indeed—his widow?"

"The conclusive proof will come when her memory returns," said Lady Castelmarten calmly. "For the time being, we are prepared to accept her as—as what she purports to be."

"Oh? Then his lordship found no actual proof?"

I bit my lip. It was Miss Esther who came to the rescue. "Was it not fortunate?" she cried madly, clapping her hands together. "Fortunate that he took with him a legal man, I mean? Yes, he was accompanied by Williams, Mr. Prys-Roberts's clerk. Gentlemen are so easily imposed upon, you know. But a sound man like Williams is quite another matter. It is such a relief to us all to have the matter settled. Of course, it was plain to me from the first that Miss Rose—Mrs. Marten, that is to say—that she could not possibly have been an imposter—even by mistake, as it were. But it is so nice to know where we stand. And for Gerry's sake, it will be a pleasure for us all to be good to his widow."

Mrs. Vaughan looked rather blank. Then she darted one of her uncomfortable glances in my direction. "I see you are wearing a wedding ring," she remarked.

I found my voice. "Yes, ma'am. It is Gerry's signet ring—rather large, as you see, but I mean to have it tightened."

"I think you had better lose no time in doing so," she said. "It would never do to appear without it, once you have assumed the name. Besides, who knows but you may be in an interesting condition, which should soon make itself apparent."

I gasped in horror. Mrs. Vaughan put her head on one side. "I see you think I am too frank; but let me warn you, *chérie*, that is the first thing that will occur to all the *vieilles femmes* here, who have nothing better to do than make such speculations—and particularly in your case, which would be so peculiarly—interesting."

"It would, indeed," said Lady Castelmarten rather faintly. "It is extraordinary, but the possibility never occurred to me. Miss—Mrs. Marten and I will discuss it later. Now, Mrs. Vaughan, there is something in which you can oblige me, if you will—"

"Oh, of course, ma'am. Anything I can do for you!"

"We are in mourning, obviously, and therefore it would be out of place for me to make an occasion on which to present my daughter-in-law to the *cantref*, as normally we should do. And the circumstances make it difficult to explain the facts either by letter of by public announcement. I would be grateful to you, Mrs. Vaughan, if you could therefore inform your acquaintance of as much as you know yourself . . . namely that Gerry was married, is dead, and that his widow is now living quietly here with us."

"*Volontiers*, your ladyship. I shall be glad to spread it about. As for the question of the memorial service, that is entirely your decision, of course. I hope at least that Lord Castelmarten was able to visit the grave at Upper Buzzard and see that all was properly in order there?"

This time it was Miss Enid who rose to the occasion. Rising, she took the visitor by the hand. In a low voice she said, "I know you are not aware of the distress such questions bring on Gerry's mother. Give her a few weeks more in which to accustom herself, I beg of you. And now, may I ring for your carriage? You see, my poor sister is quite overcome."

"And while you are waiting for the carriage," cried Miss

Esther, "I have been meaning to ask your opinion on Miss Carnaby's charity school. Has she mentioned it to you? Are you going to support it?"

Mrs. Vaughan responded to this topic, and her daughter came quietly to sit by me.

"It is hard to know just what to say," she murmured. "I suppose I should congratulate you? You are quite satisfied, no doubt, to be accepted here as a member of the family?"

"I am glad I am not to be turned out to starve," I agreed, deciding I had better not mention my moment of rebellion. "On the other hand, until my memory returns, I shall find it hard to think of myself as 'Mrs. Marten.'"

Miss Vaughan smiled slightly. "And no doubt his lordship finds it equally hard to think of you as a sister."

"What do you mean by that?"

"Why—only that he would have disapproved of any marriage in the family which he had not himself arranged—and to one who deprives him of Gerry's fortune while at the same time bringing no financial contribution of her own to Castell Marten . . . ! Well, I am sure that you can see that it would take a better man than Lucian to welcome you."

"He does not welcome me," I owned, as she seemed to expect a reply.

She leaned closer. "What did he discover at Upper Buzzard?"

"Very little, unfortunately."

She looked at me reproachfully. "You think I am as unfeeling as *Maman*, do you not? But remember that Gerry was my childhood friend, and that I am naturally agog to know what happened there."

"Yes, I sympathize with your curiosity, but I have very little to tell you. The cottage where Miss Merridew— where I used to live, I mean, has been quite burned down."

"Oh! What a pity. Then you cannot even bring that as your dowry. But perhaps the land is worth something. Ah, the gig is ready for us, it seems. Farewell, Mrs. Marten. Take good care of yourself!"

I stared after her as she left the room. There had been a decidedly warning note in her voice, and I remembered that this was not the first time Miss Vaughan had let me see that she thought I was in danger here at Castell Marten.

Lady Castelmarten beckoned to me as she left the Parlour, and I followed her to her bedchamber where she questioned me delicately. Presently she informed me that not only could I not be in a family way but that it seemed to her very unlikely that I had been married.

"Indeed, I feel as if I am unwed—but since the marriage lasted only a few hours—if there was a marriage—" I broke off, gazing at her unhappily.

"Well, for the moment we must assume there was, and that you are Mrs. Marten, since my son wishes you to be seen to be accepted as my daughter-in-law."

Lady Castelmarten did not speak unkindly, but she sounded very sad. On an impulse, I crossed the room and dropped to my knees beside her.

"Should you dislike it very much, if I were proved to be truly your daughter-in-law?" I dared to ask.

She caught her breath.

"Bless me, child!" she exclaimed. "No, since you ask it, I would like it well enough. He could have left us a far worse inheritance, in truth." She sighed, and turned her face away. "'Tis not you I dislike, my child," she said suddenly. "'Tis the deceit—the uncertainty. Not knowing who is involved, nor whom one can trust. Even my own son..."

I touched her gloved hand for an instant. Then I stood up to leave. Parry was hovering in the doorway, her black eyes hard upon me. There was one who hated me, I thought; one—but from all appearances, not the only one.

I went down to dinner a little early that afternoon. Lord Castelmarten was just emerging from his mother's room. He frowned when he saw me, and I reflected that his rest did not appear to have greatly refreshed him. He stood back to allow me to precede him down the stairs, but as I picked up my skirts intending to hurry past, he caught hold of my left hand and stared at his brother's ring.

"You know it was agreed that I should wear it," I said rather breathlessly. I could not imagine why I should be so

169

frightened of the earl at times. It was true that he was great and powerful in this part of the world, that he was physically strong, and that he held my future in the hollow of his hand—but he was only a man, after all; and somehow I felt certain that once upon a time I had prided myself on the management of men, or of one man, at least.

"I hate to see it there!"

"Shall I take it off, my lord?"

He dropped my hand "No. There is no help for it, I suppose."

"It was your own idea, that I should be—should seem to be—accepted as your brother's widow," I reminded him.

He glared down at me. "And that suits you very well, no doubt. But don't give yourself airs, Miss Rose. For you see, I don't believe in your claim. From the first I was suspicious, and my visit to Dunstable has done nothing to reassure me—has confirmed me, rather, in my apprehensions. Well," he demanded after a pause, "have you nothing to say?"

"What can I say? I know nothing, and have done nothing, so far as I can remember, to cause your anger."

"Indeed? Yet somehow you don't look so docile as you would have me believe."

"How do I look, then?" I could not resist asking.

"Damnably alluring, miss. By far too pretty for your own good. The difference in you since I went away—but—the Devil! It is madness to be talking like this. If in fact you prove not to be my sister—"

He broke off. My heart was beating so violently that I could hardly speak. "Yes, sir? What then?" I managed to ask.

He set his jaw. "Let us hope," he said in a controlled voice, "that when you do recall your past, you find yourself able to abandon this appearance of innocence, for I find it damnably irritating in a person of your character."

"And I find you, sir, offensive beyond permission!"

"Do you, miss? Then allow me to remind you, if you have really forgotten it with all the rest, that adventuresses are fair game."

I wondered why I found it so hard to get my breath. "I

fail to understand you, my lord. You make no secret of despising me—and yet—"

"I don't understand myself," he said harshly. "Let us say, you are a mystery I would be interested to fathom at my leisure. Meanwhile, so long as there is the faintest chance that you might be my sister after all, it is obviously better for me to be content with despising you."

"Thank you, sir. You have left me in no doubt of your opinion of me. Are you interested in mine of you, or is it quite irrelevant?"

"Both irrelevant, and all too obvious," he drawled. "I have not set myself to win your interest or affection—"

"That is the greatest understatement I have ever heard!"

"You exaggerate, in your feminine way."

"Sir, my sex has nothing to do with the issue."

"On the contrary, it has everything to do with it."

"Oh! Now you are provoking me, indeed! You have no means of knowing whether I exaggerate or not the effect you have upon me, and my definition of that effect is an intellectual one. Let me tell you, sir, that from the first—"

"Say nothing that you might regret!"

"You find my so-called innocence irritating. I find your implication that you could win me if you set yourself to do so utterly infuriating. It is all of a piece with the rest of your arrogant, overbearing—"

"Hush. You will disturb my mother."

"My lord, you must allow me to say that I find you quite intolerable."

"Very well. You have said it. Now, shall we go downstairs?"

I flung up my head. He smiled at me. I blinked. It was a most disarming smile, and I was obliged to remind myself that Lord Castelmarten was merely setting out to make me eat my words, before I could regain my poise. Even then, I could not quite forget it.

Chapter Fourteen

At dinner, before the Welsh-speaking footmen, the conversation was naturally all of the visit to Upper Buzzard. I was seated on his lordship's left, and ate little, for I was both too conscious of his proximity, and too interested in his story.

The rector of St. Michael's was elderly, Lord Castelmarten told us, but he was by no means senile. He could remember Miss Merridew well enough, but could not bring to mind any stranger of Gerry's description. Certainly Lord Castelmarten was persuaded that the rector had not married Miss Merridew to anyone; and the only man he had buried in the past month was Miss Merridew's grandfather, who had died of a congestion of the lung, following influenza.

"That is what Gerry—what they said Gerry died of," exclaimed his mother. "Does this point to a connection between them? Might one of them have caught the influenza off the other?"

"There is an epidemic of it in the village," said Lord Castelmarten. "It is still raging down there, in fact, but it is not the severest sort. Two old women and some infants had died of it, but it seems that Merridew was the only man who had succumbed."

"Did you see the doctor?" asked Miss Enid.

"Dr. Rothwell. Yes, of course. He has not attended anyone like Gerry this past year, in or out of Church Cottage."

"And what had the Rector to say about Miss Merridew?" asked Lady Castelmarten of her son.

He toyed with his glass, watching the wine as it caught the candlelight in its bright depths. "He was reluctant to speak ill of her," he said slowly. I felt my heart sink, or perhaps it was my stomach that sank. At all events, the effect of his words was distinctly depressing. "To begin with, he said much the same as Mrs. Farren. But at length he admitted to me that Miss Merridew was not such a perfectly good young lady as her grandfather had supposed her to be."

"Ah!" exclaimed Miss Enid. "Did he tell you anything more?"

Lord Castelmarten did not look at me.

"The Rector said that he had seen Miss Merridew out very late alone, on several occasions last summer, and that she had hid from him, and presumably supposed herself unseen. And again, early one morning when he was returning from a deathbed, he saw her from a distance going stealthily into the cottage. He wondered for a long while whether he should tell Mr. Merridew that his granddaughter was slipping out at night. But then the old man fell ill, and he did not want to make trouble. She seemed a devoted nurse at all events, and he did not catch her out after that. But I found a groom at the local inn who recalled Miss Merridew sending off a letter by a stableboy not long ago, as if to make an assignation. Unfortunately the boy has since left to work in London, so I was not able to question him."

Absurd as it may seem, I began to feel guilty. When his lordship did turn to look at me, I am sure my face was a picture of confusion.

"Does this aid your memory?" he asked in a hard voice, but I could only shake my head.

"You visited the Morton-Johnses, you told us earlier," said Miss Esther in an overcheerful tone. "Were they acquainted with the Merridews?"

"The Colonel told me that he knew of old Merridew as a very scholarly recluse, whose only visitors seemed to be university professors and the like. Mr. Merridew was once married, of course; but his wife died long ago giving birth to their only child, a son who was himself killed in active service some years past. He left a widow and daughter who were living with the old man at the time of the

Captain's death. Two years later, the mother died of a fever; which explains how the girl—Miss Merridew—and her grandfather came to be living together. There is a cousin, it seems, who offered to join them, a capable woman who would have looked after them admirably, but there was some sort of a quarrel and she left in a rage, leaving the old gentleman to bring up Miss Victoria as best he might. The first Mrs. Morton-Johns had actually invited the girl to tea once or twice, and liked her very much. But the Colonel's second wife had not cared for the association for her stepdaughter, and cut the connection. In any case, the Colonel said, the Merridews obviously preferred their solitary existence, for they made no push to entertain or be accepted in the community, and on the whole were left alone."

"It sounds to me as if their circumstances were frugal," remarked Lady Castelmarten. "No doubt they could not afford to entertain, nor could Miss Merridew afford to dress elegantly enough to please the second Mrs. Morton-Johns."

His lordship nodded. "I had formed the same impression."

Miss Esther leaned forward. "Did you happen to mention Miss Sarah Vaughan to the Morton-Johnses? I am anxious to know if she had any opportunity to meet her brother, supposing that Ned might have been hiding in the neighbourhood."

"I did ask, for it occurred to me that it might even have been Gerry whom she hoped to meet; but it seems that Miss Vaughan never left the house alone but went everywhere accompanied by her maid. As for Ned, the Colonel assured me that he had not seen him since just after he was disowned, and had not heard from him since January."

Miss Enid pursed her lips. "I dislike dealing in the hypothetical," she remarked, "but let us suppose that neither Gerry nor Ned Vaughan has anything to do with this affair. The two persons whom we know to have been in the district at the same time are Miss Merridew and Miss Vaughan. Supposing that they did chance to meet, and that between them they concocted this tale of a marriage

174

and a burial..." her voice trailed away.

Lady Castelmarten rose. "In that case," she said quietly, "what has happened to Gerry? No, I think Lucian is right. All we can do now is to await some further development. And I feel, with him, that since some mischief is undoubtedly afoot, then we have not heard the last of this affair."

Perhaps it was not surprising that I dreamed that night. I dreamed that I was climbing a dusty curving stair to my wedding in a little dark chamber under the eaves, and that my bridegroom was Lord Castelmarten; and the vicar was none other than Mrs. Vaughan. I was nervous in the dream, starting at every sound as if in great fear of discovery, and when I heard the slow dragging step of an old person approaching in leather slippers, I knew that this was what I had feared, and that the consequences would be terrible.

The footsteps ceased, to be succeeded by a dry whisper like the stirring of ancient leaves. I strove to interpret the fragments of sound, but to no avail. Then the footsteps began again, slowly, inexorably approaching me. I began to understand that I was no longer dreaming and forced myself to awaken, lying with pounding heart trying to open my eyes.

The bed shuddered as something nudged it, and terror released my heavy lids. My eyes flew open and started wide. A head seemed to be floating at the foot of my bed.

Then I realized that an old man stood there, his long white beard illuminated by the small lamp trembling in his hand.

I drew in a breath, but before I could scream he spoke in a rambling way, in a foreign tongue, and my fear began to leave me. This was no apparition, I thought; and then recollection came and I cried out, "Lord Dyffryn! It is you! Why do you come thus into my bedchamber, to terrify me?"

"I did not mean to alarm you," he replied. "I did not think that you would awaken. I only wanted to set eyes on you again, now I hear you are to be accepted as my grandson's wife."

For a moment my confusion deepened. Had I married

Lord Castelmarten after all? No, no, it could not be—and then my pulse steadied as I recalled the other grandson, Gervais Marten.

"How did you hear it?" I asked weakly.

"Hughes, the steward, told me. He informs me either by letter in my food basket, or by calling from the boat, when anything of importance occurs in the family. I wanted to have a quiet look at you, when no one else was by."

"But," I faltered, becoming frightened again, "my door was fast."

Since the night the papers had disappeared out of my reticule, I had taken to bolting the door. Now my mouth went dry as I tried to focus on Lord Dyffryn in the dim light. Had that yellow face, that wild aureole of unkempt hair, that flowing beard, any real substance, after all?

"I found it fast," Lord Dyffryn agreed. "It troubled me...when I could not open it, I went down to the Banqueting Hall and came up instead by yonder stair."

He turned with an explicit gesture and the lamplight showed me the open door in the corner of the room and the yawning darkness beyond.

"The stair is open?" I whispered. "Can anybody come and go at will?"

"The Martens are accustomed to house their guests in this chamber for that very reason, I believe," the old man informed me dryly. "Some of their guests, that is to say. Those of whom they are—uncertain."

"So that they can spy upon them?" I exclaimed in disgust. Then I sat up, clutching the bedclothes around me. "Something was stolen from me, the first night that I was here. That must have been how the thief came and went. I wondered who would dare to enter my room from the gallery, where a light is always burning."

Lord Dyffryn put down the lamp upon a table.

"Dear me. I am concerned. Contrary to what you English suppose, the Welshman is not commonly a thief. I hope it was not valuable? The steward told me nothing of this . . ." He began to rub his hands, loosely clasped, against each other, making the dry whispering I had heard before.

"I did not publish my loss, except to Lord Castelmarten.

who informed his lawyer. It was nothing of intrinsic value... but it was everything to me."

"There's sorry I am to hear it. But perhaps you'll get it back. It must have been a member of the family, I suppose."

"Do you mean—that no one else knows about that stair?"

"Well, as to that—how can I say? And there is an outside door, 'tis true, that leads from beyond the Banqueting Hall into the gardens, and plenty of carved screens there to hide a man, supposing that he had entered earlier, before the outside door was bolted for the night. But in that case, it seems that the door must have been found unbolted in the morning, if he had left the house. There would have been an outcry."

"So, it must have been one of the family, after all."

"Yes. One of my daughters, perhaps. Sometimes I wonder if either Enid or Esther is quite in her right mind. Gwynneth was the best of them, you know. Elaine is very well, and makes a good countess; but she is somewhat remote. No, she has not the heart that Gwynneth had, misguided though the poor girl could be. None of them approaches the quality of their mother, however. And that reminds me, my dear: you should not bolt your door. What if there were a fire, and you were overcome by smoke? No one would be able to get in to help you. Better be burgled a thousand times, than to die like that."

"Thank you," I murmured with every intention of continuing to bolt my door.

"But I am forgetting that I came to warn you," cried the old man, startling me.

"To warn me, sir? Of what?"

"To warn you not to disturb the peahens," he said solemnly.

"The peahens?" I repeated blankly.

"Two are sitting... the eggs are about to hatch. I am trying to breed another white." He moved towards the door. "I am always unsettled when the peacocks are nesting." He set down his lamp again and unlocked the door with fumbling fingers.

"One moment, my lord!"

He turned, raising the lamp high with grotesque effect on the shadows of his wasted face. "What is it, ma'am?"

"Only that . . . I beg you will take care not to be seen. It would appear so very singular."

He smiled, and the yellow light and the deep shadows made him look like a mediaevel gargoyle of the Devil.

"I am not so easily seen," he said softly, hissing a little in the Welsh manner. "I come and go here as I please. I have made a study of the castle, you know. I don't like meeting people. I know where to hide in order to avoid them."

He left, shutting the door softly behind him.

I lay still, reflecting that I had forgotten to ask Lord Dyffryn if his grandson had visited him on his return from Dunstable. I got stiffly out of bed, for my back was aching from my ride, and lit the candle. I crossed over to the door in the corner of the room. It opened inwards, swinging back over the stone stairs; and I saw that its bolt was on the inside, for the convenience of any spy who chose to use it. When it was closed, the panelling matched that of the wall and made it almost impossible to detect, though there was a short string attached to the latch within. I stared at the panelling, aware that some faint echo of memory was stirring in my mind. Panelling that moved—that slid. A secret passage beside a chimney. Another secret stair . . .

I pushed the door wider now, and raised my candle to look down the worn, winding stone treads, quite unlike the steep wooden steps of my nightmare, though nearly as dusty. Ivy crept in through an arrow slit and had spread down the wall to the very edge of one of the steps. I remembered Miss Vaughan remarking on it.

I shivered in the draught, and closed the door. I thought I would not sleep again that night, but all too soon I must have done so, for I found myself dreaming that Gervais Marten in his grave clothes was the rider who had loomed up beside me in the mist—and turned from me again.

At breakfast I was handed a note from Lady Castelmarten, informing me that her arthritical affliction was keeping her abed, and asking me to be good enough to exercise the dogs for her. I put on my cloak, therefore, called both the spaniels, and went out into the garden where my lingering depression was at once dispersed, for it was a glorious spring day, not very warm but full of birdsong and flowers, lambs bleating and trees bursting into leaf. The sky was a clear light blue, and a lively breeze was chasing white clouds across it.

Mindful of Lord Dyffryn's warning, I kept away from the peacocks and went to the other end of the garden where there was a maze and a large well-planned shrubbery. I devised a game of hide and seek with the dogs, which helped dispel the remaining stiffness in my joints. I would throw a stick and while they were bounding after it, I would try to hide from them. Their delight when they found me was quite absurd, and we were all wild with excitement when I dashed round a great clump of lilacs, straight into the arms of Mr. Carnaby.

"Oh, I am so sorry, sir! I think—I think the spring must have gone to my head!"

I smoothed my hair, tucking it back under my bonnet, while the two dogs frisked about us.

Mr. Carnaby's usually pleasant expression had been replaced by one so gloomy, I felt bound to comment on it.

"I did not hurt you, sir, I hope?"

He blinked. "No, of course not. Oh, I beg your pardon, Miss Rose. The fact is that I am in a fit of the blue devils."

That was a pity, I thought, on such a lovely day.

"Is there anything I can do to help?"

"You? No—yet perhaps there may be." He hesitated, ill at ease.

"Have you come to call on us?" I asked, bending to pat the nearest spaniel.

"My parents insisted on accompanying me. I had hoped to ride alone this morning, but no—they would have out the old carriage and make a family party of it, curse them."

"Mr. Carnaby! Surely you should rejoice, that your parents have planned a joint excursion."

"Well, 'tis rare enough, I'll own. But they are both so set against my having anything to do with—with—"

"With Miss Vaughan?"

He looked astonished. "By Jove, Miss Rose—how did you guess?"

"It is not difficult to suspect there is something between you."

"Well, I wish I knew just what it was—and that there were more of it."

"The course of true love—" I ventured.

"'Tis damnable—but they say I am only infatuated. Bah, what do they know of love, who were betrothed to each other in the cradle and never even liked each other?"

"I am sure it is very sad. But what is their objection to Miss Vaughan?"

"Why, the usual fustian—that she is not worthy of me—she, who could have her pick of any gentleman in the *cantref*, I suppose!"

"You were hoping when you rode out this morning to meet Miss Vaughan?"

He nodded gloomily. "I intended to call at the Vicarage to ask if she felt no ill effects from riding in the mist. With that as my excuse, I made sure Mrs. Vaughan would let me see her—but when my mother asked where I was going, I lost courage and told her I was coming here, to see Lucian. 'Excellent,' she cried. 'Your father and I will accompany you—you may escort the coach. I am very interested to know what Castelmarten has discovered—'" he broke off, his face reddening.

"I understand," I assured him. "So you found yourself obliged to put off your visit to the Vicarage?"

He nodded. "I slipped out just now, wondering if I had time to walk down there—but now, of course—"

"I have spoilt it! I am very sorry, Mr. Carnaby. I would help you if I could."

"Would you? She is so—we get so little time alone. I don't even know what she really thinks of me. Sometimes it seems—and then—"

"I feel for you, indeed."

"You cannot know! I have admired her for years, but there was always Gerry—"

"I thought he was your friend?"

"Ay, that is what made it so curst hard. I couldn't blame

180

her for preferring him, when I admired him myself. She has all the tricks, too—used to play us off, one against the other. By God, I thought, if only I could get rid of him—"

"And now," I said softly, "he has been—got rid of."

"Yes," he muttered, "and it seems I am no better off. At first, I thought—just after he had left—that I had won her. But then she seemed as if she did not care. Lately, though, she has warmed to me again. Dashed if I know what to think!"

"How did you do it?"

He stared at me. "Do what?"

"How did you—get rid of Gerry?"

"Why, why," he blustered, "how could you think—it was nothing to do with me—Lucian was disgusted with him—the whole place was humming with his exploits—" Suddenly he sank down onto a mossy garden seat. "It's of no use, is it?" he cried, dropping his head in his hands. "Very well, then—it was partly my doing, I suppose. I helped to spread the rumours—made sure that the worst of them came to Lucian's ears. I was glad when Gerry rode away, for all we had been friends. Yes, I'll own it was the happiest day of my life. But now—"

"Now, what?" I pressed him, when he paused.

"Why, now, I believe I'd give everything I owned to see him dashing through the village on one of the those fiery mounts of his, hallooing as he went—even if it meant I lost Miss Sarah—ay, even then. Do you know," he added wretchedly, "that I was glad when I heard that he was dead? Ay, glad. And now, I've just begun to realize I'll never see him more—that when I caused him to be sent away, I sent him to his death."

"You did not contrive—that, also?"

He raised his head to stare at me. I could see tears standing in his pale eyes, but his expression was quite blank.

"Contrive it? Contrive Gerry's death?"

I bowed my head.

"Ah, no. How could you think it? Murder him? No, indeed. I was mad enough with jealousy to fight him many a time. But kill him—never."

"I am sorry," I said weakly, alarmed by something in his look. "Let us go inside, since your parents are there. And I will try to help your courtship of Miss Vaughan, indeed I will."

I called the dogs to heel and began to walk back to the house. Mr. Carnaby followed me at a distance. I wished I knew what he was thinking.

Lord and Lady Carnaby turned their faces towards me as I entered the Banqueting Hall. I wondered if they were related other than by marriage, for their expressions were absurdly alike, though one was foxy red and the other fair and with the round blue eyes so perfectly reproduced in their daughter Mathilda.

"Mrs. Marten," said Miss Enid dryly, "we were just speaking of you."

"Yes, indeed," said Lady Carnaby. "It is matter for congratulation, I collect, that your claim has been substantiated."

"Well done, well done," rumbled her husband behind his high cravat.

"Miss Enid was telling us something of Castelmarten's investigations in Northamptonshire—"

"Difficult to find out anything, at a distance, I always say," contributed his lordship. "Better to go yourself, eh, Freddy?"

"Certainly, Father. In fact, I was wondering whether I should not also travel to Northamptonshire, in the hope of discovering what happened to Gerry."

"Travelling?" cried Lady Carnaby. But her expression of alarm was almost instantly replaced by one of warm approval. "An excellent notion, Freddy! Ask your father if it is not!"

"Well, Father? What do you say?"

"What's that? What's that, my boy?"

"Mother was wondering what you would say to my riding off to see if I could find out anything further, about what happened to Gerry."

"Well, but Castelmarten has just returned from there. Don't see what sense there would be in your haring off in his footsteps."

182

"I think it an admirable scheme," cried his mother. "You have not been looking quite yourself just lately, Freddy. A change of air, new friends—you know how I have tried to persuade you to go to England."

"Ah! New friends!" echoed Lord Carnaby. "Yes, my boy, it would do you no harm to make new friends, I believe."

"But, as you say, sir, it would really be absurd to travel all that way, for what could I hope to discover that Lucian has not?" He darted a sly glance at his sister. "What do you think, Matty?"

"I think that you should go—but I know my advice will not weigh with you."

"No more than mine does with you, dear sister. Well, I think I shall stay—just as you would stay, if you were in my shoes."

At that moment Lord Castelmarten appeared in the doorway. I felt my breath catch as I looked at him. He would not want Freddy Carnaby asking questions in Upper Buzzard, I realized, whether he were innocent or guilty of concealing evidence.

Lord Castelmarten greeted the company. I watched him narrowly as he bowed over Miss Mathilda's hand, but could detect nothing beyond customary politeness in his manner with her.

Then he straightened, and our eyes met.

"I have a message for you, Mrs. Marten," he said smoothly. "Miss Vaughan has written a note to my mother to ask if you may go riding with her again this afternoon. Of course, she has refused on your behalf."

"Oh," I said rather faintly. "I should have been glad to do so . . . such a lovely day." I caught Freddy's glance, and I heard myself adding quickly, "Miss Vaughan is such a delightful companion. I should have enjoyed riding with her . . . Miss Vaughan has been so kind to me. She is so—so witty and—and lively—" I saw Miss Carnaby shaking her head at me, and deduced that my efforts were not merely too obvious, but entirely wasted. Flustered, I added the first thing that came to my head.

"Perhaps Dr. Glynn will be calling today," I cried.

"Though thanks to his efforts, I really do not need him. He is so talented—a delightful man."

Miss Carnaby blushed and sent me a look of loathing. Her parents stared at me in blankest astonishment. It was Miss Enid who retrieved the occasion from social disaster, albeit at my expense.

"Perhaps you should marry them off to each other," she said lightly, "since you think both the doctor and Miss Vaughan so admirable."

The Carnabys soon took their leave. Lord Castelmarten came to my side.

"What the deuce do you mean by it?" he demanded. "Have you no more sense than to sing the praises of that couple to the Carnabys?"

"Freddy asked my help with Miss Vaughan," I replied with dignity. "And Dr. Glynn seems a good man; he and Miss Carnaby should deal excellently together."

"Indeed?" said the earl in a somewhat ominous tone. Too late, I remembered he was on the verge of becoming engaged to Miss Carnaby. "You are extremely busy in such matters, are you not? Have you given any thought to the consideration of a mate for me?"

I recovered myself. "On second thoughts," I told him stonily, "it occurs to me that Miss Carnaby will suit you admirably."

I turned to sweep out of the room. He caught me by the arm. "Do not overreach yourself, Miss Rose," he advised me coldly. "I warn you to watch your tongue. There are matters here of which you know nothing; and I do not think your behaviour worthy of Mrs. Marten."

"It may surprise you, my lord, to hear that I do not care what you think!"

"Indeed?" He stared down at me until I blushed. "But I believe you do, Victoria, despite yourself."

Then he dropped my arm and strode away, leaving me gazing after him, my heart beating rather fast.

Chapter Fifteen

As I was crossing the hall towards the stairs, I was detained by one of the footmen. Inclining his powdered wig, he informed me that Lord Dyffryn presented his compliments and desired the favour of a visit from me, "At once, if you please, ma'am."

I recalled that Lord Dyffryn had promised to send for me so that we might have some further discussions about his family and, perhaps, their secrets. It was possible, I reflected, that something of significance had occurred to him the previous night, which had been the cause of his coming to seek me out, but that he had been distracted from his purpose.

Pulling on my cloak again, I hurried upstairs to the Parlour. Fortunately it was empty, and I lost no time in entering the secret passage. As I closed the door behind me I noticed that the stairway seemed a good deal lighter than on my previous visit, and I discovered the reason when I reached the bottom, for the drawbridge had been lowered, leaving the gap in the wall open to the fresh spring air.

I found it hard indeed to force myself to cross the ancient bridge, with its broken boards revealing horrid glimpses of deep and swirling water, but soon enough I was treading cautiously on damp stone and beginning to climb the treacherous steps that led up to the hermit's lair.

My footsteps echoed, light as they were, and I hastened them, having no wish to linger in such a place which the watery light from the archway did nothing to improve. If ever some future accident caused me again to lose my memory, I thought, surely it would never be able to erase this horrid stairway from the shrouded areas of my mind.

It was one of those powerfully ominous places which seem to breathe an air of menace, as if the unseen had taken form, and lurked in the shadows waititng to pounce upon the vulnerable.

I came up unharmed, however, though I could hardly bring myself to smile at my fancies, and I knocked upon Lord Dyffryn's door with some impatience. There came no response, and without waiting to knock again, I entered.

The room was very cold. The windows stood open and a sharp little breeze stirred the pages of the open books lying in confusion everywhere.

Lord Dyffryn was plainly not at home. Perhaps he was hiding in the tower, waiting for me to discover him, as a sort of test. At least I ought to make some search before I returned to the castle, I reflected; and in truth I was not averse to exploring the Keep. Behind Lord Dyffryn's room I discovered another stair winding upwards. I took it and found at the first bend that the inner wall of it had crumbled half away. A landing brought me to other stairs, some leading to blank walls, others to doorways opening onto nothing but the empty air, or to rooms half piled with rubble, or galleries that ran along high walls to nowhere. The upper chambers were quite roofless and birds had scattered twigs and feathers all about them. Of Lord Dyffryn, whom I had been half prepared to find lying injured, there was no sign.

Slowly I retraced my steps. Should I wait in his room? But if he had forgotten sending for me, would he not be annoyed by my apparent intrusion in his private chamber?

I decided to return to the castle. I went out and was surprised to find the stairs in darkness. Someone must have closed the drawbridge. Very warily, I felt my way forward and down the first of the worn steps.

Something moved behind me. Before I could turn I felt something small and round and hard between my shoulder blades. It gave me a sharp push and I cried out as I began to fall, tumbling down the darkness, cracking my head against the curving wall.

I did not quite lose consciousness but lay in a heap where I had fallen, gasping and sobbing with pain, trying to think what could have happened. I was aware of something fumbling against me, then of light flooding in for a while, and presently disappearing again, despite my feeble cries.

Someone had pushed me, and had gone, leaving me in the dark. I began to move, testing myself cautiously. My side was bruised. It hurt me to breathe deeply. My shoulder ached and so did my knee. My ankle hurt the most, the one that had been wrenched before. It was swelling rapidly, but no bones were broken, I decided. When I was ready for the exertion, I would be able to hobble back into the castle.

I listened, and then realized that I had been straining my ears since I had ceased to fall. But there was nothing to hear except my own heartbeat and the steady drip of water down the walls. I was certainly alone, and while I was deeply relieved my assailant had taken himself off, yet I longed for human help and comfort.

How somebody must hate me, I reflected, to use me so. And yet they could hardly have meant to kill me in such a haphazard way. Did they mean me to lie here and starve to death? Or should I expect the villain to return and finish me off at a more convenient time, after establishing an alibi elsewhere perhaps?

I found I was shivering. I would have to move, if only to get myself warm again. I found I was almost at the bottom of those evil stairs. I got down to the floor and began to crawl forward cautiously, towards the wheel that would lower the drawbridge. The light was very dim, but I could make out the bulk of its shape and pulled myself upright beside it. Then I released the catch and leaped upon the wheel. But it would not turn.

I tried it this way and that, and reluctantly accepted the truth at last. My enemy must have jammed the wheel.

I stopped struggling with it at last. I hobbled back to the stairs and sat down to think. I had sat on stairs before to think, I remembered. Once, long ago, I had had a favourite place on the turn of a stair, where I had watched motes of dust sliding down sunbeams while I sat and thought . . .

Wearily, I forced my mind back to the present. I could climb up, I supposed, and shout from a window. No doubt someone would hear me in the end, and would come to rescue me. Or there was the possibility that Lord Dyffryn would return and find me here. Except that he would not be able to get in, if I could not get out. And where could he be? Was it possible that it was he who had devised the whole? Could he have lured me here, hidden and pushed me, and gone away? If not, where was he? Perhaps he had been enticed out of the Keep as I had been tricked into it; but still, he must be expected to return sometime. In fact, the more I thought about it, the more absurd became the plot. Naturally, I would be found to be missing, the alarm would be raised, a search made, and I must inevitably be discovered. Even if it were impossible to lower the drawbridge, someone could always row a boat across the water to rescue me.

But then I began to wonder if it would be so easy to find a way into the tower. It had been built, after all, for the very purpose of keeping itself inviolate from invaders.

I shook my head. This train of thought would not do. My business now was to get upstairs and make sure that my whereabouts was known.

When I reached Lord Dyffryn's room, however, I found that none of his windows overlooked the castle. They commanded only an oblique glimpse of the carriageway which led to the bridge and gatehouse. The direct view was to the north and west, the river valley and over to the right beyond the Dower House, the high wild mountains of the Snowdon range.

I closed the windows. Suddenly I realized that I was thirsty and looked about for something to drink. I found a leathern bucket with a ladle beside it, and helped myself to the smoky-flavoured water. Standing by it was a crock containing the heel of a loaf and a ham bone, so at least I was not in immediate danger of starvation. That reminded me that I must watch out for the footman bringing his lordship's supper. He would row round under one of these windows, I supposed, and I would only have to call out to him. It was somewhat comforting too, to reflect that food would arrive twice daily, even if I were to be forever a prisoner in the tower.

I was determined to raise the alarm as soon as possible, however, and set out to climb the crumbling fragmented stairs that were now even more difficult to negotiate. I breathed like an old woman, with a knife of pain striking into my lungs with every gasp, making me wonder if I had not after all broken at least one of my ribs. When I reached the window I had remembered as overlooking the castle, I found it was so narrow a slit at the outside of so thick a wall that I could only just wave my hand through it. It was most unlikely that anyone would notice my signal, I thought. If they did observe the movement they would probably suppose my hand was a pale bird nesting there. It would be better, I thought, to hang something out of the window—a white cloth, like a sheet. But I could recall nothing suitable in Lord Dyffryn's room. I knew I would not be able to undress myself without assistance in my present state, but I was carrying my reticule and inside it were my embroidery scissors.

It did not take me very long, by cutting and tearing, to remove a wide strip from the bottom of my petticoat. I thrust it through the window and weighed the end of it with a rock upon the narrow sill. It was only when replacing the scissors that I realized that they, a handkerchief, and my slender purse, were the only contents of the reticule. The gold bracelet and, more ominously, Rose's letter had been stolen.

Slowly, I retraced my steps to Lord Dyffryn's chamber. Who would want that letter, to the extent of risking my broken bones to steal it? Who even knew that I had received it? Sionedd and the children; but I could not believe that they had anything to do with the predicament in which I now found myself. Ysolt? But how could she have known that Sionedd had given me the letter—albeit reluctantly, as I now recalled. Who else could possibly have known of it?

And then I remembered Lord Castelmarten watching me from the doorway while the blind harper played his music. There was no way of telling how long he had stood there, or even if he had spied through the window earlier.

Supposing that he and his brother Gervais were in the plot together? Unbidden, the thought came, and though I resisted it, it continued to torment me. They were brothers, after all—though they had appeared to quarrel. What if Gervais was still alive, and Lord Castelmarten knew, or had helped to plan, whatever had happened at Dunstable? What if there was some hint of the truth in Rose's letter, some hint that must be destroyed, if possible, before I could have time to read it? What if that shadow I had glimpsed in the upstairs window, and which Lord Castelmarten had denied—what if that had been Gervais himself?

I shuddered and sank down upon the uninviting bed. Lord Castelmarten, I suddenly remembered, had owned to being in the vicinity when the stagecoach was overset... but if one of the Martens—or even one of the Dyffryns—and not a casual thief were responsible for my present predicament, then the golden bracelet must, as I had feared, be of some sinister significance for it to have been stolen as well as the letter. As I considered the unwelcome implications of this thought, there came a sound upon the stairs of booted feet. I cowered back. The door burst open, and there stood Lord Castelmarten, with the sound of other footsteps behind him.

In the first moment of relief at seeing the earl, I flung out my hands towards him, and the colour rushed into my face. But then he spoke in a quick rough voice, and my delight died as my suspicions came flooding back.

"What the deuce are you doing here?" he cried. "We have been searching everywhere—and here you are upon my grandfather's bed, quietly enjoying a nap! Get up at once, and come over to the castle before Aunt Esther flies into hysterics."

I stared at him, trying to read his real thoughts.

"How did you find me, sir? Did you see my signal?"

"The white cloth up there? I thought it was some crazy

190

notion of my grandfather's until he told me it must be yours."

"You have seen him? What happened to him?"

"I am here, my dear." The old man entered and sat down heavily beside the table. "It was all a jape it seems. The peachicks had not hatched though they will do so at any moment."

"He heard someone calling up to him," Lord Castelmarten explained. "He thought it was Hughes, telling him two white peachicks had hatched out."

"Hughes? Of course it was Hughes," said the old man testily. "Do you think I don't know the steward's voice, after all these years? Only he denies it now. I don't understand why he should play such a trick on me."

"He is incapable of it," Lord Castelmarten declared. "And why should he interfere with the mechanism of the drawbridge?" The earl stared at me. "Was it you who did that?"

"No, of course not. I left it open when I came into the Keep, as I had found it."

"But why did you leave no word of where you were going?" he demanded. "My mother sent for you quite soon after I left you, and first my aunts and then the servants were drawn into the search. The place was in confusion when I got back from the sheepfolds."

"Pray don't blame me for it," I cried. "I had a message from one of the footmen that Lord Dyffryn wished to see me. I could not find him, and on my way back down the stairs someone pushed me with a stick. By the time I was able to crawl to the wheel, it had been rendered useless."

"You are hurt!" he cried angrily. "I told you to take care! What has happened? Your ankle?"

"Yes," I muttered, staring at it and realizing it was now quite swollen. "And my ribs ache so that I can hardly breathe."

"I don't like it," complained Lord Dyffryn. "It is most upsetting. I wish everybody would go away."

"Very well, Grandfather," said the earl in a grim tone. "Come, Mrs. Marten. Allow me to assist you."

He began to help me up.

"Have you still got the message?" he asked suddenly.

"What message, sir?"

"The one you say the footman gave you. I might recognize the hand."

"Oh, it was not a written message. The footman told me that Lord Dyffryn had asked for me—"

"He told you?" Lord Castelmarten's voice was dangerously soft. "But none of my footmen speaks a word of English."

"Quite right," remarked Lord Dyffryn in the silence that followed. "Preserve the purity of the language ... and besides, 'tis more comfortable if they cannot understand what is said while they are in attendance, especially in the dining room."

"They don't speak English?" I had known it, of course, but it had not occurred to me to question the authenticity of a man in the Martens' green livery, with a powdered wig.

"You mean—" I faltered, "someone disguised himself, to lure me here?"

"It begins to look uncommonly like it. I warned you this was a dangerous business. Have you learned your lesson now?"

"I have learned that someone means me harm. I am not certain that they mean to—kill me." How absurd it sounded. Rather quickly I detailed some of the reasons why I felt it unlikely my death could have been seriously intended without mentioning the theft of the letter and the bracelet, for I wished to reflect on that a little longer before I spoke of it.

Lord Castelmarten half carried me down the stone stairway. He was very strong, I noticed.

"You do not think it might all have been an accident, however?" he demanded.

"No, sir. Someone raised the drawbridge after I had passed inside the Keep. And I felt the stick between my shoulders. Oh, and someone lowered the drawbridge again, and raised it behind him to bar my escape."

"It was wedged on the other side," the earl remarked. "From that end, it was not hard to undo the damage. But certainly this English-speaking footman has much to answer for."

He put me down at the foot of the narrow stairway leading to the Parlour.

"Why do you sigh?" he asked. "Is that rib hurting you? Dr. Glynn has already been sent for."

"Not that—it is hurting, of course—but I was wondering if we will ever know the answers...and do we want to know them?" I added softly.

"You may be afraid of the truth," said Lord Castelmarten firmly. "For myself I am determined to get to the bottom of the whole affair. I shall find out every detail, even if I have to carry you to Dunstable and Lichfield myself, even if it takes ten years and obliges me to mortgage Castell Marten to the hilt—"

The secret door to the Parlour was opened, and the shaft of lamplight enabled me to hobble up the last of the steps and fall into Miss Esther's arms.

"Oh my dear!" she cried, in a half-scolding tone. "I have been searching from the attics to the cellars! I could not believe you would go to the Keep again without one of us. But you are hurt! Leave go of her, Lucian. Your mother is asking for you, and we shall manage well enough without you. Mrs. Marten must go to bed at once...oh, your ankle! And just when your foot had mended so well..." Somehow she swept me on a tide of breathless exclamations to my door, where Ysolt assisted her to undress me and put me in the great apostle bed.

Dr. Glynn appeared eventually, rubbing his hands together briskly, in his considerate way, to warm them before touching the patient.

"Well, well," he exclaimed with a sympathetic look, "in the wars again, ma'am? Just as you had recovered from your last accident, too. Fell down some stairs, is it? Onto stone, they tell me. Did you hit your head?"

His examination was thorough, and left me exhausted. I submitted to his ministrations as I had to those of Miss Esther and Ysolt, but when Miss Enid appeared with one of her inevitable tisanes, I tried to revolt. In the end, however, I saw that beneath her stiffly disapproving look,

Miss Enid was hurt at my rejection of her potion, and I drank some of it unwillingly, contriving to spill some in the saucer and to leave a quarter of it. Before it took effect both my rib and my ankle were hurting enough to make me thankful that I would soon be removed from the pain they were causing me. But then, I thought despairingly, I would be alone in a room which anyone could enter, and in no condition to raise the alarm or attempt to escape a determined assailant. Perhaps it was this combination of circumstances for which the person who had attacked me in the Keep had been hoping. For my enemy, I knew, had access to the castle.

As the shadows closed about me, I made a determined effort. I reached out for Miss Esther's mittened hand. "Please stay," I whispered.

"Oh, my dear!" Miss Esther seemed quite overcome. "Are you sure you don't mean Miss Enid?"

"No—you. You are my friend."

Miss Esther blushed slightly. She pressed my hand. "Of course I will stay, if you really want me. There is a comfortable chair, and it won't be the first time I've sat up ... Gwynneth couldn't be left before the end, and it was only her sisters she wanted about her ..."

I heard her voice coming and going as she made herself comfortable. It seemed a long time that I lay in a half sleep, incapable of movement but still conscious. Then I was waking again, and yet I seemed to know that it was hours later in the night and that I had been deeply asleep.

It was the panelled door opening that had woken me, I thought. I lay slackly, gathering my wits. The door to the secret stairway ... yes, without moving my head, I could see it opening inwards. Slowly the gap widened and was filled with something black.

Lord Dyffryn was coming to visit me again, I supposed; but this time he would find that I had company and a lamp lit to receive him, low though the flame was burning.

Then someone glided through the gap into the room, and I saw at once that it was not Lord Dyffryn. It was a much younger person by the way it moved—but I could tell nothing else about it because it was clad entirely in

194

black, with a black hood pulled down over the head with slits for eyes, and some sort of black cloak wrapped about the body. Even the hands wore black gloves.

I found I could not scream, or even move. I was only able to lie and stare beneath my lashes at the dim, appalling figure.

It took three steps towards the bed and paused. Then it bent to pick a velvet cushion off a chair, the only cushion in the room that Miss Esther had not placed about herself. The figure stood a moment, its black hands kneading the cushion, turning it a little as if to get a better grip of it. Then it paced on, the cushion held before it like a weapon—a weapon meant, I knew, for me.

"A-ah!" I had managed a shuddering breath. Miss Esther stirred. The figure stopped, its hooded head turned towards her sleeping form, which must have been hidden from it by the bedcurtains until that moment. With a gesture of relinquishment, it let the cushion fall; then with infinite care it stepped back on silent feet, slipped through the opening in the panelling, and closed the door with a slight click behind it.

Only then did I come to life.

"Quick," I cried, shaking Miss Esther by the shoulder. "Run to that door! Someone came—see who is there!"

By the time she understood what I was saying, I knew it would be too late. She stumbled to the door and looked down the winding stair. Then she turned with a puzzled look.

"Are you sure you did not dream it, dear? No one is there."

I pointed to the cushion with a shaking hand.

"Someone came to kill me," I panted, through dry lips; and this time the statement did not sound absurd, for I knew it to be true.

Chapter Sixteen

Miss Esther helped Ysolt to dress me when morning came. She was still somewhat bewildered by the night's events, and seemed glad when a message came that Lady Castelmarten wished to see me. She assisted me to hobble down the gallery to the Royal Bedchamber, where her sister was still recumbent on her pillows, Miss Enid bending over her solicitously.

"My dear child," Lady Castelmarten greeted me in a sympathetic tone. "What ordeals you have been through! I have heard all manner of extraordinary stories, and only beg you to let me hear the truth from your own lips. But sit down first, and make yourself as comfortable as may be."

When I had finished, Lady Castelmarten sent for her son.

"It is out of the question for our guest to be exposed to further danger while under our roof, Lucian," she declared. "I know you had your reasons for wanting her to be in the Stair Chamber, but I must tell you that I can no longer allow it."

He was very pale as if he, too, had not slept well. He inclined his head.

"Very well, Mother. You know I believed that some approach would be made to Miss Rose, and I did not wish to hinder it. But if murder was intended then indeed it is a very different matter."

He turned to me. "You were certain yesterday that no great harm was meant to you when you were lured to the Keep and pushed downstairs. Surely now you have changed your mind?"

"I did not tell you the real reason for my attack," I said in a low voice. I did not know if I was being wise, or a great fool, but I had suddenly determined that I might as well make a clean breast of all I knew. My position, after all, could scarcely be worse than it was already, and if my enemy had motive enough to kill me now, then surely it hardly mattered whether I spoke out or kept silent about all the other incidents that troubled me.

Lord Castelmarten took a seat opposite the sofa on which I lay. He pulled the chair forward so his face was close to mine.

"What was the real reason, then?"

"It was a letter which Sionedd gave me. It was taken from my reticule while I lay half-stunned in the Keep."

"What letter?" he said quickly. "A letter from whom?"

"A letter Mrs. Nanny Jones had promised me, from her niece Rose." I turned to explain to Lady Castelmarten. "While I was at the Castell Marten Arms, I was so concerned with my loss of memory, and with the—the mystery, that Mrs. Jones promised to write and ask her niece if anything unusual had occurred in Upper Buzzard; for her home, it seems, is very close to the Parish of St. Michael's."

"No one spoke to me of this," exclaimed Lord Castelmarten.

"In truth, I had forgotten it myself, until two days ago in the Evans's cottage. Mrs. Jones had sent the letter to Sionedd by her husband, to give to Ysolt, and the boy, Davy, remembered it while I was there and fetched it for me. Sionedd—" I hesitated.

"Yes?" said the earl quietly. "What of Sionedd? Let us hear it all."

"She seemed—reluctant to let me have the letter," I admitted. "But the children knew about it, and that it was meant for me, so she was obliged to give it to me." I raised my eyes to meet those of Lord Castelmarten, dark and inscrutable. "Apart from Sionedd and the children, there was only the blind harper present," I said in a low voice. "Then a few moments later, I noticed you were there, my lord."

There was a silence in the Royal Bedchamber, until one of the spaniels, too close to the fire, began to scratch.

Lady Castelmarten turned restlessly on the great bed. "Are you suggesting, child, that it was my son who went to such lengths to get that letter off you?"

"I think she could not be suggesting that," remarked Lord Castelmarten. "She knows well enough I could have taken it from her at any time."

"But not without betraying your interest in it, my Lord."

He frowned at that, and his colour rose.

"What was in this—important document, then?" he asked. "You read it, I suppose?"

"Yes, when I got home—"

I paused on the word, which had slipped out. Lord Castelmarten did not miss it. One of his black brows lifted, and he gave me a curious look.

I hurried on. "It seems that Mrs. Jones had asked her niece particularly if any strange young men had been seen in Upper Buzzard." As well as I could recall them, I related the details of the letter. When I mentioned the burglary at the Morton-Johnses, Lord Castelmarten brought down his fist upon his knee.

"Ned!" he cried. "Ned, for a certainty! He would know where to find the hampers, and he would certainly know how to use the costumes. I have always felt that Ned was in this somewhere, and now I'm sure of it. Why—I even thought I glimpsed him in the upper gallery, at a window, two days ago."

"You told me no one was there," I cried hotly.

"I was not sure then—but now I am." He glared at me. "Who else could it have been?"

"I thought perhaps—your brother Gervais."

Lady Castelmarten cried out at that, and one of the spaniels got up and waddled to her side.

"Gervais is dead," said the earl emphatically, and with a reproving look.

"We cannot be certain of that," cried Miss Esther.

"It is foolish to build our hopes on fancies, when we have not heard news of Gerry for so long," Miss Enid declared. She turned her inimical glance on me.

"And it is cruel to raise our hopes, without evidence," she concluded.

"I—am sorry," I said, with truth. "I thought that—that the time had come to tell all my—my fears and suspicions, everything that haunts me."

"You were correct," Lord Castelmarten said, staring at me. I wished I knew what he was thinking. Sometimes he appeared to make no secret of his thoughts regarding me, showing me unmistakably that he admired me against his will, or more often that I angered him; but at this moment he was utterly inscrutable.

"What else is there?" he asked, his eyes intent on mine.

"I did not tell you, but—Lord Dyffryn visited me two nights ago, by the same stair that last night's intruder used," I faltered.

Lord Dyffryn's daughters gasped in unison. Then they all spoke at once.

"Father! No, really, it is too bad!"

"Of course, it is the spring—"

"What did he say? What did he want?"

It was Lady Castelmarten who asked that, and I told her what I could remember of my conversation with her father. Her sisters looked quite sympathetically upon me, knowing what a fright the old man must have given me. But the earl was unreasonably angry.

"How could you not have made any mention of this before?" he demanded. "Don't you trust us to protect you from such ordeals?"

"Of course she does not," said his mother, smiling faintly. "How could you expect it, when you make no secret of your suspicions of her—when you are prepared to use her as a bait to entice robbers and murderers into your lair?"

Lord Castelmarten looked quite disconcerted at this unexpected attack. He ran a hand through his hair, ruffling it.

"I admire a great deal about Miss Rose," he muttered. "Her courage..."

"Well, let us not try her courage too highly," retorted his mother. "Tonight she shall sleep in the Blue Room, and you, Lucian, will make sure there is a satisfactory bolt upon the door."

"What else have you to tell us?" asked Lord Castelmarten. "Has Miss Vaughan said anything out of the common?"

"Miss Vaughan?" I queried, startled.

"Yes. If her brother is in this somewhere, it is possible she knows about it."

"She warned me against you," I murmured. "And..."

"Well, what?"

"It seems so impolite to repeat it," I objected.

"More impolite than what you have just said?" he demanded. "Come, Miss Rose, this is no time for niceties."

"Well, she also warned me against...these ladies."

"Really, that Vaughan girl is quite impossible," Miss Esther cried.

"Sarah is hot at hand," said Lord Castelmarten thoughtfully. "She is wild enough—but no one could think Ned capable of violence, any more than Mathilda Carnaby might be."

"Well, there you are quite out," Miss Esther cried triumphantly. "I have seen Mathilda lose her temper with a horse, because it had frightened her. People hide their worst sides from the world, Lucian. One should never say that a person is not capable of violence. Everyone is capable of surprising those who thought they knew them, when under sufficient provocation."

"Ned would vomit at the sight of blood," Lord Castelmarten insisted. He turned back to me. "Miss Vaughan has never mentioned her brother to you, I suppose?"

"Yes, I believe she has. When we went to Plas Celli—"

"What is it?" he said quickly, when I paused and put my hand to my mouth.

"I had quite forgotten—not that it signifies anything, probably. Only the other day when we were riding through the wood we passed an old woman who called me Mrs. Marten. I was excited at the time and thought she might have valuable evidence to give; but then we thought it was probably only that I had been pointed out to her under that name."

"What sort of an old woman was this? Describe her to me."

"She was gathering wood, and smoked a pipe." I strove to think of something more particular. "She had a stick with a bird's head carved upon it."

Lord Castelmarten rose. "We will go to see her straightaway, in case she has anything to tell us. I will order the curricle."

"But really, Lucian, I do not think the child is fit to drive," Miss Esther protested.

Lord Castelmarten looked down at me. "Is that true?"

Something in his eyes insisted I must deny it. Weakly I heard myself declaring that a drive would be the very thing to hasten my cure, even while I wondered why I should wish upon myself what promised to be an awkward interview, together with the disturbing company of Lord Castelmarten, at a time when I was feeling far from strong.

He rang the bell, ordered the curricle in a rhythmic burst of Welsh and, taking me entirely by surprise, stooped to lift me in his arms.

"You will need warmer clothes," he said, interrupting my protests. "You have no time to hobble to your room—and your weight is inconsiderable."

I said no more, and he strode down the gallery with me.

"If you are—Mrs Marten," he said suddenly, "then you will have to find somewhere else to live."

He spoke harshly, and I glanced at him in surprise.

"I am only warning you that you must not think of Castell Marten as 'home,'" he continued. "Once you are acknowledged, it would be better if I were never to set eyes on you again."

I gasped. He lowered me to the ground outside my door and pushed it open. "You might as well know how matters stand," he said brusquely and strode away.

My hands were shaking as I put on my bonnet and rather shabby cloak. I was still before the mirror staring at my pale, unhappy face, when Lord Castelmarten returned for me. He looked large and commanding in his caped greatcoat and tall hat, but he said not a word as he carried me downstairs and lifted me into the two-horse curricle that was awaiting us in the stableyard. He arranged a rug considerately about my knees, took the reins from the groom, and sprang up into the carriage.

"Now," he said as he swung the horses expertly round, "we will see what the old woman has to say about you."

"Do you know her name?" I asked as we rattled over the bridge.

"No, but I know the woman you mean, and where she lives, a little way out on the Llangollen road. She'll be a Jones, or an Evans, or perhaps a Parry."

The horses trotted between the stone walls of the village, the sound of their hoofs echoing in our ears. Children ran out to look and to wave at us, and I felt an unexpected elevation of the spirits at being seen in such a dashing equipage, with Lord Castelmarten for my coachman.

We drove by the inn, bright with fresh whitewash, and the smithy, where our horses pricked up their ears and danced at the ring of the hammer on the anvil, until Lord Castelmarten brought them sternly back under control.

Next we passed behind the old wing of the Vicarage, with its barred windows and somber yews, and then the churchyard, green with the new spring grass except where the raw earth was piled from a newly dug grave. The road ran on a little longer between some fine beech trees, and then a few more cottages appeared.

Here Lord Castelmarten drew rein, and called a question to a man mending a wall.

The man looked round in a startled fashion and touched his hat. He seemed disconcerted, I thought, and gestured with an appearance of relief towards a plump elderly woman just leaving one of the cottages, a black shawl over her head.

"Wait here," commanded the earl curtly, and handed the reins to a sallow youth chewing on a straw, who leaned back against the wall, never taking his eyes off me. I looked away, and saw Lord Castelmarten speaking earnestly to the woman in the shawl. After a moment he took her by the arm, turned her about, and marched with her into the cottage.

A few minutes passed. A little girl and her big sister paused to stare at me. The little one held a ragged doll she was dragging by the hair. I beckoned, wishing I had a ribbon to give the child. She responded to my smile and lifted her doll for me to admire. The other girl was shyly approaching when I heard a door banged shut. I looked round to see Lord Castelmarten on the cottage path. He pressed something into the woman's hand. Then he returned to me, gave a coin to the youth, and got up into the curricle while the children scampered to a safe distance.

"Well, sir?" I asked, waving good-bye to them. "Did you see her? What does she say?"

He began to turn the horses.

"She is dead," he replied bluntly. "That woman had just finished helping to put her in the coffin. The new grave in the churchyard is for her."

I felt a terrible chill steal over me.

"How did she die?" I asked.

"She appeared to have died in her sleep," he said harshly. "Everyone was surprised, Mrs. Wynne the midwife told me, in spite of Mrs. Parry's great age, for she had never a day's illness in her life."

"You said, 'appeared.'" I clasped my hands together and bent my head. "You sound as if you do not think her death a natural one."

"I had a look at her. There is some bruising of the eyelids which seems curious to me. I intend to talk to Glynn about it. In the meantime, I beg you not to mention it."

"No, I will not. Thank you for telling me," I added uncertainly.

"I want you to be aware of danger," he retorted. "I cannot be with you every moment of the day ... but I mean to move into the Stair Chamber, so at least I shall be within call at night."

I stared at my hands. "But what will everybody think?"

"Good God, does it matter?" he replied with the

impatience of one so accustomed to servants that their opinions were a matter of genuine indifference to him. "It was my mother's suggestion. Her approval is all that need concern us. I only hope the villain does not get to hear of it, but I doubt if my people are in touch with him."

"Do you not think, if Mr. Vaughan is truly in the castle"—I dared not suggest again that Gervais might be there—"that he has not some friend among the servants? One of the footmen, perhaps, if he was able to borrow livery."

"It is possible, I suppose," he conceded grimly. "But I prefer to think my servants loyal. He could have borrowed the livery himself without the permission of its owner."

"Supposing that another attempt is made—?"

"Then I shall be there to surprise the intruder," he said grimly. "I shall enjoy unmasking the villain, I assure you."

I stared at him. Was he assuming a part, or was it possible that I had been mistaken in him and that he was not, after all, the man I had to fear? At least it could not have been he at the upper window, I reflected.

"What are you thinking?" he demanded abruptly.

Confused, I shook my head. How could I have told him that I was wondering if I could trust him, after all?

But it seemed my hesitation was unnecessary.

"You don't trust me," he said bluntly. "Well, that suits me for I don't trust you, either. Who and what are you, Miss Rose, and why have you come to meddle in our lives? Until I have the answers to those questions, the less our paths cross, the better, I believe. All I ask of you is that you stay quietly and safely in your place until you have served your function here. No heroics, Miss Rose. You may leave me to deal with any untoward visitor from now on."

I found some difficulty in getting my breath.

"If you believe that I enjoy being thrown downstairs and—and frightened half to death, then, my lord, allow me to inform you—"

"No need." He pulled up his horses before the great front door. "We are neither of us fools, Miss Rose. The only thing of which I desire you to inform me, is whether you have told me everything that I ought to know."

He waited until a stableboy had taken the horses by their bridles and then descended from the curricle. As he turned to help me down, his eyes met mine. "Anything," he insisted. "No matter how trivial it may seem to you. Those notes, for instance. Have you had any more of them?"

"Yes, in a way. There was a message written in the dust upstairs..."

He held me tightly by the arms as he swung me to the ground.

"Upstairs? You mean in the upper rooms, above the gallery?"

"Yes. I went there while you were away."

I was glad I could not see his face, but I could tell that I had angered him again.

"You can show me," he said grimly. "We will go there now."

Without warning he swung me up into his arms and strode across the chequered marble hall towards the stairs.

"There is something else perhaps I ought to tell you," I said impulsively. "You remember the gold bracelet in the reticule? That was stolen, too, with Mrs. Jones's letter."

Lord Castelmarten stood quite still. He made no comment but I saw his jawline tighten before he strode forward again to carry me up the two flights of stairs.

Once on the upper gallery, he put me down but kept his arm about me, and I hobbled with his assistance to the room where the warning had been written in the dust. The bed chamber was empty, the floor now gleaming softly between the rugs.

"It has been cleaned," I murmured apologetically.

"You are sure it was in this room?"

"Yes, I think so. First I went to your brother's room..."

"Let us go there."

He helped me back along the upper gallery. I wondered if it were only my imagination, or if our progress was being watched. I had the sense of eyes upon me and tried to increase my speed. But my ribs ached, and so did my ankle. I felt bruised all over and rather cold.

Lord Castelmarten halted before the first door on the gallery. He threw it open. There was an impression of sudden furtive movement within the room, which was rather dark, the curtains drawn together across the windows. The bedcurtain, I noticed with a chill of horror, quivered slightly.

I stood quite still, all my senses straining. My hand crept out and touched the earl upon the sleeve.

Disregarding my mute appeal, Lord Castelmarten stepped forward and gazed down at the bed. He placed his hand upon the cover for a moment, and then beckoned to me. I tiptoed into the room, and obeying his gesture, put my own hand flat upon the bed.

It was warm.

I snatched back my hand and stared in horror at the earl. A little sound made me jump, but it was only the draught setting the door swinging.

Suddenly Lord Castelmarten clapped his hands together. I jumped again, more violently. There was a frantic scrabbling noise, and a big grey cat ran out from under the bed. It leapt up on the window seat. Finding the window shut, it doubled back and ran between us, out of the open door.

"A cat," I breathed, feeling quite weak with relief. I leaned back against the bedpost. "For an instant, I really feared . . ."

I stopped, wondering at Lord Castelmarten's stern expression.

"The door was closed when we came in," he reminded me. "How did that cat get in here?"

"Oh! But wait, if the other room was cleaned, it is likely this one was also. In fact, I am almost certain it has been—the hair brushes are in a different place."

"They are in want of polishing," he remarked. He began to look about the room, searching in a somewhat desultory manner. He opened another door I had not noticed in the panelling and stood on the lintel, staring down.

I hobbled to his side and found he was looking down a winding stair, exactly similar to the one in the room I had been occupying, though this was in the corner of the building. Seconds passed. Just as I was opening my mouth to ask Lord Castelmarten what he was finding so absorbing, he stooped and picked up something very small between his finger and his thumb. He stared at it closely and then sniffed at it. A look of surprise came into his face. He pulled out a handkerchief and shook whatever it was that he had found into its center. Then he folded the kerchief carefully and restored it to his pocket.

"What is it?" I asked in a frightened voice. "What have you found?"

He turned to look at me, and I was alarmed by his expression.

He said in a low voice, "Proof, perhaps, that all my guesses have been wrong."

"But—what did you guess?"

He did not seem to hear me. His eyes were on the staircase wall, and his lips moved as if he were counting. Then he leaned forward and pressed upon one of the great stone blocks, near the edge. It resisted him for a moment, and then swung slowly open to reveal a niche or small cupboard snugly within the wall. In it was a bulging soiled sack.

I glanced at the earl. He seemed as surprised as I to find the hiding place thus occupied.

"What the Devil—?" he exclaimed, drawing it towards him. It did not move all in one piece, like a sack of flour, but clanked and sagged as if it contained a variety of objects.

Lord Castelmarten looked grim as he untied the cord at the mouth of the sack and pulled it open. He peered inside and then, with a sudden violent movement, tipped out the contents onto the cupboard's floor.

I stared for a moment uncomprehendingly at what appeared to be a pile of limp little bodies, some plump, some skinny; some leather, some velvet; some embroidered, others netted—purses! And in between and all about the purses were other objects: little boxes, pocket watches, chains and fobs and rings and necklaces—a robber's hoard.

Lord Castelmarten, stony-faced, picked up an enamelled snuffbox and flicked it open with a practiced hand. He sniffed the contents cautiously.

"So that explains it," he murmured.

"What does it explain? I wish you would explain to me!"

"It explains the presence of an alien snuff in Gerry's room. There must be ten snuffboxes here, or more."

"And why would your brother be collecting snuffboxes—to say nothing of purses?"

"God knows. Anything of value he would have taken with him when he left for England. This was his secret hiding place. I believe I am the only other to know of it. We found it not many years ago, when he was foxed and slipped on the stairs while I was trying to help him to his room without the servants hearing. He put out his hand to steady himself against the wall and the stone swung back..."

"And you know nothing about—all this?"

"Lord, no," he said blankly. "Where can it have come from? There are things here belonging to men, women, rich, poor, and the middle sort alike. You would think Gerry had turned highwayman—"

I heard a roaring in my ears. I recalled the face that had looked in at me as I lay helpless in the Castell Marten Arms, the masked face which had reminded me of some similar experience. My lips moved. Distantly I heard myself saying, "He did! Your brother was a highwayman!"

And then I slid down the wall and into darkness.

Chapter Seventeen

The next morning, I woke in the Blue Room to hear the cuckoo call.

I lay in the wide bed listening to the hesitant, nostalgic sound. Through the open window the sun and the breeze and all the scents of early summer entered. I had lain often so before, I knew. I did not have to search my memory for that: the past was absorbed in the present, a part of me. Yet I knew that I still dared not probe too deeply. If I began to wonder where it was that I had lain before while the cuckoo called, then the old misery and fear would engulf me, as surely as it had done yesterday when the earl had shaken me into consciousness, demanding an explanation of my having accused his brother of being a highwayman.

"I don't know," I had repeated over and over. "I tell you, I don't know why I said it—or if it was indeed your brother that I seemed to recall. It was as if it all fell into place. But of course it could have been another highwayman—or any robber, come to that. A face with a mask—but that is all I can remember."

At length, he had relented and left me to my rest. Later in the day Dr. Glynn had visited me, his manner heavy and his forced joviality failing to hide the trouble in his face.

"What is it, Dr. Glynn?" I had asked, when he had pronounced me a little improved upon the previous day, despite my swoon. "Did Lord Castelmarten mention the old woman to you—Mrs. Parry?"

"Yes . . . ay. But she is buried now, and no sense in stirring up a hornet's nest. Besides, who would have cause to do such a thing? No, it was just a chance—a trick of light, or of the way she lay."

"What was, sir? Did you find evidence of—foul play?"

He looked quite shocked—at my importunity, no doubt.

"No, no, indeed to goodness. Else I could not have signed the death certicate. Only it is not impossible—improbable, mark you—but not impossible that such an appearance of petechiae could have been caused by suffocation."

"Suffocation!" I recalled the figure in my room, picking up the cushion, and must have looked aghast, for he cried quickly that he had spoken foolishly and I must forget it.

"Of course," I agreed, to calm him. "As you say, who would do such a thing?"

"No one, to be sure. Only she had a great tomcat that might have lain against her face."

"A cat! Could it have suffocated her?"

"There are cases—babies—" he said unhappily. "But as for murder—no, that is quite out of the question. Oh, by the way," he added suddenly, as if eager to change the subject. "Miss Carnaby has news for you, Mrs. Marten. It seems, she says, that you are being enquired for."

I stared at him. "Enquired for? May I ask, by whom?"

"Miss Carnaby was telling us, downstairs just now. She said it was some old woman in a donkey cart, who asked of Jennings, the butler at Hafod Hall, if the young woman was there, that had been in the coach accident. When she was told there was none such at Hafod Hall, it seems the woman cried that she had mistaken the place for Castell Marten, such a great house as it was; and off she went, no doubt to follow his directions here. Perhaps she had been here and is now gone again. If Hughes saw her before his lordship did, he will have sent her to the rightabout."

"What has his lordship to do with it?" I asked faintly.

"Why, he spoke of wishing to interview the woman, in case she knew you." Dr. Glynn looked puzzled. "But I had thought the question of your identity was no longer in doubt."

"The mere fact of one's identity is not all one would like to know about oneself," I suggested vaguely. "I certainly ought to talk to the woman."

In fact, I realized, I was extremely reluctant to do so.

210

My heart was thumping at the mere thought of such a meeting, with its possibility of implicating me in some frightful plot. Nevertheless, I knew it would be impossible to avoid the confrontation.

"So his lordship thought," Dr. Glynn agreed. "He said, if the woman did not call here, then he would have a search made for her. It should not be hard to find her . . ."

Dr. Glynn had left soon after, leaving me to lie uneasily, a prey to unhappy conjectures, until a knock announced Lord Castelmarten, with one of the Welsh-speaking chambermaids by way of chaperone.

"You have heard the news, I see," he remarked, staring down at me. "Our friend Glynn is not the most discreet practitioner, I fear."

"He certainly is not. He as good as told me Mrs. Parry had been suffocated—and then this tale of the woman and a donkey cart, enquiring of me. Oh, sir, what do you suppose it means?"

In my distress I reached out to lay my hand upon his sleeve. I would have given a good deal not to have done so when he shook it off with what seemed like involuntary disgust.

"How should I know what it signifies?" he returned coldly. "No doubt we shall discover for ourselves soon enough. She may be carrying a message from one of your accomplices, for all I know. It is essential that you should interview her, and appear to be alone while you do it."

My hands were cold. "I think I am afraid," I murmured.

"Good! For fear sharpens the wits, and you will need all yours about you."

"You are not very sympathetic," I cried. "One would think you hated me!"

"I hate—" he broke off and strode to the window. "I hate the mystery, the uncertainty," he resumed in a quieter voice. "I would give a great deal to have this tangle resolved."

"I suppose you would like to know whether you are justified in mistrusting me," I suggested. "I wish you would tell me exactly what you do suspect."

He turned, folding his arms, and stared at me across the

211

room. "I do not know," he said at length. "You are an enigma. You are like two people."

"Perhaps I am two people," I cried. "Perhaps I am both Mary Ramsey and Miss Merridew—and mad into the bargain. Perhaps my adventure in the Keep was only an accident after all, and I imagined the man I thought was there. Perhaps I did write those warning notes to myself—and then forgot it. Perhaps I have been a highwayman, and hid that sack myself!"

"I don't think you are mad," he said flatly. "And it is hard to believe you are anything worse than an adventuress of a kind that is often found among young women. Indeed, at times you seem too young and innocent for even that to be true."

I burst into tears, astonishing myself. "Oh, go away," I sobbed.

"Now, how can I leave you in such a state? Please control yourself. I detest tears."

"You are a brute. Do you—do you think I like crying like this?"

"Then stop it."

"I—can't! It is all so terrible. You do not know how terrible everything is!"

"You are overwrought. I should not have disturbed you so soon after your faint."

The chambermaid came forward, looking concerned. She sat on the bed, glanced nervously at Lord Castelmarten, and then put her arms round me. He gave a snort of what I assumed to be disgust, and left the room. Once he was gone, I found it quite easy to stop crying, and soon I was able to manage a watery smile and a few halting words of thanks in Welsh to the maid, who patted me sympathetically, and presently left me to enjoy a night of unbroken sleep.

Ysolt entered now, putting an end to my reflections.

"Miss Enid sends to say, are you well enough to come down to help her in the garden, ma'am?"

"Yes, indeed," I cried, beginning to get out of bed at once. It was an inspiration on Miss Enid's part, I thought.

Garden work was exactly what I needed on this glorious day, to distract my mind from all those things I did not wish to contemplate.

Ysolt assisted me to dress. She was pale, I noticed, and looked as if she too were troubled by haunting thoughts. But she had also an air of wariness, and I believed she did not want me to probe into her preoccupations. I wondered how much the servants knew and talked about me, and about the disappearance of Gervais, the younger son of the house. Lady Castelmarten would have announced his marriage and his death when first she heard of it, I suppose; and since then they would have gossiped about my loss of memory, and the times that Dr. Glynn had been called in to see me. Parry, her ladyship's maid, thought me to blame for everything, I knew. But of what did Ysolt suspect me, and did she, too, wish me gone from Wales?

I was glad to hobble out into the sun and put all these fruitless cogitations behind me for the moment. I felt better at once out in the fresh air, and when Miss Enid handed me a sackcloth apron and motioned me to kneel beside her, I soon was able to absorb myself in the fascination of the work.

I thrust my hands into the crumbling earth, and was pleased to find it faintly warm. Tenderl,, I took out the first small cucumber plant and laid it in its place, pressing the earth about the hairlike root. I glanced up after a few minutes to see Miss Enid looking at me with a positive expression of approval.

"Perhaps you are Victoria Marten after all," she murmured.

It was the first time she had admitted the possibility, and I must have shown my surprise at her choosing this moment to make such a statement, when my hair was blown by the wind under my bonnet, and my ungloved hands were stained with earth.

"It is my opinion," she explained, pushing in her trowel, "that such a person as Mary Ramsey would take good care not to soil her hands, for in her circumstances I believe she would be careful to maintain the appearance of a lady so far as she would be able to do so; and the same applies, only rather more strongly, to an imposter."

"I enjoy the work," I said, after a moment.

"I see you do. It is plain to me that you are accustomed to gardening."

"Yes, indeed. When I was little, I used to love to pull out the weeds in the gravel paths—" I stopped abruptly. "I remember," I said with a feeling of awe. "I remember that garden. The large one was for vegetables, and we had a lawn, and a smaller flower garden. There was a long border against a wall...hollyhocks, delphiniums..."

Miss Enid caught in her breath, but she did not speak or pause in her work.

"I can see that garden now...but not the house."

"Town or country?" asked Miss Enid gently.

I shook my head. "But there was a dog...I am nearly sure there was a dog. The sun was warm on his coat. I used to put my hand on him as I worked, from time to time. He was so smooth and warm. Oh, Miss Enid, do you think my memory is coming back?"

"It appears to be doing so." Miss Enid frowned as she picked out a cluster of seedlings and began to separate them delicately. "Let us consider a little at a time. Let me see, now. You once mentioned a basket of blackberries, did you not? Did you grow blackberries in your garden?"

"No—that was in the wood. Someone came running to tell me something terrible. I dropped the basket and the blackberries spilled in the grass. The sun went in. Everything was dark. I think...I think someone had died."

"Your mother, perhaps?"

"Yes. I think it must have been. I felt so lonely. So terribly, terribly lonely. But then later, he was there—and he said God loved me; and it was true, I felt protected then. And after that I never felt quite so alone."

"He?" queried Miss Enid gently.

"The old man. Oh, I don't know who he was, nor where, nor when—though it seems as if it were a long time ago. I don't know who those people were—"

"Hush, my dear. Nothing will be accomplished by

becoming overwrought. Even such a fragment of memory is better than nothing, do not you agree? Pass me the watering pot, if you would be so kind. Shall we put in the new potatoes today, or wait until the weather is a little more settled?"

I looked about me dazedly. "Oh, let us do it today. The lilacs are already out, it must be late enough."

"Very well, call the boy there to bring them from the shed. And do, pray, put in the rest of your cucumbers before the poor dears give up hope."

The morning passed. Absorbed in my work, I forgot my fear of lifting the veil and spoke aloud my thoughts, just as they came. My memories were all of gardening, of wallflowers and stocks, lilacs and pansies, tomatoes and apples. Now and again Miss Enid nodded to herself, but she made no comment until we stood up and stretched our aching backs before going in to wash our hands. Then she said quietly, "It is a pity . . ."

"A pity—what?"

"Why, my dear, only that you cannot remember one name out of your past. Only a single name."

"Well, I can't," I said flatly. "But I can remember feeling happy—and surely Mary Ramsey can't have been a happy child."

"Why not? Children may be happy in every circumstance, from time to time. Mary Ramsey may have had access to a garden, and we know there was an old man in her life, Mr. Cliffe, to whom she was attached—and that he died. She must have had some happy moments with him. But no matter. Though all that you have said could apply to either girl, I fancy it applies more aptly to Miss Merridew than to that other, and indeed I am prepared to accept you now. Furthermore, I shall inform Lucian at once that it is my considered opinion that you are, after all, his sister-in-law."

I stood still. It seemed minutes before I was able to move again, and when I did so, I felt numb; for I was stunned to discover that such a relationship to the earl would be utterly abhorrent to me—and not because I

215

hated him. I realized in that moment that I would rather be proved Mary Ramsey than Lord Castelmarten's sister-in-law.

I am in love with him, I thought dazedly. And yet, how could I be? Oh, he was a very fine and powerful young man, and in other circumstances it would surely be no wonder—but in mine! He had done nothing but insult and despise me from the moment that we met, he seemed to impute the worst of motives to me, and though he acknowledged some kind of attraction between us, it was obviously against his better judgment. And yet I could not help myself! The damage was done. Even if I could find nothing to admire in him, I would still long to be with him. How absurd! But it was tragic, too, I feared, for I felt as if he had aroused in me a hunger that could never be appeased.

I made myself follow Miss Enid into the house. In my room, while I was washing my hands, a burst of weeping overtook me until I was struck by the appositeness of tears splashing into the basin and weakly laughed. When I had regained some measure of control, I realized that what I needed most at that moment was to escape from Castell Marten. I would order a horse, I thought, and ride to Mrs. Jones at the inn by the Afon Ystwyth. I longed for her quite desperately, and it seemed to take an age to change into my habit, and for the groom to saddle Juniper, while I sat impatiently upon the mounting block.

At last I was mounted, and with Emrys himself escorting me, I rode out through the village and down the wooded road towards the inn. It was much closer than I had expected or remembered from that first drive. I drew rein in the cobbled yard and paused a few moments to stare up at the turn in the road where the accident had been. There was no doubt of the place, for the fall of the coach was still plainly written on the mountainside in a trail of torn bushes and broken saplings.

"Why there is Miss Rose, or Mrs. Marten, should I say, my dear!"

I looked round. Mrs. Jones was bustling towards me

her hands outstretched. A wave of feeling overcame me. I slipped my foot from the stirrup and dismounted. Then, turning, I fell into her comfortable arms.

"There, then! Why, you're shaking! 'Tis a shock to you to return here, doubtless. Come you inside, into the warm."

I soon found myself in her little parlour, behind the taproom.

"This is my 'snug' as I call it," said Mrs. Jones, poking up the fire, although the day was warm and I was no longer shivering. "Sit down in that comfortable old chair, and tell me how you do."

"I had another fall, so I am black and blue again," I told her. She clicked her teeth in sympathy and I continued, "Strange things have happened to me. You remember the note I had, warning me to leave Wales? I had another when my papers were stolen..." The words came tumbling out of me, like the river in spate. Mrs. Jones made no comment. She just sat there, looking wise, pursing her lips, nodding or shaking her head as the recitation demanded, while I talked on and on.

"Well, my dear, there is someone means you harm, no doubt of it," she pronounced at length, when I had stumbled to a halt.

"Oh, Mrs. Jones—then you believe me?"

"And why shouldn't I, my dear? After all my years' experience, it would be a queer thing if I couldn't tell when a girl was speaking truth, I think. You visited my sister-in-law Sionedd, you said? Master Gerry was very fond of her. If anyone knows about his marriage, it is very likely to be she."

"But she can't speak English. She could tell me nothing."

"She gave you the note I had from my niece Rose, you said. It seems to me..." Mrs. Jones paused and frowned. I held my breath. "It seems that 'twould be best if you were to go secretly to Upper Buzzard, as soon as may be, even if you are not yet quite well. You could stay with my Rose down there; she lives in the next village, and she could keep you safe while you were making your enquiries. Then you could find out if you are a Merridew, for certain."

"Oh, but I—"

I pressed my glove against my lip. Mrs. Jones stared at me, her beady eyes very bright. "Don't you want to prove it, after all?" she asked.

I shook my head.

"Well, well," she said, after a moment's thought. "So that's the way the wind blows! Deary me! There's a complication, then. Not but what one ought to have expected it, a sweet pretty girl like you, and a fine gentleman like Master Lucian. But all the more reason for your leaving, miss, if you'll forgive my saying so."

I gazed at her with pleading in my eyes. "Am I so foolish, Mrs. Jones? I did not mean to love him, indeed I thought I hated him!"

"Hush, my dear. Don't put it into words—not yet. And don't despair, neither. Even if you did marry Master Gerry, perhaps—well, perhaps it could be annulled. But the first thing is to get you out of danger, and the second thing must be to find out for certain who you are."

"But—if I am so far away—I will never see him again!"

"If he loves you, my dear, losing you will convince him of it. He'll find you out, never fear. Besides, he is sure to unravel the mystery, however long it takes him, for he was never one to give up soon; and he always felt responsible for Gerry." She looked at me thoughtfully. "The best thing would be for you to take the coach from Holyhead when it comes through here this evening. Never mind your bags—Rose can supply you with everything you need, and I will lend you one or two necessities for the journey, and the money for your fare—"

"Oh no," I cried. "I could not possibly—I must go back to the castle first. I could not leave without speaking to Lady Castelmarten, certainly. Tomorrow—tomorrow, I will come."

"Ay, God willing. Very well, then. I shall send to book your place—"

"I have not enough money for the ticket," I confessed.

"There are only three sovereigns in my purse, and I must leave something for Ysolt, and for food upon the journey."

"I will lend you what you need, as I said. I trust you, my dear, if nobody else does. I know that you will repay that money, be it a shilling at a time. And if you do not, why, I fancy his lordship will reimburse me."

"I pray you will not need to ask him," I muttered.

The clock upon the wall struck, startling me, for I had grown so accustomed to the silence of the castle that I had forgotten other clocks had chimes.

"You had better go," said Mrs. Jones. "You won't want to be late for your dinner, I dare say."

I felt as if she disapproved of me for wishing to return to the castle for no better reason, as we both knew, than a last glimpse of Lord Castelmarten. I rose reluctantly.

"Mrs. Jones," I said impetuously, "who do you think is at the bottom of this? Who could it be that means me harm?"

She shook ' ̃r head. "I wondered if it might be Miss Carnaby. She ̃ powerful jealous of you, so I have heard; and it could be she who drugged the posset Miss Enid gave you. But then she is not a good enough horsewoman to ride alone."

I stared at her. "Are you thinking of the person I saw in the mist, when I was lost?"

"No, my dear. You had not heard? One of my nephews, a young shepherd, saw someone riding from the road above the *pistyll*, just after the accident. We wondered if that rider might have caused it—thrown a stone at one of the horses and caused the coach to overset. But that could never have been Miss Carnaby—besides, it was a man young Evans thought he saw."

"Mrs. Jones, you don't think ... his lordship ... ?"

She put her arms about me. "You should know better than to ask me that, who was his nurse. Now don't fret yourself. All will come out in the Lord's good time, I reckon. Get you back to Castell Marten, and I'll be looking for you tomorrow, in the afternoon."

I rode back in silence, my thoughts in turmoil. Could anyone be so wicked as to cause on purpose such an accident as that which had befallen the Llangollen coach? What must be the overwhelming motive of such a person? Or were they deranged, their madness only appeased by killing? Yet it could not be that, I thought, or there would have been other killings, long before I came to Wales. And then the notes of warning I had received seemed to show that the malice of the murderer was directed at me personally.

I changed for dinner in a daze, yet I was not so distracted that I did not choose the most becoming of the gowns which Lady Castelmarten had given me, and I urged Ysolt to pay special attention to the dressing of my hair. I went downstairs slowly, leaning on the bannister like an old woman, for my ride had not improved my injuries. I reminded myself as I went that I must be on guard, not only against betraying my intention of leaving, but above all against revealing my interest in Lord Castelmarten. It would be unbearable if he guessed at the change in me, I thought, feeling my colour rise at the mere suggestion. Supposing that he did already know of it—had suspected before I did? With embarrassment I recalled the moment when he had repelled my touch upon his sleeve. How dreadful if he had known the truth even before I had realized it myself!

"Rose, you are quite well?" demanded Lady Castelmarten.

I looked at her almost in horror. Had I given myself away somehow? Had I spoken aloud?

"I addressed you twice, but you did not seem to hear me," said Lady Castelmarten reprovingly.

Behind her, I could see Lord Castelmarten entering the hall.

"I am very sorry, ma'am," I stammered. "I believe I might have a touch of fever—just a touch."

"You certainly look rather flushed. Would you rather dine in your room?"

"Oh, no—that is, I am sure it will pass off."

"What is this?" cried Miss Esther. "Rose has a fever? There—I thought it was foolishness for her to be out gardening in the hot sun as she was doing this morning.

Very well for Enid, perhaps; but Rose, who is barely risen from her sickbed—"

"Miss Rose was quite well this morning," said Miss Enid dryly. "I expect it is merely that she is a little sunburnt."

"Dreadfully so," agreed Esther. "She looks like a gypsy. We must see what we can do with sliced cucumber, after dinner."

Lord Castelmarten raised an eyebrow. "Do you propose to make her into a salad?" he enquired frivolously.

I stared at him in fascination. How handsome he was! How could I have thought him dark and ugly when I first set eyes upon him? Now his darkness seemed dramatic, especially with the black coat he wore. But there was much more than looks to his appeal for me, I feared.

We had gone in to dinner and began to eat. I found I had lost my appetite and only toyed with my food. I wondered if I should tell Lady Castelmarten that I was leaving, or if it would be better just to leave a note to say that I had gone. Yes, that would be best, for then she would have no chance to dissuade me. For if I told her, she would insist on Lord Castelmarten knowing of it, I supposed, and would probably refuse to allow me to leave without his permission. Would he be angry when he found me gone, I wondered then. Sad, perhaps? Or relieved?

Hughes, the steward, entered the dining room at that moment, and approached the earl.

"Excuse me for interrupting your lordship at your dinner; but it was your lordship's desire to be informed if a certain person should demand admittance."

"The woman Miss Carnaby mentioned," he said quickly, while I almost dropped my glass. "Is she here?"

"A person with a donkey cart, my lord, and a young Welsh boy with her. The person is English, my lord, as well as I can tell—but she suffers from a disfiguring disease and has several veils over her face, so it is not altogether easy to make out what she says."

"And what does she say, so far as you can understand it?"

"Why, my lord, she is enquiring for—'for the young

woman who had the accident last month.' Those are her words, my lord. 'The young woman who had the accident.'"

I took a deep breath in an unavailing attempt to steady myself. If only, I thought despairingly, I had taken Mrs. Jones's advice and left on the coach this afternoon! How could I have forgotten the possibility of this hateful meeting?

I realized that Lord Castelmarten was staring at me. His face was set, and I derived no comfort from it.

"Very well," he said at length, turning to Hughes. "You may show her into the library, and inform her that Mrs. Marten will shortly join her there."

I must have made some sound of protest. Lady Castelmarten leaned forward. "I believe I should be with Miss Rose during the interview. I would like to see this person on my own account, and I believe you should do so as well."

"And I," said Miss Esther eagerly. "I should certainly like to see her. I have a particular interest in any matter that concerns Miss Rose."

Lord Castelmarten frowned.

"This is a delicate matter," he said soberly. "We do not want to frighten away this woman, who may be about to help us solve the mystery of my brother's disappearance. I believe she will be off her guard if she thinks she has only Rose to deal with; but it is my intention to stand outside the door and listen to what passes within, and to be at hand should Miss Rose require assistance, which I do not at all anticipate," he added with a quick glance at me. "I should not have told you I would be listening," he exclaimed, with an air of annoyance. "I hope you are a good enough actress to appear to forget it."

"Really, Lucian," cried Miss Esther in a flutter. "Listening at doors! Is that proper behaviour for an earl of Castelmarten?"

"In this instance, I believe it is, Aunt Esther."

I licked my lips, which felt very dry. "You desire me to speak to this woman on my own, my lord?"

"Yes. I want to hear what she can have to say to you,

believing you to be alone and, I hope, ignorant of your loss of memory. Come now, for we must not keep her waiting overlong. She may become overawed by the place and decide to leave before we can discover what it is she has come to say."

"That would be a pity," I managed to say, though my lips were trembling. I stood up and essayed a smile. "Please excuse me, Lady Castelmarten, Miss Enid, and Miss Esther. I hope we shall be back presently with—something of interest to report."

"Are you quite sure you are all right?" Miss Esther cried.

"I do feel—rather nervous," I owned. "But I have every confidence in his lordship's power to protect me." I spoke the truth, but when I glanced at him, he was looking very stern and avoided my eye. Did this mean that I could not rely upon him after all, I wondered, and felt as if I stood in a cold wind.

Lord Castelmarten held the door, but he was silent as I passed him. Each of the ladies murmured something, but I scarcely heard them. I limped reluctantly down the stone passage to the library. What I expected, what I feared, I did not know. I was certain only that this meeting would be significant beyond the common.

Mr. Hughes had gone ahead. He was waiting for me with his hand upon the doorknob. I realized that he had not cared to leave the person within unsupervised for long. I smiled at him faintly, and he let me in.

"Mrs. Marten," he announced, and discreetly closed the door—only I did not hear the click of its closing fast behind me.

The fire had not been lit so late in spring. The room was chilly at this hour of the day, and perhaps that was why the person standing with her back to one of the windows seemed as if she had chosen to be overburdened with clothes and shawls. But looking at her closely as I walked towards her, I realized that she was stout, in addition to wearing several gowns or coloured petticoats, one upon the other. Her head was crowned by a monstrous feathered bonnet that had seen better days, and her features were concealed behind thick veils.

She seemed to be as lame as I and hobbled forward supported by a stick to stand quite close to me, her head upon one side. Her clothes gave off an unpleasant smell, as if she had worn them continuously for months, so that quite involuntarily I took a backward step.

"Ha!" she cried suddenly, peering up into my face. "You've fallen on your feet, I see! Mighty grand you've become since flying out of the nest, you naughty girl! Mrs. Marten, indeed! But you can forget all that nonsense now. Send that little Jack-in-office up for your baggage, miss, and we'll be on our way—for it ain't yet quite dark, and we can make a league or so before night falls."

"Who are you?" I breathed.

"Ho! So that's your game, is it? Pretending you've forgotten me—who should I be, pray," she cried, wagging her gloved finger right beneath my nose, "who should I be—but Mother Cliffe?"

Chapter Eighteen

"Mother Cliffe!"

I had feared it all along, I realized. I had supposed I would rejoice to find I was not Lord Castelmarten's sister by marriage, but now I knew that I had been indulging a wild hope that there was a third and a more acceptable solution to the problem of my identity.

So I was Mary Ramsey, I told myself, and at the mercy of this odious woman—unless Lord Castelmarten chose not to allow her to take me away.

"Ay, that's better," said the woman affably, assuming by my exclamation that I had chosen to acknowledge her. "Come, Moll, and let's waste no more time. I've a good-for-nothing lad out there with the donkey, and 'tis odds of ten to one he'll be too lazy to walk him about, and I don't want the ass to catch a chill."

She caught my hand in a strong grip and began to pull me towards the door.

As we reached it, Lord Castelmarten opened it.

"Ho!" cried Mother Cliffe. "Here's my lord himself, I'll lay me life! This girl is my runaway apprentice, your honour, so I'll thank you not to stop us."

He ignored her, but looked gravely at me.

I said in a small voice, "Sir, it appears that I must be Mary Ramsey after all, and must go with—with—" I swallowed. "With my foster-mother. It seems that your brother's widow must have been the unfortunate who died in the accident . . . that should please you, in any event. I mean, I heard you say that you wished the corpse were Mrs. Marten . . ." I tugged his brother's ring off my finger and unwound the wool that had held it tight, while waiting breathlessly for his response.

"Yes, it pleases me," he said in an expressionless voice, taking the ring and dropping it in his waistcoat pocket. "I have sent for your clothes," he added coldly. "Ysolt is packing for you."

I felt myself stagger, and Mother Cliffe caught me by the arm. "None of your vapours now, me girl! And tell his lordship just a bag will do—no trunks, mind. My donkey has work enough without overloading him with your fripperies—not that you took much away wth you, Moll, now that I come to think of it."

"Here is Richard now with your necessities," observed Lord Castelmarten. "The rest can be sent on later. Now I must ask you to excuse me. Hughes will show you out. Good-night, Miss—Ramsey."

He turned on his heel and stalked away. I watched him go through a haze of tears.

"Come on, girl," said Mother Cliffe, shaking my arm. "Why, are you mooning after him? Lost your heart to him, have you? You'll not be the first, I wager, and you should know as that's the road to ruin for a wench like you. Don't dawdle, Moll. Let's be off."

So I left Castell Marten in a worse state than I had come to it, with one bag and my reticule with the purse in it that Hughes handed me as I went past him. All my other possessions were left behind: the rest of my clothes, most of my memories—and my love.

I stumbled into the stableyard and, at Mother Cliffe's insistence, climbed up into the cart. Emrys stood by, shaking his head, as Mother Cliffe pushed the lad aside and took the donkey's rein herself.

"Gee up there," she cried, and we were off.

I wondered if Lord Dyffryn were looking out of the tower in the moat, and what he would make of our little company. What would the village make of it? But to my immense relief I was spared the ordeal of driving through the village. Mother Cliffe led the donkey down a track that bypassed the houses and entered the wood, joining a ride that I rather thought was the one that led to the water mill. I was too numb with misery to wonder why she had taken us this way. Every now and again I looked behind me, in the vain hope of seeing Lord Castelmarten riding after me.

"He did not say good-bye," I kept reminding myself. "He only said good-night!"

After a mile or so under the trees, I was surprised when the lad climbed in the cart beside me. He was roughly dressed, with a shapeless hat pulled low over his brow.

"Can the donkey carry us both?" I asked. "Would you like me to get down?" It occurred to me that when it got a little darker I might be able to run away—except that my ankle was still weak. But perhaps I could slip out of sight behind a tree and hide.

The lad chuckled. He said something in Welsh, and then added in singsong English that we would soon be stopping for the night.

"Why—where are we going?"

"You'd like to know, would you?" he asked in a teasing manner. "Where do you think that you are going, then?"

"I don't know! I don't know!"

"All right, no need to squawk—not yet!"

I felt horribly afraid. "What do you mean by that?"

"Ah, wouldn't you like to know! Well, soon you shall."

I gulped. "I am sure two of us are too heavy a burden in this cart. Why don't we get down and let Mother Cliffe sit up here, while you lead the donkey."

"Mother Cliffe?" said the lad, grinning. "Who is Mother Cliffe?"

"Why—why, she—that woman, of course."

"So that's what you think, is it? Well now, miss, do you really think such a one as Mother Cliffe would trouble herself to travel all over the country looking for you?"

"W-wouldn't she?"

The lad spat over the side of the cart. "Not she! Well, I've never met Mother Cliffe, if you want the truth, but it stands to reason, she could get a dozen girls from the workhouse at any time to replace a runaway apprentice, just as good as you—or better, for that job."

"Then—who is that woman?" I gasped, my senses whirling.

"Ah! That would be telling, indeed it would."

"Oh, please!"

"Confused you, have I? Beg pardon, miss, but it's such a game to tease you. I've a reason for it too, as you'll find when you know all—and you shall know all, I swear it, before this night is through."

That was doubtful comfort, I thought. I wondered if I were going mad—or if the youth was some sort of lunatic. Almost in the same moment I realized that it was nearly dark, at least beneath the trees.

I took a breath, surreptitiously caught up my skirt—and then leapt off the cart and hobbled away as fast as I could go. I could hear the others crashing in pursuit, getting closer. My ankle ached, and my breath seemed to sear my lungs. Suddenly I was seized and thrown against a tree by Mother Cliffe, who could not have been so lame as she looked, and was certainly a good deal stronger. She easily held me prisoner until the lad ran up, brandishing a pistol.

"Put that away," said Mother Cliffe.

"Be quiet," said the lad gruffly. "Haven't we agreed, this is my night?" He pressed the muzzle to my ribs. "How dare you try to escape," he cried passionately. "Don't you realize how little it would take to make me kill you?"

"No! No—I don't believe you!"

"You shall believe me! Do you want to hear about the people I have killed?"

"Hush, for God's sake," cried the woman. "No need to tell the young lady all your secrets," she added in a different tone.

"She must respect me! We cannot afford to lose her."

The woman took her hands off me. "You'd best do as—the lad—tells you," she said. "He would shoot you, if you ran again."

"Ay, that I would—but I'd prefer not to do it, see. What do you say? Will you be a good girl and walk back to the cart?"

I pressed my cheek against the rough bark of the oak tree, and said nothing. The lad bent closer.

"You still don't believe me, isn't it? What of that old woman in the wood, with kindling on her head? Wasn't it I who smothered her, because she knew too much?"

"You!" I gasped.

"Yes, indeed. And the old clergyman, Evans Plas Celli, didn't I trip him by the millpond and hold him under with a long stick, until he drowned?"

"That's enough of talking," grumbled Mother Cliffe. "Let us get her to the house. I don't feel safe out here, so close to the village."

"Oh, you always were easily alarmed—but don't fret, we'll go to Plas Celli now." He thrust the pistol closer in my side. "You believe me now, don't you?"

"I—I don't know—"

"You don't know?" he repeated incredulously. "Wasn't it I in your room the other night? I thought you saw me there."

"You?" I gasped. "It was you—in my room—with the pillow?"

"You don't think it was her, look you," said the lad, gesturing towards Mother Cliffe who cried out, "What is that about a pillow?"

"Never you mind," snapped the lad. "Didn't I tell you not to be surprised at anything you heard?" he hissed.

"But why—did you come to—smother me?" I faltered. "What have I done—how have I harmed you?"

"Ah. That will take a while of telling—but you shall know, miss. I mean for you to know it all."

I tripped on a root, and the lad's bony fingers dug into my arm.

"Have a care," he hissed, but my mind was grappling with the implications of what he had admitted.

"Was it—could it have been you—who caused the coach to overset?"

"Ay, simple that was. But it failed, mind you. The wrong young woman died."

I forced my numbed brain to reflect on this. "How do you know that?" I whispered.

"Why, I knew as soon as I set eyes on you that night. I'd have finished you off, too, if old Nanny Jones hadn't been beside you. But you saw me, didn't you?"

"I saw—a man in a mask."

I stood still. When I spoke, my lips were stiff. "You say you knew me? You know my true identity?"

"Certainly," said the youth good-humouredly. "I'll make you a present of it, if you like. You were born Victoria Merridew, of Church Cottage, Upper Buzzard..."

"So I am not Mary Ramsey, after all!"

"No—nor never was. Now, along the path with you."

"His lordship will come after me," I said in a feeble voice.

"Not he! What, try to get you away from the person he believes to be your rightful owner? No, he is too upright, too law-abiding for that."

"You sound as if—you despise him for those qualities."

"Despise him! I hate him. I threw myself upon his mercy once, and he laughed at me—" the lad broke off, as if he had not meant to say so much.

"Was it you who left the notes?" I asked, a few minutes later.

"Notes?" he said sharply. "What notes?"

"The notes warning me to leave Wales, because of danger."

"Never mind that," interrupted Mother Cliffe nervously.

"Ah, here's the donkey. I thought he might have wandered off..." She handed me up into the cart and took the reins, the lad walking beside her.

In silence we passed the quiet waters of the Melin Llyd. I glanced at the mill house, but it was shuttered and dark. The lad got on the cart beside me.

"One squawk out of you," he hissed, "and I'll blow out your brains!"

Slowly the donkey drew the cart across the narrow bridge and up the gentle hill beyond. The lad drew a length of black cloth from his pocket, and turning away, took off his hat and pulled the cloth over his head. It was the hood, with slits for eyes, that the intruder in my room had worn.

I was shivering by the time Mother Cliffe stopped the donkey and hitched it to a tree stump outside Plas Celli. The youth prodded me. Stiffly, I got down from the cart. The woman took me by the arm and began to lead me towards the square grey building. The lad went ahead, opening a side door without difficulty. As we followed him into the house, he fumbled on a table for a tinder box, struck a light, and lit an oil lamp, which he handed to Mother Cliffe. She carried it down a short passage to a bare damp parlour, in which a few pieces of decaying furniture stood forlornly.

"Are you sure the shutters are fast?" asked Mother Cliffe, looking about her. "We don't want a glimmer to be seen."

"Certain sure," said the lad brusquely. "Turn down the lamp and put it here, where it will shine into her face. Now you, miss, sit up here on this high stool, so that I may watch your face."

"For God's sake, be careful what you say," muttered the old woman.

"Careful? It is too late for that. Besides, you know I have looked forward to this moment, to bringing back her memory piece by piece, for my revenge!"

"Revenge?" I whispered faintly. "Revenge—for what?"

"Let us see if we can prompt your memory, shall we?" said the lad, straddling a chair and resting his arms along the back of it, the pistol hanging limply from one hand. "One night—it was not so long ago—you were in your cottage parlour in faraway Northamptonshire. You were setting the room to rights before retiring. You plumped up some cushions, picked a book up off the Turkey carpet, spread out the fire with the poker, and put the fireguard in the hearth. You were frowning, for upstairs your grandfather lay sick. Your mind was on him, for he was very ill and must at all costs be kept free of any worry and disturbance. And then came a sudden scratching on the door..."

"Go on," I breathed, clutching the sides of the stool.

"You do not yet remember?"

"No...and yet, there is a certain familiarity about it. I can picture the scene, as if it were a play."

"See, then, your hand, hesitating upon the latch. You decide—and open it. How dare you open the door to a stranger, when you were alone, so late at night?" he demanded in a curiously irritated tone.

"It was not . . . very late," I said defensively, before I had time to reflect. "And I hoped it might be Sirius, our dog. He had disappeared a few days earlier."

"Ah! So it's coming back to you . . . but what is this about a dog?"

The hood turned towards Mother Cliffe, sunk in apparent depression upon the sofa. She nodded. "He thought it wise to poison the dog," she murmured. "It was one of those silly spaniels, too curious and quick to bark."

I stared in horror. "Sirius was poisoned?"

She shrugged. "It was as well, as matters turned out."

The lad turned back to me. "Well, girl—what did you see, when you opened the door?"

"I saw—I saw—" My eyes narrowed as I looked back into the past and felt again the chill of that frosty night against my cheeks. "I saw a man. I was afraid, for he was masked—not a hood like yours but a narrow eye mask. He was leaning against the porch, and and his arm was thrust inside his coat."

"You were afraid?" hissed the lad. "Are you sure you were not glad to see this man? Was it nothing more than fear you felt?"

I hardly heeded him. "I was afraid at first, but when he saw I was only a woman, he took off the mask and revealed his face. Then I felt concern, for I could see that he was in pain. He was pale and sweating, gasping for air. I knew there was not another house nearby where he could find shelter, and I could neither leave my grandfather, nor allow him to be disturbed. He spoke. He spoke . . . and I was so surprised . . ."

For I had thought him a young labourer at first, in his round hat, rough country coat and breeches, and his unpolished boots. But his voice had been gentle. Gentle and musical . . .

"Good evening, Miss Merridew. I am sorry to disturb you so late. The truth of the matter is that I have met with an accident and must throw myself upon your mercy—or bleed to death—" And then he had swayed and I had found myself helping him into the house before I knew it. When I had seen how much blood was seeping from the wound in his right arm, my own senses had almost left me.

"You should be in bed," I warned him. "The spare bedchamber is empty . . . do you think you are fit to climb the stairs?"

"With your assistance, I am fit for anything," he assured me, with the glimmer of a smile in his white face. "But I dare not lie where I may easily be discovered. Have you not some outhouse where I could hide? For I may have left traces of my coming here, and if they search the house and find me, I am as good as gallows meat."

"If I am to take you in, then I must know what you have done."

"Very well, ma'am, I will not attempt to deceive you. I am a common highwayman."

I remembered staring at him aghast. "An uncommon one, I think!"

"I see that I have shocked you," he murmured. "But needs must when the Devil drives . . ."

He swayed again, and I pulled myself together, for his lifeblood was draining away before my eyes and there was no time to be lost.

"This cottage was once part of a much larger old house," I told him. "There is a priest's hole here, that no one would suspect." I helped him towards the fireplace and fumbled with the panelling upon the chimney wall. I had not opened the secret door for years, though it had been my childhood refuge once; and I wondered for a moment if I had forgotten the way of it. But suddenly I felt the wood move under my hand, and in an instant more it had slid back to reveal the dark beyond. I picked up the lamp and carefully stepped inside. Holding the light high, I looked up the dusty winding wooden stair.

"Follow me," I bade him. "But have a care. I do not know if these steps will bear your weight . . ."

I blinked, finding myself in the parlour at Plas Celli, with my head smarting. The lad had leaned forward and tugged my hair.

"Don't keep it all to yourself," he said sourly. "He spoke—and then?"

"Why, then—I took him in and hid him up in the priest's

233

hole. I knew he would need careful nursing for a while, and I dared not treat him where he could be discovered, not only for his sake but because the confusion of his arrest would have been enough to kill my grandfather. I had to dismiss our maid—"

"Did he tell you his name?" the lad demanded.

"No, not then. He said only that I could call him Dick. He was thinking of Dick Turpin, I believe. It was the next day, when he was tossing in his fever, that I asked him again. I told him I must know his proper name, in case he died, for I would have to inform his kin. He said—he said—"

"Well, what did he say?"

"He said, 'You will not trick me so! Besides, I have no kin. I have no friend now at Castell Marten—only the silliest of my aunts. And even she would be finished with her dearest Gerry if she knew he had been reduced to robbing the common stage...' and so, by degrees, I discovered he was Gervais Marten."

"And what else did he tell you, this handsome wounded highwayman, during those long days and nights you nursed him?"

"I did not spend a great deal of time with him. I had my grandfather to attend to—and Grandfather grew worse... but Gerry told me he had been turned out by his family, and he had a pressing need to acquire money—a great deal of money. He had a friend who had found him a hiding place in a disused quarry, and who had procured him a couple of good horses. This friend had a system of discovering what coaches were due, and their first attempts at—at highway robbery were all successful. The friend promised to sell the jewelry they—took, in some place far from Dunstable, and they used only the change from the stolen purses which could not be traced. They should have moved from the area while their luck still held, but they were afraid of unknown country. Their reputation spread, of course, and on this last occasion the guard was armed and ready for them, with his pistol cocked. He shot on sight, and Gervais was wounded. His friend knew of—of our cottage and its isolated position.

He helped Gervais to my door and left him there, after looking through the window to make sure I was alone."

I put a hand to my throbbing head, which seemed to be bursting with memories now that the barrier was broken.

"Very well," said the lad in a hard tone, "but how did you come to marry him?"

"It was when—when my grandfather died." I swallowed and regained control of my voice. "Gervais improved after the first few days, you see, though he was still weak. But Grandfather—Grandfather died. Suddenly it occurred to me that I was alone in the house with a young man—and my Cousin Prentice was expected shortly." I shivered at the very thought of that overwhelming woman, whom even the loss of my memory had not been able entirely to obscure. "I was afraid of Cousin Prentice," I explained, "for she used to beat me when she lived with us after my mother's death—until Grandfather caught her at it and sent her away. I knew she had only to step through the door to discover our secrets . . . I told Gervais this, and he laughed . . ."

"He laughed?"

"He said, 'Why, Miss Merridew, I would not see you distressed for the world. Allow me to offer myself in return for your kindness to me. You need not then be obliged to live with this cousin of yours, who sounds quite tedious, and if after all we do not suit each other, it would be no great matter to have our marriage annulled.'"

"And you agreed," said the youth flatly.

"Oh no! Not at first. But he was very persuasive, and in truth the alternative was distressing to contemplate. Besides, I liked him. He was the first man to compliment me—and there was something very romantic about his situation. I began to think it not impossible that we should deal together well enough. I was already halfway in love with him." I sighed, realizing just how young I had been those few weeks ago.

"He assured me that with a roof over his head he would give up the high toby, as he called it, and we would be able to live off our four acres. I weakened, but I was still afraid of the scandal that would follow on my marrying this stranger, so soon after Grandfather's death. He told me then that he knew a clergyman who would marry us secretly—he asked me to send a message to this man to attend him to discuss it. I thought—I thought, if the clergyman did not think it wrong, I would agree."

The lad gave a short laugh, though he did not sound amused. "Well, go on."

"I had a letter from Cousin Prentice in reply to mine. She could not come for Grandfather's funeral, she said. She trusted I was well chaperoned . . . She was setting her affairs in order and hoped to be with me on the first of the month. I was greatly relieved . . . I took Gerry's message to a groom at an inn not far from us, and the next night the clergyman came . . ."

The lad raised his hand to stop me there. Then he gestured to the woman, who got to her feet and shuffled forward into the circle of lamplight. I stared at her uncomprehendingly as she unwound the veils from her face, pulled off her gloves, and dropped her shawls and reticule upon the floor. Nodding and chuckling, she began to unhook her skirt. When she stood revealed in her grey petticoat, she pulled out a pillow that had padded it.

I bit my lip and glanced at the lad, but naturally his hooded face could tell me nothing.

When I looked back at the woman she was lifting off her monstrous hat. Next she untied her yellowed cap and pulled it off, together with her wild grey hair, which must have been a wig beneath it. A moment later her petticoat flew across the room.

And that, I thought, was the end of Mother Cliffe.

In her place stood a slim young clergyman, neatly attired in full black suit and bands.

I gaped at him.

"Mr.—Mr. Fremantle!" I exclaimed.

He bowed. "Your servant, ma'am," he declared in a grave and educated voice.

He was the clergyman who had married me to Gervais Marten.

Chapter Nineteen

The lad gave a short laugh. "How about..." he
mumbled. "Well, go on. Go on. Get on with it."

"I had a letter from Church Cottage in
Tewkesbury," said the..."

"I see you remember me," the clergyman went on. "The
Reverend Edmund Fremantle. I came in answer to your
summons to Church Cottage, as you recall. You conducted
me upstairs to the secret chamber where Mr. Marten lay.
We discussed the question of your marriage. I thought it an
excellent notion, for propriety must be preserved. Besides,
Mr. Marten was set on it, and he was ever a hard man to
cross. Then it occurred to us that we would need a witness
for the ceremony, and I bethought me of Mrs. Farren..."
He broke off, looking at the lad.

Slowly the boy stood up. He laid down his pistol on the
chair and sauntered across the room to pick up the
discarded wig and cap. He turned his back to me, pulled
off his hood, and put the wig and yellowed cap upon
himself. Then he picked up one of the voluminous shawls,
draped it about himself, and threw a fold of it across his
head. Half-turning, he slipped his lower lip beneath his
upper teeth in a manner I instantly recognized, and
simpered with averted face.

"Thank 'ee kindly, sir—and where do I sign the paper,
your honour?"

I shivered. "You were the witness to the wedding?"

"Oh, yes, I was the witness, ma'am—may it please you,
ma'am," he piped, edging towards the door. When he was
safely in the shadows, he turned his head towards me.
"Werry surprised I was, to be asked—werry surprised. But
there—I do love a romance, and a wedding above all
things. I could not help myself—that I could not. I had to
see it with my own eyes." He chuckled rather horribly.
"Mr. Marten did not question it—he had entrusted the
reverend gentleman to find a suitable witness, you

see—werry sober and discreet; and his confidence was not misplaced—no, not for a minute! For you may rest assured, ma'am, that I never spoke of it to a living soul—no, never, not until this moment, and never will again."

I looked wildly from one to the other. "But wait—you are not Mrs. Farren, our maid! Who are you both? What is all this charade?"

It was the clergyman who answered me in a measured, reasonable tone. "Softly, ma'am, I beg of you. There is no cause—no immediate cause for alarm. My friend here, under the name of Mrs. Fanner, which would look like enough to Farren if the certificate had ever to be shown, insisted on our enacting for you this little drama. We struck a bargain between us, and this was her price. I thought it best to humour her, and I swear you should be grateful for it."

"Perhaps, perhaps," lisped "Mrs. Fanner" from the doorway. "Confess, though, that you have enjoyed playing your part? But the child is still curious, I see, so we had better make haste to oblige her with the rest of the explanation."

"Yes, let us be done with it," agreed the clergyman, on a suddenly weary note. "Tell her the rest."

"Well, so you were married, ma'am, in that little secret dusty chamber; and afterwards we left discreetly, the reverend gentleman and I. But I soon returned alone, for of course I could not allow the marriage to be consummated. Oh, no, that would not have done at all. I had drugged the bridegroom's wine, to be sure, but I had to make certain he was—incapable. So I slipped back, intending to burn down the place that very night, with you young lovers snug inside it."

The clergyman turned suddenly away, as if this statement had been as much of a shock to him as it was to me. I forced my attention back to "Mrs. Fanner" and, clinging to my stool, concentrated upon committing to memory the incriminating details of her story.

"Oh, yes, ma'am, I crept back to the cottage—but I was interrupted in my work. Had quite a narrow shave, I had, to avoid being caught. For as you will remember, ma'am, that was the werry night the militia chose to come out to hunt for the young highwayman again. They looked here and there, and then they searched the house, and talked to you, ma'am—for hours it seemed. It was awkward—werry awkward it was, for my time was not my own, as you might say. But they went at last, bless 'em. Of course, I dared not fire the place after that, while they were in the area, so I got inside, and seeing that you'd gone to your own room, I looked in on Mr. Marten as he lay sleeping, innocent as a baby, or so you'd think. Did you never wonder why he slept so sound after his wedding? It was only laudanum—just enough to make sure he'd give no trouble. And I am bound to say, he did give none. I picked up the pillow—a fussy sort of an affair, it was, all lace and frills, the best in the house, I dare say—and pressed it down upon his deceitful lying face—"

"I wish you would not tell her this," said the clergyman in a low voice.

"Mrs. Fanner" turned on him. "I know my business best, sir, I believe." She sidled across the room and picked up the pistol again, stepping quickly back into the shadows.

"You—smothered Gervais?" I repeated numbly. "I thought—I am sure I thought he had died of the influenza. He got over his bullet wound, but his constitution was lowered. He caught the influenza. He did have a cough and something of a fever..."

"Yes, that was fortunate."

I tried to stand up, but "Mrs. Fanner" pointed the pistol at me, and I sat down.

"You found him in the morning," the clergyman reminded me. "You went out to the inn, to send for me again. I don't know how you passed the day—packing, perhaps? At all events, I came as soon as it was dusk—as soon as I could. You remember this?"

I nodded, incapable of speech.

"We agreed—" He broke off. To my amazement, he brought out a handkerchief, turned away, dabbed at his eyes, and blew his nose, as if the memory caused him acute distress.

"We agreed," he continued rather huskily, "as to the cause of death. It was fortunate you did not realize that a doctor should properly have been called. You accepted my offer to bury him quietly, almost with gratitude. I hardly needed to persuade you. Partly it was, I think, because you were afraid of the scandal coming to your cousin's notice, of your succouring a highwayman and subsequently marrying him in clandestine circumstances. Also, I believe you were so shocked by—by Mr. Marten's sudden death that you would have agreed to anything. You certainly seemed quite unlike yourself. I dare say I, too—but never mind that. I stepped round to the churchyard, then, on that same night, and took the wheeled bier out of the shed. It was locked, of course, but I am clever with locks. Then my assistant and I—" He gestured towards "Mrs. Fanner," who dropped the gown and took off her wig and bonnet, to become "the lad" again.

"Yes," said the clergyman, with a sigh. "This is my assistant. I could see you were wondering earlier if you had ever met him before. Well, we had quite a task to get the body down that narrow stair and onto the bier, but after that it was no great matter for us to wheel it to the churchyard. The ground was hard with frost, which made it easier for us to push the bier; but it also made it out of the question for us to dig a grave. We were obliged to slip the body into one already recently prepared. It was unfortunate that it happened to be your grandfather's ... but no harm would have been done by that if you had not disobeyed my suggestion to stay at home. Alas, you followed us, and saw what it was we did. I believe your senses left you from that moment. If only I had realized it then, how much trouble would we have been saved! As it was, it seemed best to give you a certificate of burial, which you accepted as meekly as you had the marriage certificate—both papers stolen from this very house, as it happens—and to lead you home."

"Very solicitous, we were," went on the lad. "Tucked you up we did, in a manner of speaking, and I made so bold as to bring you a drink of the same soothing brew with which I had quietened Mr. Gervais. We left you with it in your hand, and went our ways. I came back later when the coast was clear, and set my fires. It was a fine dry night, and the building caught in no time. I stayed to see the cottage well ablaze, and then I left. The next morning I set out for Wales. It was quite by chance that I discovered in Dunstable that you had caught the early stage for Birmingham. You must have got out of bed as soon as our backs were turned—ignored your sleeping draught and left the house by a back door before I returned to it."

I shook my head. "I remember nothing of it," I murmured.

"You must have walked and begged rides to Dunstable through the night—"

"Rides," I echoed, memory stirring again. "I used to ride secretly by night, bareback, whenever I could find horses left out to pasture . . . I had not ridden sidesaddle for years, until I came to Castell Marten . . ."

"Well, perhaps you stole a horse and rode to town. In any event, I guessed then, of course, that you were on your way to Castell Marten. Thanks to a loan from this gentleman, I was able to hire good horses and travel a good deal faster than you, so that I reached Wales a day ahead. I made plans and lay in ambush for the Highflyer coach. You know how well my plan succeeded, beyond my hopes—but for one thing. You survived the accident. So then I contrived to climb up to your room, intending to hit you over your head—wound you with the poker so that you would appear to have died of your accident after all. But Mrs. Jones was there, so I was obliged to wait. Then we heard you had lost your memory. It seemed like a reprieve. We had only to steal the certificates from you, having drugged your tisane on your first night at the castle, and await the perfect opportunity to dispose of you—for I am sure it has occurred to you by now that those certificates were false, and our signing them was a capital offense."

"So—I was not really married, after all?" My tongue felt thick and numb, and I was shaking as if I had the ague.

"No, Miss Merridew, you are still a maiden. Next, then,

241

for I can see this tale interests you, we heard that his lordship was to travel to Dunstable, and we rejoiced, for we knew he would find no proof that Gervais had married there, and thought he would reject you as an imposter. But, alas for him, he must have fallen in love with you by then, and could not bear to part with you, even if he had to pretend you were his sister. It must have been hard on him. Was he very ill-tempered wtih you? Ah, well, you understand it now ... I did try to kill you once or twice when the opportunity arose, although not in earnest until after this gentleman had rifled your bag of its interesting contents in the Keep—but I failed, unfortunately. And all the while this gentleman was living in the castle, watching your comings and goings, your riding and your gardening. Not that you had aught to fear from him, for he's a gentle creature, despite his naughtiness. He does not want to kill you, nor to see you killed. It was his idea to pose as Mother Cliffe and take you to Lichfield, to see you into slavery as it were. Probably it would have been an effective obscurity, but, alas, I am sure you will agree we could not take the risk of merely delivering you to Mother Cliffe just as you were. After all, it is not impossible that his lordship might overcome his pride and come riding after you—so I determined to make sure of your discretion. If this evening's entertainment has persuaded you that I am to be feared, that my reach is long and my vengeance sure, then perhaps I can trust you to go free—or at least into such limited freedom as apprenticeship to Mother Cliffe must be. If not—then, my dear, sometime before dawn, you will surely disappear."

"So—so that is why—you told me everything?" I felt somewhat relieved. I had feared that, indulging themselves by revealing the whole plot to me, this mad pair could not have intended my survival. If on the other hand all that they had said was only to frighten me, perhaps the half of it might not be true ... but, of course, I must pretend to believe it.

"Not quite, my dear," said the lad. "I wanted to present you with a charade that no one else would credit if you did ever speak of it. But more than that, I particularly wanted

242

you to know why Gervais died. I wanted you to know your marriage to him was false—that you were never Mrs. Marten—and above all, I wanted you to know that, for his amusement, he deceived you."

"You mean, I suppose, that he connived at a sham ceremony?"

The lad shook his head. "It could have been conducted in Westminster Abbey by the Archbishop of Canterbury, my dear, and still have been invalid. Gervais deceived you, poor dupe, because he was already married."

"Married?" I gasped, for his words had the sure ring of truth.

"Yes, sweet Victoria—to me!"

And the lad tugged at the black ribbon that held back his hair, and stepped out into the light.

It was Miss Vaughan.

The clergyman giggled. It was a shocking, inapposite sound, and he seemed aware that it was not in the character of his part for he passed a handkerchief over his face as if to wipe away his glee.

"It was her expression," he explained to Miss Vaughan. "As you know, I did not approve of what you had in mind for this evening, but you were quite right to say there would be moments that I would find amusing. Besides," he added with a sharp glance at me, "she really deserves to be teased a little, for ignoring the warnings I was kind enough to give her. Three times I urged her to leave Wales. No doubt Mother Cliffe will make her wish she had paid heed to me."

"I could be very angry with you for warning her," remarked Miss Vaughan. "However, it does not matter now. But I should have known better than to trust you."

"Oh come, Sal," he protested. "Don't I always do just as you ask?"

"Indeed—and a great deal that you know I would never ask. I have not yet forgiven you for helping Gerry plan that false marriage with this wretched girl," she added coldly.

"Well—well, never mind that. It seemed expedient at the time, to make sure she would not betray him. But should you not be changing now? You know you should get home. Supposing that *Maman* takes it into her head to bid you good-night?"

"And you know as well as I do, Ned, that I have bought my maid, she is my faithful creature and will hide my absence, whate'er befalls." She turned her shoulder on him—her brother, as I now realized he was—and smiled cruelly at me. "You see, Miss Merridew, I understood early on in life that I would have no freedom unless I could be sure of the absolute loyalty of my maid, and fortunately *Maman* never guessed that Polly was not the most trustworthy of jailers, for she permitted her to chaperone me on all my journeyings."

My back ached, I realized. I straightened on the narrow stool, and shut my eyes for a moment.

"I also gave you fair warning, did I not?" Miss Vaughan said softly. "I told you, when first we met, that I was two people: one, the daughter of the Vicar, named Sarah; the other, Sal—a wild girl."

"Were you truly married to Gervais?" I asked faintly.

"Oh, yes." She pointed to Mother Cliffe's reticule. "I have my lines with me here—and they are not forgeries, I promise you."

"You have them with you?" exclaimed her brother in surprise. "I thought you would have decided to forget that marriage, now that you are sure of Freddy."

She looked at him impatiently. "I had to bring them to convince Miss Merridew, if necessary. Besides, when all the gossip has died down, I may yet proclaim myself as Gerry's widow and claim my inheritance. I shall go sobbing to Lady Castelmarten, tell her I was too frightened of *Maman* to own to it before—tell her that I never saw Gerry after he left Wales, and show her my marriage certificate. I will be able to explain how it was to Freddy, and as for Lady Carnaby, she will certainly find Gerry's widow a more acceptable connection than a mere Vicar's daughter would have been."

"But why did it have to be a secret marriage?" I persisted. "Surely your parents would have encouraged the match?"

"It was that Devil, Castelmarten, who stood in our way. At first, I thought I would oblige *Maman* and marry him rather than Gerry, for he had the title and the position, after all. And I would be close enough to Gerry, then ... But Lucian called me a child, and either teased me or ignored me. Last autumn, after his father had died, I set out to compromise him. But he laughed at me, curse him, and said that nothing would induce him to wed a wildcat. A little later, when Gerry made it plain that he was in love with me, Lucian told him in so many words that he would never allow his brother to marry such a girl as he knew me to be. Not that he knew the half of me, of course."

"But did your brother need Lord Castelmarten's permission to marry whom he pleased?"

"He could have married without it, but he was afraid that Lucian would cut off his allowance, as he had the power to do; and until he came into his fortune, Gerry could not afford to offend his brother by openly defying him. We were married in secret here, in this very room. Evans Plas Celli performed the ceremony, Ned and Mrs. Parry, his deaf old maid, were the witnesses. I did not think I could trust my Polly with *that* secret, you see."

"'Mrs. Marten!'" I exclaimed. "It was you then, and not I, whom the old woman was addressing when we passed her in the wood."

"Yes, did I not tell you that she knew too much? Well, Gerry and I tried to keep our secret, but it was hard. Lucian almost caught us once—and *Maman* accused Ned of encouraging me to meet Gerry. It was plain that she suspected something ... it was then they had their great division. Ned left home. He stayed with Sionedd for a while, and then here, 'til Mr. Evans, clergyman, was drowned. But he and Gerry were desperate for money. At last they decided to go away together, and make enough for us to live on until Gerry attained his fortune. I contrived to visit the Morton-Johnses after a while, so that I could be at hand to join them when the time was ripe ..."

I was beginning now to understand the plot. I stared at Mr. Vaughan. "So you and Mr. Marten became highway-men?"

"Yes, Miss Merridew," he owned, after a glance at his sister to obtain her approval. "We made an admirable team, I think, while our luck held. He supplied the courage, I the cunning. And of course my turn for playacting was a great advantage. We chose Upper Buzzard because I knew that country well, from staying with my cousins there. I had discovered an old hut long before, in a quarry, all grown over with brambles so that it was quite invisible, and thought at the time that it would make an excellent hiding place. We hollowed out the bank behind it, and there we kept our horses secretly. I did not attempt to see my relatives, of course, but I broke into their property to borrow some costumes which I thought might be useful if we were obliged to effect an escape. I struck up a friendship with a boy in a coaching inn, who let me know what carriages would be passing down the road—the only danger we were in at first was from your dog, which had stumbled across our hiding place, but Gerry saw to that."

I turned my mind from that, for it would do no good to let him see what I thought of the poisoning of my beloved Sirius. "Why did you bring Gervais to me, when he was wounded?" I asked.

"I had heard of you as being a devoted nurse," he said, looking wry. "I had a very different picture of you in my mind from what you actually are. I believed that you would not turn away a person in distress—and I intended to make sure you did not slip out to warn the constable that he was there. I helped Gerry to the cottage, then knocked on the door, and took his horse to a little distance. I saw him go in and returned to my hiding place. When I had that note from Gerry, I hardly knew what to do. He persuaded me, however, that an appearance of marriage to you was his only chance of being allowed to stay at the cottage in peace until he was fully recovered. I knew Sal would not like it, but—"

"I could kill you for it," said Miss Vaughan.

"Don't say that, Sal," her brother cried. "I know you like to pretend, but—"

Her mood changed again. "At least you told me what

246

was in the wind," she conceded. "I decided to play my part
in it, unknown to Gerry. I wanted to see this country
wench who seemed to have ensnared my husband. I stood
by meekly, biding my time. But when I saw Gerry take
your hand—" She paused, and I realized for the first time
just how cold the room was. "That was when I decided to
kill him."

"Oh, but, Sal—"

"Be quiet, Ned. You are a very good actor—almost as
good as I am—but amazingly foolish in real life. Do you
not think he made a convincing clergyman, Miss
Merridew?"

"Yes, indeed," I murmured, anxious to humour her.
Besides, it was true. I could still hardly believe he was not
in orders.

He looked up eagerly. "The role of clergyman was, of
course, a comparatively simple matter," he informed me.
"I had long studied it, under my father and later, Mr.
Evans. Myself, I am more pleased with my Mother Cliffe.
I own, I was uneasy in the part, until I had tried out my rôle
on Jennings at Hafod, without his suspecting me. But
facing Lucian! That was another matter. I delayed till dusk
to give myself a better chance, but I was nervous, I
confess. He had glimpsed me once when I was dressed as a
footman in the castle—yes, I was the one who sent you to
the Keep of course, for I had to recover that letter from
Dunstable—but I had yet to fool him face to face.
However, I did pretty well, I think."

"You pushed me down the stairs and took the letter?" I
exclaimed. "Was it you I saw riding in the mist, up on the
mountain? Were you staying with Sionedd then?"

"Yes, that was a narrow escape. Not only did you see
me, but I nearly knocked down poor Evans the shepherd a
few moments later. I was afraid he might forget his
promise and mention my name to you—Sionedd had
made him swear not to betray me, you see, for I was once
her dearest nurseling. Since Gerry died I have been staying
either in the upper storey of the castle or in the cottage
under Sionedd's wing. I had to have somewhere safe to
stable my horse, you understand, and the shepherd

provided it. He also kept my donkey and cart until I needed it. I was able to pay him well, of course."

I nodded, remembering the treasure hidden in the castle wall.

"Sionedd showed me the letter from Mrs. Jones's niece," Mr. Vaughan explained, "but she would not let me have it. She is loyal, but stubborn in some ways, alas. I hope you will believe that only desperation obliged me to maltreat you as I did?"

"You would have let me ride into a bog," I reminded him. "I suppose that would have pleased your sister, though."

"I felt it was too much to hope for," said Miss Vaughan calmly. "I did what I could, and left the rest for fate, for the time being. Well, I believe that is enough talking for one day," she went on in a different tone. "I have enjoyed it—you have an expressive face, Miss Merridew. The experience has been all I wished for. But now the time has come for action."

"Action?" said her brother, rising from the sofa. "I should have thought rather for sleep. You should be at home, and if I am to conduct Miss Merridew out of Wales in the morning, we must make an early start—or shall we trust to her good sense to keep silent, and release her?"

Miss Vaughan smiled mockingly. "My dear Ned, the final plan is quite different from the one I told you. Tomorrow you are going to leave Wales for a while, disguised as an itinerant preacher, mounted on a donkey. You will make for London and get taken on as an actor in some theater for a few months. By next Christmas it should be safe for you to return, if you wish to do so."

"Indeed?" he said meekly. "London, is it? I never got so far. I confess I should like that. Well, then, an early start is more than ever necessary."

"Of course it is." His sister smiled. "You can think of me, playing the part of Miss Sarah at her most docile during the next few weeks, while I am luring Freddy Carnaby into the meshes of my net."

"And—what of Miss Merridew?"

"Ah, yes, Miss Merridew will be where I tried to put her during the first part of our ride the other day—at the

248

bottom of the millpond, with her donkey cart."

My fear returned, engulfing me. I stared at the pistol in her hand, but it pointed unswervingly towards me.

"Sal?" said Ned in a weak voice. "Sal, you cannot mean it?"

"Hush, Ned. If you had an ounce of sense, you must have known I could not let her go now that she knows more than enough to hang us both."

"But I thought we agreed—all the evidence is gone— she fears you now—she will not talk—who would believe her?"

"No one, probably, but it is not worth the risk."

"But, Sal—you sound as if you really want to kill her! Tell me it is not so!"

She flung up her head, her nostrils flaring, like a mad charger my father once rode off the battlefield that had to be shot.

"Is it not?" she cried, as if her courage had been called into question.

He gazed at her fearfully. "I must know the truth," he said in a low voice. "I have hidden from it long enough. Did you—did you—kill my poor old friend, Evans, of this house?"

"Lord no," she said scornfully. "Why should I? He was as close as a clam, and quite useful to us, too. He tripped over his knitting, doubtless."

"Thank God! And then the old woman, Mrs. Parry?"

"Of course I had to kill her," she said reasonably. "I knew it when she greeted me in the wood by my real name. By then I was almost sure of Freddy and had decided to forget my wedding and Miss Gwynneth's fortune in favour of the Carnaby estate."

"You—murdered her!"

"I only helped her out of this world. She had not long left in it, doubtless, and I don't suppose she suffered. It took longer than I would have expected, though," she owned. "Longer than Gerry took to die. But I succeeded in the end."

"Not Gerry?" Ned cried in a terrible voice. "Say you did not kill Gerry?"

"But why should I say it," she demanded, her eyes

249

glittering, "since it would not be true, as anyone but you, poor Ned, would have realized long ago? But you were always adept at believing only what you wished to believe, were you not? Yes, I killed him. Ned. For his treachery, he had to die. But you admire me, don't you? You respect my planning and my resolution? I don't ask you to do anything you would find too difficult—the hardest part I take for myself, and for that you are bound to love me."

"I—never knew you," he gasped.

"You chose to blind yourself, perhaps. You will soon become accustomed to the idea," she promised him. "I was bound to kill Gerry, just as I am bound to kill his flirt."

She raised the pistol again, and with a sick plunge of the heart I realized she was aiming it at me. I had lost my chance of snatching it from her while she was distracted.

"Well, girl," she said smiling, "won't you kneel to me and beg for mercy? It will make no difference, of course, but I should like to see you grovelling. Have you nothing to say in your defense?"

"Only that—I was wrong—to agree to marry Gervais," I declared. "I did not love him." I flung up my head, determined to say it once before I died. "I love—Lucian—and it is an entirely different matter."

Her eyes rounded incredulously. "You love Castelmarten? I would never have guessed it." The pistol wavered in her grasp. Out of the corner of my eye I saw her brother move forward with his hand outstretched as if to take the gun.

"No, Ned!" she cried, and at the same moment a voice shouted from the doorway.

Instantly there was a flash, a roar. Something knocked me to the ground, where I lay winded by the crushing blackness that engulfed me. There was a female scream, and a horrid gasping sound.

Gradually I felt my wits returning as the weight upon my body lessened. My vision cleared, and I found myself staring into Lord Castelmarten's eyes, only a few inches from my own. I was aware that my face hurt. I put my hand up to it and brought it away, dripping with blood. I stared at it uncomprehendingly.

"You are all right," said Lord Castelmarten in an odd voice. "You are only bruised. It was Ned who was shot. That is his blood. He stepped in front of you; she shot him, and he fell back on top of you."

He helped me up onto the sofa. I became aware that the room was full of people; Mrs. Vaughan, stooping over Ned; Sir Caerleon ap Owen; Emrys, the groom...

"Oh, no! Oh, no!" Miss Vaughan was sobbing. She had dropped the pistol, and her face was in her hands. She had no need to simulate grief, she was indeed distraught. "What have I done? What have I done?"

"You have shot your brother, but he may yet live," said Lord Castelmarten grimly. "You have committed two murders, by your own admission—more if you upset the Highflyer coach. You killed Gervais."

She stared at him through her tears. Then an expression of cunning crossed her face. "No, no—I only said that just to frighten Miss Merridew. Ned will tell you I make up such things—Ned—"

"Gerry—" came a choked voice from the wounded man in answer. "She—Sal killed..."

"He does not know what he is saying. Why should I kill Gerry? He was my dear husband, after all."

"So you say, but can you prove it?"

"Oh yes," she cried quickly. "I have my marriage lines always with me. Where is that reticule? Ned was carrying it when we first came in. Oh, there it is."

She picked up the reticule and pulled the strings.

"Here, sir," she cried in triumph, dragging out a folded paper. Something flashed and fell, rolling across the floor to rest beside my feet. It was a gold bracelet, finely engraved with fleurs-de-lis.

I picked it up and stared at it, the hairs rising on my neck.

"Give that to me," said Miss Vaughan sharply.

"By no means, for this is evidence." I cleared my throat. "I recognize it, and his lordship will also, for I showed it to him after I found it sewn into the lining of my reticule. Your brother took it from me in the Keep. I knew it meant something evil, but I could not then recall where I had seen it first. Now I remember that it was caught in the lace of Gerry's pillow, when I found him dead. I saw it at once, as soon as I approached the bed. You had thrown the pillow on the floor, after the murder. The bracelet must have caught in the lace and been pulled off your arm. It fell with the pillow. I remember now that I stared at it and thought—so it is a woman who has murdered my husband. That was the shock, I am now convinced, which caused me to lose my memory. I set out to tell Lady Castelmarten that her son was murdered, as soon as I had seen him buried; and I determined to discover who it was who owned that bracelet, for I knew that person must have been the one who killed him."

"But how do you know the bracelet is mine?" asked Miss Vaughan in a little voice.

It was her brother who answered slowly, between painful gasps. "I brought it to you, Sal, with Gerry's love—when I rode back to Wales in February—with our plunder—he took it off—a screaming Frenchwoman— especially for you..." He groaned, pressing his face against his mother's shoulder.

"Hush, hush," said Mrs. Vaughan, stroking his hair. "You must not strain yourself—don't think about that wicked girl—I shall not call her my daughter. You must save your strength to live, for you are my only child now. You need me, Ned," she crooned. "I shall not let you die!"

And her overwhelming love would be his punishment, I thought, for years to come.

"Dr. Glynn is coming now," said Sir Caerleon, turning from the window. He coughed. "Miss Sarah Vaughan, I arrest you, in the name of the Law..."

It was a ghastly moment. Dr. Glynn entered, and I fastened my thoughts on him instead. Dr. Glynn and Miss Carnaby... perhaps they would be allowed to marry now that Freddy would be free to make an eligible match... I must help them all that I could, for Miss Carnaby had warned me several times against Miss Vaughan, and I had sadly misjudged her. Besides, I owned, I did not want her marrying Lord Castelmarten—and I did not think he would be heartbroken to lose her.

"Are you willing to let me take you from this place?" murmured Lord Castelmarten in my ear. "Will you ride pillion with me once again? Have you forgiven me?"

Sarah Vaughan was walking proudly across the room, without so much as a last glance at her mother, or at the brother who had betrayed her in the end. But her step faltered as she passed her gentle father, hesitating in the doorway, and heard his quiet and final blessing, "May God have mercy on your soul."

"Forgive you?" I repeated numbly to Lord Castelmarten. "For misjudging me?"

He shook his head. "I doubt if I was able to do that almost from the first, although I tried. No, I wondered if you could forgive me for letting you leave Castell Marten for this last ordeal without a hint that I was following you closely."

"You—did not reject me, then, when you thought that I was Mary Ramsey after all?"

"I did not think so—though I could only have been glad to know we were not related. But I had recognized poor Ned—I was expecting him to appear in some disguise. It was of no use to think of unmasking him, however. I knew he was not Gerry's murderer. I had once had a taste of Sarah's violent temper and feared at an early stage it might have been she who killed him. But proof was lacking. Then when you showed me that bracelet, I knew I had seen it somewhere. Later I recalled that Sarah had worn it one evening at Hafod Hall when her mother was not there..."

No one seemed to notice as Lord Castelmarten lifted me and began to carry me out of the room.

"What would you have done if I had proved to be your lawful sister?" I asked him breathlessly.

He looked wonderfully stern. "I should have taken you, I fear, to live sinfully in Morocco, or in Timbuctoo. Close your eyes, my love, for I don't want you adding this scene to your memories."

I received a brief impression of Miss Vaughan being dragged into Sir Caerleon's curricle and averted my eyes.

But I kept them open, for now that I was able to understand Lord Castelmarten's enigmatic expression, I could not have enough of reading it. He glanced down at me, and I gazed into his dark eyes, rejoicing that they were no longer inscrutable to me.

"We will be married soon," he declared, striding towards his waiting horse. "There may be objections, but I shall overcome them. We will retire to the Dower House for our honeymoon and wait for the scandal to blow over. All this, of course, can never be forgotten; but at least we shall have the knowledge that out of this tragedy, our happiness was born. Did I tell you that I have loved you passionately ever since that wretched Mr. Thomas threatened to take you away from me? Did I tell you that—"

But then his eyes again met mine, and lingered there, and there was no more need for words.